Black Valley Farm

Sheila Bugler grew up in a small town in the west of Ireland. After studying Psychology at University College Galway (now called NUI Galway) she left Ireland and worked as an EFL teacher, travelling to Italy, Spain, Germany, Holland and Argentina.

She is the author of a series of crime novels featuring DI Ellen Kelly. The novels are set in South East London, an area she knows and loves.

She now lives in Eastbourne, on the beautiful East Sussex coast. Eastbourne is the location for her series of crime novels featuring investigative journalist Dee Doran.

When she's not writing, Sheila does corporate writing and storytelling, she runs creative writing courses, is a tutor for the Writers Bureau and is a mentor on the WoMentoring programme. She reviews crime fiction for crimesquad.com and she is a regular guest on BBC Radio Sussex.

She is married with two children.

BLACK VALLEY FARM

SHEILA BUGLER

First published in the United Kingdom in 2023 by

Canelo
Unit 9, 5th Floor
Cargo Works, 1-2 Hatfields
London SE1 9PG
United Kingdom

Print ISBN 978 1 80032 734 4
Ebook ISBN 978 1 80032 733 7

Cover design by Black Sheep

Cover images © Shutterstock

Look for more great books at www.canelo.co

Printed and bound in Great Britain by Clays Ltd, Elcograf S.p.A.

1

To my Suzie Lou. This one's for you, darling!

Prologue

The wind whipped in from the North Sea, rippling across the mud-coloured hills and whining into the car as Rosemary opened the door. Peter had parked at the entrance to the farm, in front of the wooden gate that was held in place by a chain and padlock. As Rosemary unhooked the lock with one of the keys the estate agent had given her, the chain fell to the ground and the gate swung open. Behind her, she could hear the others getting out of the car and she willed them to stay quiet, not to ruin this special moment by saying something stupid.

She walked through the open gate towards the house. It was an ugly building, but she hadn't bought it for its kerb appeal. For what she had planned, this squat grey farmhouse situated on the side of a hill overlooking a remote valley in the Lincolnshire countryside, was perfect. It would need work, of course, but that wasn't going to be a problem. Thanks to her parents, she was a wealthy woman. All those years being a dutiful daughter, never once stepping out of line, had been worth it in the end.

It was nine years ago today since Mummy and Daddy died. A tragic accident, the inquest concluded at the time. Although in truth, her parents' deaths had been neither tragic nor an accident.

'It's going to cost you to get this place the way you want it.'

Peter's voice was an assault on the silent beauty all around her. She hated him then, more than any other time since she'd known him. If she could have found another way to do this, one that didn't involve him or any other man, she would have done it. But for now, unfortunately, he was necessary.

Ignoring him, Rosemary walked closer to the house until she was able to read the wooden sign over the door: *Black Valley Farm*. This was it, finally. All these years of planning and here she was, standing outside her new home. The place where she would finally be able to have the children she so desperately craved. Here, in this remote farmhouse, she was going to fix what her father had broken.

Already, she could picture it a year from now. Transformed from this desolate, deserted farmhouse to something utterly different. The thriving heart of her new family, a self-sufficient community of women and children living their lives untouched and untarnished by the conflicting demands of modern society. With Rosemary as their adored leader, the matriarch of this special place.

'Open the door, would you?' Peter said. 'This wind is freezing my nuts off.'

She swung around to face him, pleased when she saw the flash of fear behind his eyes.

'Go back to the car.' She looked at the women standing behind him, each one with blonde hair, blue eyes and fair skin. They were good-looking, she wouldn't have chosen them otherwise, although not one of them could have held a candle to her own startling beauty. 'You three come with me.'

The women looked relieved and Rosemary was glad she'd allowed them this moment. These broken women were vital to her plans. It was important to keep them happy, even if most of the time she'd rather kick them than pretend she cared about them.

Inside, it was exactly as she'd remembered. A wide hallway, far bigger than the outside of the house would have led you to believe, with three doors leading off it. The air smelled musty and when Rosemary breathed in, she imagined she could taste the motes of dust dancing around her in the dim light.

Beside her, one of the women started to speak. Rosemary held her index finger up to silence her. This wasn't a time for mindless chit-chat or endless questions about how they were going to get everything ready in time, or how many people could live here comfortably or blah, blah, blah. The effort it took to deal with people was exhausting. If Rosemary could have done this any other way – without involving tiresome people who utterly lacked her vision – she would have done.

But she couldn't think about that now. If she did, she would start to remember the reason she needed them. And now was not the time to think about Daddy and those nights when he came into her bedroom, or all the things that happened after that.

Today was about the future. Her future. Rosemary Fry, the woman on the brink of her very own Utopia. Her eyes filled with tears and her chest felt as if it might burst from the rush of joy bubbling up inside her.

'Come on.' She gestured for them to follow her back outside. 'Here's where we'll build the church. We'll extend the house, of course, and build a separate annex at the side for me and Peter. See that shed? That will be a classroom because the children will need an education.'

She kept talking, faster and faster, her vision for the future pouring out of her. And when she'd finished, and she was out of breath from speaking, she threw her hands in the air and looked at each woman in turn, taking a moment to gaze into every pair of blue eyes before moving onto the next.

'It's going to be perfect,' she said.

There was a pause, where she thought for one terrible moment one of them was going to disagree with her. Then, suddenly, they were all smiling and telling Rosemary how wonderful it was and how they couldn't wait to move in. As they continued speaking, their voices got higher until they sounded more like birds than people. They were saying and doing all the right things but there was something about that pause that worried Rosemary. These women had been carefully chosen. She had put time and effort into her relationship with each of them, ensuring they perfectly understood what she wanted to achieve here in this special place. In every single conversation, she had felt that the women understood her vision and shared it. She realised now this might not be true for all of them. And she wondered, for the first time, what they talked about when she wasn't with them.

She would have to be more careful in future, do everything she could to ensure total obedience. There would be rules, lots of them, and she'd make it crystal clear what happened to anyone who broke those rules.

She had told the women – these second-rate imitations – that the farm was going to be a place they could be safe. It wasn't a lie, because they would be safe. As long as they did exactly what they were told.

Part One

Chapter 1

The boy moves so fast I almost miss him. A flash of colour out of the corner of my eye, no more than that. His trousers are blue, and that's what catches my attention. They're the same colour as the bus he's running out in front of.

Suddenly, I'm running too. The world races past in a blur of sounds and images. People's faces; a man shouting; the blare of car horns. Above it all, louder than anything else, a woman is screaming.

I'm on the road now, my eyes focused on the boy as I swerve through the traffic that clogs this stretch of Sheffield during the morning rush hour. Then I have him, my hands wrapping around his waist as I scoop him off the ground. He's heavy. I stumble beneath his weight and almost fall, but somehow manage not to.

The air is hot from the heat of the bus, and stinks with the sickly smell of diesel. The screaming is louder now. I don't know if it's coming from me, or the boy or neither of us. He's a dead weight that tugs on my lower back as I throw both of us forward towards the pavement. We hit the ground, so hard my teeth clatter together.

The honking of a horn rips through the air, too loud and too close. We're going to die. I squeeze my eyes shut, waiting for the weight of the bus to press down on us but it never comes.

There's a moment when everything is still and silent. Then the pain kicks in, sharp and shooting in my elbows and knees. A buzzing sound in my right ear and, when I try to sit up, a drum starts pounding behind my eyes. *Tharum, tharum, tharum.*

I look around for the boy, but he's gone. A man is leaning over me, his face too close to mine. He's speaking but I can't understand what he's saying. A gobble-gobble of words that get lost beneath the thumping drumbeat. The man is holding my arm and trying to pull me up but I shake him off. The boy. Where's the boy? I thought I'd saved him. I remember how he felt in my arms, but maybe I only imagined it. I swing my head around, looking back to the road, half-expecting to see him squashed beneath the blue bus that's blocking out the sunshine.

But the boy's not there, either. Then I see him, and the relief is warm and it fills every part of my aching body. A woman is holding him, tears rolling down her face as she says 'thank you, thank you' over and over again.

There are more people now crowding around me. It's all too much. The push of the crowd, the dark shadow of the bus, the stink of burning rubber, the voices and the pain and the shivery shaking that runs through my body like a waterfall.

'You were amazing,' the man says, as I haul myself off the ground. 'You saved his life, do you realise that?'

I try to step back, away from him, but there are people behind me too. Before I can stop him, the man has taken hold of my arm again and is guiding me through the throng of bodies. I want to tell him to let me go, but I don't know how to do it without seeming rude. Besides, he's actually trying to help me and I need someone to get me away from all these people.

He takes me to the café that has tables outside on the pavement. I've never been here before, but I walk past it most days. It has cakes in the window that look amazing – pink and white and blue and there's one that's shaped like a princess castle – but it looks way too expensive for someone like me. A woman wearing a white apron pulls out a chair and gestures for me to sit down. The man disappears inside the café, comes back a few minutes later with a white mug.

'Sweet, milky tea.' He puts the mug on the table in front of me. 'Good for shock.'

I try to say thank you, but my mouth isn't working properly. When I lift the mug to sip the tea, my hand is shaking so badly I have to put it back down again. The man sits down and stares at me. I wish he'd go away.

'What's your name?' he asks.

'Clare.'

I lift the mug again and, this time, manage to get it as far as my mouth. The tea is good. Not too hot, and very sweet. After a few more sips, the shaking isn't so bad and I'm starting to warm up a little.

'Good to meet you, Clare. I'm Howard Jenkins, journalist with the *Sheffield Herald*. If it's okay with you, I'd like to ask you a few questions. I've already got some footage of you in action. This will make an incredible story for our readers. How do you feel about becoming a local celebrity?'

I slam the mug down, so hard the tea sloshes out.

'I don't want you writing about me.'

'Hang on,' he says, as I push my chair back and stand up. 'No need to be shy, Clare. You've done something incredibly brave. People ought to know about it.'

'She said no.' It's the woman with the boy. She's still holding onto him, like she's afraid to let him go in case he runs out in front of another bus.

'She doesn't have a choice,' Howard tells her. 'The story will run whether she likes it or not.'

'You can't do that,' the woman says. 'It's not right.'

Howard Jenkins starts saying something, but I don't wait to hear what it is. I'm already walking away as fast as I can without running because I don't want anyone to notice me. I hate Howard Jenkins and men like him: men who pretend to be kind but they're only being nice because they want something from you.

I'm almost at the end of the street when someone touches my shoulder. I swing around, expecting to see Howard Jenkins. But it's the woman. The boy is beside her, holding her hand, and they both have red faces and are breathing heavily.

8

'I'm sorry,' she says. 'I couldn't let you go without thanking you properly. You saved Freddie's life. If there's anything I can ever do for you, please just let me know.' She opens her red handbag and pulls out a white card that she shoves into my hand. 'My business card.'

When I see what's written on the card, my stomach twists into a tight knot.

'You're a policewoman?'

'A detective,' she says. 'I've tried my best to scare off the journalist, but I'm not sure what good it will do. I'm truly sorry if it causes you any problems.'

I can't work out if she's being sincere, or if she's chased after me for another reason. There's a voice inside my head, screaming at me to run. But I don't do that because I have to act as if everything is okay. I can't let her know that a police detective is the very last person I want to be talking to, now or ever.

'I also wanted to check you're okay,' she says.

Her name, on the card, is Helen Robins. Detective Inspector.

'Why wouldn't I be?'

'The way you reacted when that journalist said he was going to write about you. It made me wonder if you're trying to hide from someone.'

'I have to go.'

She reaches out, as if she's going to try to stop me.

'Leave me alone.' It comes out angry and aggressive, but it does the trick because she steps back, as if she's scared I might hurt her. Good. I want her to believe I'm dangerous.

This time, when I walk away, she doesn't try to follow me. And I let myself believe, for a moment, that this might be the end of it.

Chapter 2

Leo Bailey speaks fast and walks faster. Up ahead, he can see the hotel. When he goes inside, he'll have to end the phone call and start making tedious small talk with the people he's come here to network with. Which means he needs to slow down his walking and speed up his talking. The person on the other end of the line is his right-hand man, Harry, who has been with Leo since the beginning. Harry knows more about Leo than most people. Although Harry's knowledge of his boss is limited to the edited bits of Leo's life he's been willing to share.

'Gotta go, Harry,' he says as he joins the groups of men and women surging towards the hotel, all of them here for a monotonous networking event for entrepreneurs in the food and drinks industry. 'I'll call you when this is over.'

There are few things Leo hates more than networking events. Most of the time he avoids them altogether. But today he's made an exception, because according to Harry, Joe Luciano will be here today. Joe runs a chain of upmarket gastropubs that Leo's keen to invest in. If he can grab ten minutes with Joe to set up an initial meeting, it will be worth the effort of showing up.

Inside the hotel, he doesn't need signs to tell him where to go. The hubbub of conversation, punctured by bursts of laughter, is enough to guide him towards the event. As he walks towards the noise, his resolve falters. He'd forgotten quite how awful these sorts of things are. He can't stand any of it – the pointless small talk, and the egos and the air thick with the stink of overpriced perfume and cologne. But he's here now, so he'll just have to get on with it.

He's at the entrance to the large ballroom, where his fellow entrepreneurs are gathered, when he sees her. Their eyes connect and he freezes. Someone bumps into him from behind. Bodies jostle against him and people mutter as they swerve past him. He ignores them all, as he stares at her face across the crowd. The world stops. Despite all the people, it feels as if there's no one except the two of them.

As the initial rush of panic and fear subsides, he realises that it's not her. It can't be. Yet somehow, it is. He'd know that face anywhere. The eyes, blue and piercing, staring at him; the hint of a smile playing at the corners of her mouth.

There's a man with her, someone vaguely familiar from a business lunch Leo attended last summer. Leo can't remember his name and it might not be important, anyway. Right now, the only thing that matters is getting away from here.

He swings around and starts running, elbowing his way past men in suits and women wearing shoes that click-clack against the hotel's marble floor. All thoughts of finding Joe Luciano have left him. A man shouts at him to watch where he's going. A woman bares her teeth through blood red lips.

He thinks he's not going to make it then, suddenly, he's outside. Breathing in mouthfuls of grimy London air that tastes beautiful, because there was a time in his life when he thought he'd never taste city air again.

He hurries past the hordes of people making their way home after a day spent sitting at computers, wasting precious hours of precious lives doing mindless tasks that could, and probably soon would, be done by a machine. He's tried hard to be more than that. To make the most of every opportunity that's come his way, never once allowing himself to forget how close he'd come to living a very different sort of life. One with no choices or opportunities.

He swings right, into Thirleby Road. It's quieter here. Fewer people. Red bricked mansion blocks on either side of the street, communal gardens running along the centre. Homes for rich people. Prettier, but less impressive, than the modern, riverfront building he calls home these days. A light-filled apartment with floor-to-ceiling windows, two landscaped terraces and a clear view of the Houses of Parliament from his living room.

A woman is walking towards him. Tall and slender, wearing a black fitted dress and red shoes. The tap-tap of her heels on the concrete pavement is too loud. The sound follows him as he turns into Francis Street, and stays with him long after the woman is gone.

Click-clack, tap-tap. Shoes. Black and white and red shoes, all laid out in neat rows at the end of her bed. *Click-clack, tap-tap.* The sound grows louder. It's inside his head, mixing with the other things that he's spent so many years pushing to the furthest corners of his mind.

He realises, too late, that he shouldn't have run. If he'd stood his ground, stared back at her until she was the one to turn away first, she might have thought she'd made a mistake. That the man she saw in the hotel this evening wasn't him. Couldn't be him. That man had died years ago. Just like her.

Chapter 3

I wake up, fear crawling beneath my skin and my breath coming in short, sharp gasps. My face is wet because in the dream I was crying. I'd been dreaming about the day we found out Leo had died. Mother was angry, blaming me for what had happened, even though I'd had nothing to do with why he'd run away or how he'd died. And even though it was a stupid dream and not real, the injustice of the punishment stays with me. I know it will darken the rest of the day, making it harder than ever to drag myself through the endless hours until evening comes around.

From my bed, I can see straight out the window to the rooftops of the houses on the other side of the street and the blue sky above them. There are no curtains in the room. I like to lie in my bed at night and watch the stars, twinkling white and bright in the black sky.

Each time I dream of Leo, it's like losing him all over again. Even now, all these years later, his absence is an ache in my chest that never fully disappears. And when I remember what his voice sounded like, or the way his eyes crinkled at the sides when he smiled, and how he made me feel special in a way no one else ever did, it hurts so bad I sometimes think it would be better if I didn't remember him at all.

I force myself to get up. Once I'm showered and dressed, I sit in front of the dressing table and carefully dot concealer over the birthmark beneath my left eye. When I'm finished, I check my face from different angles to make sure the tear-shaped stain is invisible.

My room is on the top floor of a three-storey house in Ecclesall, Sheffield. This converted attic with its own en-suite has been my home for the last eight months. It is, by quite some way, the nicest place I've ever lived.

My landlady, Kath Dinsdale, lives on the floor below mine. As I start walking down the stairs, her bedroom door opens and she looks up at me.

'Good morning, Clare. It's going to be another lovely day. Can't believe it's still this warm. We're almost into October. A quick coffee before you go?'

'I won't have time,' I tell her. 'Don't want to miss my bus.'

Kath looks disappointed, and I feel bad. I hate disappointing Kath who's been nothing but kind to me and lets me live in the attic room for free. Kath says she doesn't charge me rent because of what I did for her, but we both know that's not the real reason. She lets me live here in her lovely house because she's lonely.

'Just a quick word,' Kath says. 'It won't take a minute, I promise.'

She takes her phone out while she's speaking and, as I reach the bottom step, she presses it into my hand.

'Have you seen this?' she asks.

I'm not sure, at first, what I'm meant to be looking at. It's a video. A recording of a street nearby. I recognise the Nando's on the corner. Then I see the blue bus and the boy running out in front of it and I realise, with a sick lurch in my stomach, what this is. A woman appears, and she's me. I'm running towards the boy and scooping him into my arms.

I don't want to keep watching but I can't drag my eyes away from the video. When I see how close we were to being run over by the bus my skin grows hot. The video ends with a close-up of my face. Whoever recorded this must have had a good camera on their phone, because you can see the freckles across the bridge of my nose, the flecks of dark black in my blue eyes. Clearest of all, though, is the tear-shaped birthmark beneath the outer corner of my left eye.

'Why on earth didn't you tell me?' Kath says.

I stare at her, unable to speak.

'You're so brave, Clare. First you face up to that horrible man who stole my bag, and now this. I'm glad the whole world will finally get to see what a hero you are.'

Three weeks after I moved to Sheffield, Kath got mugged on a street in the centre of the city. I'd already met her the previous week at the homeless shelter where I went most evenings to eat and get cleaned up. On the afternoon of the mugging, I was wandering around the city when I heard someone calling my name. I looked up, and saw Kath waving at me from across the street. At the same moment, a man came up behind her, pulled her handbag off her shoulder, pushed her to the ground and ran off.

Before I even knew what I was doing, I was chasing after the man. Somehow, I caught up with him and, in the grapple that followed, the ring finger on my left hand got broken. I screamed and I think it must have scared him off because the next thing I knew I was standing on the street with the bag in my hand and Kath clucking over me. She insisted on taking me to hospital and staying with me while my finger was X-rayed and bound up. Later, she took me back to her house for dinner and invited me to move in with her rent-free. It was only meant to be a temporary arrangement but I've been here for eight months already.

'How did you find this?' I ask, handing back the phone. 'Did someone send it to you?'

'It came up on a local Facebook group I'm a member of,' Kath says. 'Why? Are you worried someone from your past might see it?'

'What do you mean?'

Kath knows almost nothing about my life before Sheffield. The little bits I have told her are all lies. So why does she think I'm hiding from someone?

'When we first met you were living on the streets,' she says. 'People who end up homeless often do so because they're running away from something or someone. I've always assumed that's the case with you.'

'Well you're wrong. I don't like being the centre of attention, that's all.'

'It says here this happened on Friday,' Kath says, and it takes everything I've got not to scream at her to shut up. 'That was three days ago, yet you never mentioned a word about it. You're too modest, you know that? You hide yourself away, as if you're ashamed of something. But you're a good person, Clare Brown. One of the best. I wish I could get you to see that.'

It's so far from the truth I can't bear it. I push past her, mumbling something about not wanting to be late, and get out of there as quickly as I can. As I hurry down the hill, away from the house, I run through the different things Kath thinks she knows about me.

She thinks I'm twenty-seven-year-old Clare Brown, an only child, originally from Hereford. I've told her that both my parents were killed in a car crash when I was nineteen, and I used to have a black cat called Ollie. None of these things are true.

I don't like lying to Kath, but she can never know the truth about me. So I lie to her instead, as I've lied to every single person I've met since I left the farm ten years ago.

Chapter 4

The award sits on the shelf in Nuala's bathroom. When she first received it, she wanted to put it on display in the sitting room. Two things prevented her from doing that. One, she has enough self-awareness to know that it would look too much like boasting. The placing of the award in her tiny bathroom hints at her not taking the achievement too seriously, which isn't true but she likes that people might think it. The second reason she decided to relegate it to the bathroom is simpler: the award is hideous. The thought of it sitting on the mantelpiece, in between the Murano glass candle holder that was a present from an ex and the framed photo of Josh taken on his first day of school, is inconceivable.

There's no doubt that winning the Best True Crime Podcast award has been the highlight of her career so far. The podcast, *Black Valley Farm*, has been described as 'storytelling at its best', with one judge praising Nuala for 'the sensitive and intelligent way she approached this difficult subject'.

Nuala had believed that night, at the glittering awards ceremony in a fancy Central London hotel, that the success of the podcast would be the springboard to other work. She'd even managed to convince herself that the pain of her break up from Liz had been worth it, after all. Now Nuala knows, too late, she was wrong.

Despite the award and the thousands of downloads and positive reviews, Adrian Addenshaw's power over Nuala's life hasn't gone away. Say what you liked about him, but Adrian was a man of his word. He'd told her she would never find another job in the media and here she was, three years after telling him what she really thought of him, jobless with her prospects narrowing as each day passed.

She wants a better life than this hand to mouth existence, as much for Josh's sake as her own. Her son doesn't deserve to lose out because Nuala decided to be a single parent instead of shacking up with a man she'd had a one-night stand with and had no interest in ever seeing again. But apart from one award and a handful of advertising deals that have kept food on the table and the bills paid, success has so far eluded her.

Despite this, Nuala tries to stay positive. She tells herself, repeatedly, that she should feel proud of what she's achieved. And she is, most of the time. When she's able to ignore the guilt that never quite disappears, no matter how often she tries to convince herself that what she did wasn't really that bad.

The problem is, with Josh at school now, she has too much time on her hands. Time spent thinking about what might have been, instead of focusing on what's next. Most mornings are spent like this one – sitting at her computer, scrolling through her social media channels before sending emails to the few contacts she's got left, hoping someone might take pity and throw some work in her direction. They never do and she's resolved that if she still has nothing by the end of this week, she'll go back to temping again.

She hates temping, sitting in an office with people she's got nothing in common with and doing work she doesn't care about. But the rent is due and Josh is going to need new school shoes soon. And, although it's only the end of September, Christmas already feels as if it's just around the corner. It's taken on a whole new level of importance since Josh started school and spends his days with children whose parents seem to have endless amounts of money to spend on presents and parties and holidays.

Nuala opens Instagram and scrolls through the latest photos posted by the people she follows. One post is a photo of a house that is instantly familiar. Nuala pauses, zooms in, as she tries to figure out why it's suddenly appeared in her feed. The photo shows the house before the fire that destroyed it. A long, low grey stone building with a modern annex built onto the side. Surrounding the farm in every direction are rolling hills that Nuala knows, although it can't be seen in the photo, stretch all the way to the North Sea.

The photo has been posted by a user called *truthfinder*. Nuala doesn't recall following an account with this name. Then again, she follows all sorts of accounts on Instagram. She knows there's no obligation to follow back, but it's something she does most of the time because not doing so seems rude. The downside of being polite is that her feed ends up being full of photos from people she's never even heard of.

She clicks on *truthfinder*'s profile, hoping this might jog her memory. When she reads the single sentence bio, a chill runs down her back. *The truth will out.* Abruptly, she shuts down Instagram and stands up. As she crosses the room, she notices her hands are trembling. She tries to tell herself it doesn't mean anything. There are all sorts of weirdos out there, and social media is their playground.

She puts the photo out of her mind as she tidies the flat, and goes into Josh's room to make his bed. His room is a mess. Pieces of Lego scattered on the floor beside a crumpled heap of clothes. She finds an empty crisp packet and a half-eaten piece of toast under his pillow, and wonders how on earth the food got into his room when she's always been so strict about that.

But all the tidying and cleaning doesn't help shift her unease, and an hour later she's back in front of her laptop again. She has opened Instagram and is taking a closer look at *truthfinder*'s account. Whoever this person is, they've managed to accumulate 158 followers, despite only posting one image: the photo of the farm.

Nuala opens her messages and creates a new chat between herself and *truthfinder*. Of course, she doesn't have to do this. She could ignore whatever's going on here, close the laptop, call the temping agency and say she's available for work from next week. But if she did that, she might never find out who this creep is and why he, or she, is invading her Insta feed. Yeah, she could do that, if she lived in some alternate universe where she was a different type of person. Someone who avoided conflict instead of running headlong into whatever battle presented itself.

She's barely started typing when the message arrow at the top right-hand corner of her screen turns red. She's got a new message. Right away, she knows it's from *truthfinder*. She can feel the pull that's drawing them closer together. There's a fizzing in her stomach, a buzzing in her head and the room is suddenly too hot. The words on the screen move and merge and it feels like forever before they settle into place and she can read them:

> You lied.

Chapter 5

I push open the front door and step inside the house.

'Hello?'

No response. No Kath, moving about in the kitchen or upstairs in her room. There's no one else here. Instantly, I feel lighter. I like Kath but it's always an effort, at the end of a long day cleaning other people's houses, to put a smile on my face and carry on pretending to be someone I'm not.

Upstairs in my room, I put my earphones in so I can listen to the new playlist I created last night. The first time I heard music was the day I moved into Jasper's flat. We were hardly in the door when he picked up what I now know is a remote control and pressed a button on it. Sound burst out of two over-sized speakers, terrifying me.

When Jasper saw me putting my hands over my ears, he thought I was joking. After I'd begged him to turn it off, he tried to get me to see what was good about it. He told me about lyrics and guitar chords and bass and drum, and played different pieces to demonstrate what he was talking about. Jasper made me fall in love with music. Because of that I thought, for a short time, that I loved him too.

After I left Jasper, my access to music was limited. I had to be somewhere with free Wi-Fi, so I could watch YouTube music videos or listen to the radio. But Kath subscribes to a music streaming service and she's given me her username and password. Now, I can listen to music whenever I want, which is pretty much all the time.

With the Foo Fighters blasting through my head, I sit in front of the dressing table and start the transformation. Outside the house, I'm boring Clare Brown who never wears make-up – apart from the concealer to cover her birthmark – never makes eye contact with people, and does everything she can to make sure no one notices her.

It's only here, in this room at the top of Kath's house, that I can become someone else. Someone different in every way to Clare Brown, with her horrible clothes and her pale skin and hair the colour of cow dung that's faded beneath the heat of a summer sun.

I love playing around with make-up, seeing the different ways I can make myself look older, prettier, more interesting. Tonight, I choose dark red lipstick, inky black eyeliner, smoky grey eyeshadow and an electric blue mascara that makes my lashes seem longer than they really are. The final touch is the blusher I bought last month. I've had to watch a few YouTube tutorials to work out how to apply it properly, but I've pretty much nailed it now.

When I'm done, I take a photo with my phone. I have hundreds of photos of my face. Whenever I'm feeling down, or bored or petrified about what's going to happen to me, I scroll through the photos. They remind me of who I really am, the person hiding beneath dull Clare Brown.

Sometimes, the birthmark is invisible in the photos. But other times I like to play around with it, pretending it's a gangster tattoo and using black eyeliner to make it really stand out.

It should have been hidden the morning I saved the boy. Most mornings, I make sure to cover it before leaving my room. But I'd been running late and had taken the concealer with me, planning to do my face once I was on the bus.

It's not a mistake I'll make again, although I'm starting to think I'll be okay. It's been four weeks since Kath showed me the video. So far, no one seems to have recognised the girl in the video as the person whose face was plastered all over the news ten years ago. The girl one newspaper described as 'the most wanted woman in Britain'.

The video is still out there, available to view from the *Sheffield Herald*'s YouTube channel. When I last checked, it had been viewed over two thousand times. There are comments beneath the video but they're all about how brave I am. Not one of them mentions the farm.

As each day passes and no one has made the connection, I worry a little bit less. It's been ten years, after all. My face must have changed during that time, even if I can't really notice the differences myself. Plus, in those earlier photos, my hair was long and blonde; not short and brown like it is now.

I study my face in the mirror, trying to work out if I'm pretty or not. It shouldn't matter, I know that. If anything, it's better not to be pretty. There's less chance of people noticing me, or remembering me. Yet I can't help it. I want to be the sort of pretty that means people will be kinder to me simply because of how I look.

I'm so caught up with staring at my face from different angles, and listening to Dave Grohl singing about never wanting to die, that I don't hear Kath come into the room. When I see her face, appearing beside mine in the mirror, I bite back a scream. Ripping the earphones out, I stand up and back away from the dressing table.

'Sorry.' Kath puts her hands in front of her, like she's half afraid I'm going to hit her. 'I didn't mean to startle you. I knocked on the door, but you didn't answer. You look amazing, by the way. What's the special occasion?'

'What do you want?' I sound rude, but I don't care. She shouldn't be in here. This is my private space and when she invited me to live with her, Kath said she'd respect my privacy.

'There's someone I'd like you to meet.'

This is a surprise, and not a good one.

'His name is Arnie,' she says. 'He started helping out at the shelter this week.'

Three days a week, Kath volunteers at the homeless shelter where I first met her. Lots of other people work there too, but Kath's never invited any of them back to the house. I don't understand what's special about this Arnie. But before I can say this, Kath is speaking again.

'I've told him about your wonderful singing voice. Arnie has a friend who owns a pub in the city centre. A live music venue. He wondered if you might be interested in doing some gigs there. Apparently his friend is always looking for new acts.'

My heart is beating hard and fast. I can feel my face growing hot, the way it does when I'm stressed or angry. Right now, I'm both.

'You've never heard me sing,' I tell her.

'Of course I have.' Kath laughs. 'You're always singing around the house.'

She beams, like this is perfectly normal. Like she hasn't obviously been spying on me all the time I've been living here, and she has no clue how angry I am right now. The more I think of Kath listening to me as I move around up here in my own private space, the angrier I become. She has no right, none at all, to be spying on me like that.

'I've told you before what a beautiful singing voice you have.' The smile has slipped and Kath's starting to look confused. She has, in fact, spoken to me about my singing. But that was only one time when she came home and I was in the kitchen making myself a cup of tea. She'd tapped me on the shoulder, making me jump then too, and told me I had the voice of an angel.

'It's kind of you,' I say, when I can trust myself to speak without shouting at her. 'But I'm really not interested in singing in a pub, or anywhere else.'

'Such a shame.' Kath sighs. 'A voice like yours deserves to be heard. Well, at least come down and say hello, won't you?'

She doesn't wait for an answer. Instead, she leaves the room and goes back downstairs. It's clear she expects me to follow her and, even though I really don't want to, I go anyway.

They're in the kitchen, his voice loud and alien in a house that's normally so quiet.

'Here she is,' Kath says, smiling at me as I push open the kitchen door.

She's sitting at the table beside a man I've never seen before. He's about the same age as Kath, fifty-five or thereabouts, and he has a completely bald head and grey eyes that are staring at me in a way I don't like.

'Arnie Cummins,' he says, standing up and walking towards me with his hand out for me to shake. 'Good to meet you, Clare. Kath's been telling me all about you.'

As he gets closer, I catch the smell of his cologne. Something flickers at the back of my mind, a half-remembered feeling that's too vague for me to make any sense of.

'I showed Arnie the video,' Kath says.

He's still got his hand out and, after a moment, I shake it as quickly as I can.

'What you did was extremely brave,' he says.

He's standing a little too close, the smell of his cologne clogging the inside of my nose and the back of my throat.

'It was nothing, really,' I mumble, taking a step back to put some space between us.

He starts telling me I'm heroic. Says that most of my generation are so self-centred he can't imagine them throwing themselves in front of a bus to save someone else. He's smiling as he says all of this, but his eyes remain cold and hard.

I don't like him. The thought lodges itself inside my head. I don't like him, and he's here in Kath's house and there is not a single thing I can do about it.

'We're heading to the pub,' Kath says, when Arnie finally stops speaking. 'Would you like to join us, Clare?'

'No thanks.' I force myself to smile at her. 'It's kind of you to invite me, but I'm really tired this evening.'

'Come on,' Arnie says. 'It'll be fun. Besides, I want to get to know Kath's secret tenant.'

He hasn't stopped looking at me since I came into the room. I glance at Kath, to see if she's noticed, but she's beaming at Arnie like he's the best thing that's ever happened to her. I feel it again, then. The flash of anger that makes me want to scream at her until my face hurts and my throat is red raw.

I repeat that I'm too tired to go out, then I say goodbye and get out of there as quickly as I can. Upstairs, I lock my bedroom door and lean against it while I wait for my heart to stop pounding and the anger to roll back down my throat.

Kath's been telling me all about you.

Kath never has visitors. I've always assumed this is because she's like me and doesn't want to get close to people. But of course Kath is nothing like me. She volunteers at the shelter because she cares about helping people. She's kind and interested in the people she meets. She has this big house that she owns, and a man she's not afraid to invite over because she doesn't spend every minute of her life hiding from the world.

And she's been telling people all about me. Showing the video to anyone who'll watch it, even though she knows I wish it had never been recorded. For a moment, I don't try to push the rage back down. I let it rise up inside me, filling me with its heat and its energy.

I close my eyes, giving in to the rush of feeling, willing it to stay with me. But it never does. Moments later, it's gone and I'm hollowed out, empty. It's the worst sensation, like there's a big black hole inside me.

There's only one thing that eases this emptiness. I've promised myself I won't do it again, but right now I need it. Quickly, I cross the room and open the drawer of the small bedside table. Inside, there are four shiny new razor blades. I select one, hold it between my teeth while I roll up the sleeve of my shirt and find an unmarked section of skin. There's a rush of pain, a hot gush of blood, followed by a blissful release. My breathing slows, my body relaxes, and the noises inside my head quieten.

Downstairs, Arnie and Kath are getting ready to go out. I hear voices in the hall, followed by the sound of the front door slamming shut. I look out the window and see them crossing the driveway. Arnie opens the gate and gestures for Kath to go first. As she does, he turns his head and looks at the house, staring right up at me. I step back, away from the window and those cold eyes. When I get the courage to look out again, there's no one there.

Chapter 6

In the weeks and months after I left the farm, it was the birth-mark that made me so recognisable. It jumped out at me from every newspaper and TV story about the farm and the people who died there. The photo in the papers was taken from a selection the police found in the days after a man named George Fisher discovered the nine dead bodies.

George Fisher was hiking alone in rural Lincolnshire when he made his gruesome discovery. He'd run out of water and went to the farm to see if he could refill his water bottle. In the interviews he's given, he claims he was traumatised by what he found that day. Although at the time, he seemed happy enough to tell his story repeatedly to any journalist who asked for it.

These days, George Fisher lives in Nottingham. He's married with two children and his wife's name is Beverley. I know this because I've looked him up on the internet many times over the last ten years. He writes a blog about hiking, which includes lots of photos of himself and his family wild camping in various places around the UK. He must have grown tired of talking about the farm, because there's no mention of it anywhere in his blog posts.

When the police searched the building and the surrounding area, they found a bag of photos in a van abandoned near the property. The police and the press assumed the photos were of the people living on the farm, and they were right. The police were able to match the photo of me with a description provided by the woman who'd picked me up the morning after the fire. The photo they chose for the media shows me standing alone at the front of the farmhouse. My long blonde hair hangs loosely around my face, and the birthmark is clearly visible – a tear-shaped brown mark beneath my left eye.

Jasper showed me how I could use concealer to cover up the birthmark. He came back to the flat the evening after the story broke, and presented me with a silver tube. When it was clear I had no idea what it was, he explained that women used make-up to make themselves look pretty, and that included hiding bits of their faces they didn't want people to see. He stood behind me in the bathroom, while I stared at my face in the mirror, watching the birthmark gradually disappear as I dabbed dots of concealer onto it. At the time, I thought Jasper was trying to help me. It was only later I realised this was just another way of controlling me.

Later, after I'd left Jasper and moved to London, I became lazy about concealing the birthmark. By then, there were other stories taking up newspaper space and TV time. No one seemed to care anymore, about what had happened at the farm.

I liked living in London. It's easy to disappear in a big city like that. I scraped a living doing cash-in-hand jobs – cleaning houses and doing part-time catering for people who were happy not to ask questions about why I didn't have a bank account or a national insurance number. I rented a room in a house with a couple from Latvia who let me pay cash in exchange for me taking care of their two children a few evenings a week. It wasn't a good life, but it was better than anything I'd had before.

Then one day, nine months ago, I was cleaning Brenda Marlowe's apartment in Butler's Wharf. Brenda runs a TV production company and she lives in a fancy apartment by the river. I used to clean for her two days a week and, each time I was there, she followed me from room to room, talking to me. It used to drive me mad but I never said anything, because she paid me £10 an hour and never complained if it took me four hours instead of three to clean the apartment the way she liked it.

Brenda liked to tell me about the TV programmes she watched in the evenings and the podcasts she enjoyed listening to on her daily runs. On this particular day, she could barely wait to tell me about a new podcast she'd discovered a few days earlier. I was only half-listening, busy trying to clean a layer of limescale from around the taps in the bath, when I heard her say the words 'Black Valley Farm'.

I didn't hear anything else after that. I told Brenda I felt ill and I got out of there as quickly as I could. Half an hour later, I was sitting in Whitechapel Library downloading the entire podcast onto my phone.

In the first episode, the host Nuala says that the podcast is an attempt to 'uncover the truth about the deaths at Black Valley Farm'. By the final episode, she claims to have done what she set out to do, although that's not quite true. There are a few things she got completely wrong.

The podcast has been a big success. This is good news for Nuala Fox, but very bad news for me. A few months ago, it won some big award and Nuala spent weeks bragging about it and reposting links to the podcast on her social media channels. I hate Nuala Fox and wish something bad would happen to her.

She talks about me in every episode, and constantly mentions my birthmark which she describes as my 'distinguishing feature'. Because I'd stopped wearing concealer in London, there were a lot of people who had seen my birthmark. I couldn't risk one of them matching me with the woman in Nuala's podcast.

There are eight episodes in total, each one presented by Nuala Fox, who I now know — because I've read the bio on her website and Insta page – is 'an Irish journalist and documentary film maker'. That afternoon in the library I listened to all eight episodes, one after the other. When I'd finished, I knew it was time for me to disappear. Again.

Chapter 7

It's two days since Nuala received the message from *truthfinder*. She replied straight away, saying she didn't understand what their message meant. Thirty minutes later, *truthfinder* responded with a single sentence: *You know exactly what I'm referring to.* That time, Nuala didn't respond, and she's heard nothing since then.

The silence should reassure her. Instead, it's had the opposite effect. Her anxiety has shot through the roof and she finds herself constantly checking Instagram for new messages. Last night, she woke up four times and had to check her phone on each occasion to see if there was anything from *truthfinder*.

There are only two people in the world who know Nuala lied. Liz is one. The other is Lydia, the chief suspect in the police investigation into the deaths at the farm. Nuala doesn't believe Liz would ever do anything as underhand as creating a false identity and sending her threatening messages. Which means *truthfinder* has to be Lydia.

When Nuala first came up with the idea for the podcast, she was determined to do what the police had failed to: she was going to find Lydia. But despite her best efforts, Lydia remained elusive. More than once, Nuala has wondered if Lydia might have died at some point over the last ten years. The messages from *truthfinder* imply otherwise. Lydia is still alive. She's listened to the podcast and she knows Nuala's dirty little secret. Each time she thinks of it, Nuala feels the familiar flush of guilt that no amount of self-justification will get rid of.

This morning, after dropping Josh at school and making inane small talk with the other mums at the school gates, Nuala hurries home and logs onto her computer.

Finding Lydia has become an obsession. At least when Josh is with her, Nuala can push thoughts of Lydia to the back of her mind and focus instead on her son. But during the long hours while he's at school, she has nothing else to do except sit and try to get to the truth. Which is ironic, because it was her inability to get to the truth the first time round that caused this mess.

Before she started recording the podcast, Nuala had researched the ethics of making a true crime documentary. She believed she'd understood how to create something honest, fresh and insightful while remaining true to the story itself. Except, it turned out, Nuala's principles were about as solid as ice cream on a hot summer's day.

With her laptop open, Nuala goes to the files she created during the making of the podcast. She scrolls through the photos first, starting with the images of the house itself. A squat, grey building, it sits alone on the side of a hill over-looking a valley in the remote Lincolnshire countryside. There's a wooden sign over the front door with the words *Black Valley Farm* written on it.

To the left of the house, and a few feet behind it, is a wooden barn with a pitched roof and a cupola. The barn is painted red and, to Nuala, it looks out of place in the rolling green hills of England. It's more like the barns she saw during her time in the States, where she spent six months living with a woman she'd never really loved on a farm in Montana.

In the first photo, the house looks a bit run down but perfectly habitable. When Nuala clicks on the second image, she sees the building as it was after the fire. In this photo only the barn remains intact. All that's left of the house is an empty shell.

A decade ago, nine people died at Black Valley Farm. Five adults and four children. Three of the adults and all the children were killed from the fire that ravaged the house while they were sleeping. The other two victims, both women, were found outside the house. One had died from the blast of the explosion caused by the fire. The other had died from a single stab wound to her stomach.

In total, Nuala has six photos of the farmhouse and the people who lived there. None of them are the originals; they're scanned images of the photos found in a bag inside a van abandoned near the farm in the aftermath of the fire. She's looked at these images countless times, yet she examines each one again this morning. Looking, always looking, for something she's missed.

She opens the photo of the woman and baby. The woman is holding the child, who looks no more than about three months old. She's dressed plainly in a white dress with long sleeves. Nuala estimates her age as somewhere in her early twenties. In the photo, the woman is smiling, but Nuala thinks she sees a trace of sadness in her blue eyes. The first time Nuala saw this photo she was struck by the woman's beauty. Despite the plain clothes and the sad eyes, there's no disputing the fact that this woman is stunning.

Next, Nuala opens the photo of the children. There are six kids in total, ranging in age from about twelve to toddler. Nuala guesses the youngest is no more than eighteen months. The children are all dressed identically – the girls in white blouses and long white skirts, the boys wearing white collarless shirts and black trousers. Nuala zooms in on one of the children. A girl somewhere between the ages of four and six, Nuala thinks. Blonde hair, blue eyes, pale skin with a sprinkling of freckles across her nose. A tear-shaped birthmark beneath her left eye that clearly identifies her.

'What do you want from me, Lydia?' Nuala whispers.

She opens Instagram and checks *truthfinder*'s profile. No new posts, zero activity. Suddenly, the urge for action overtakes the need for caution. She cannot sit here another day waiting for Lydia to make her move. She types a new message:

33

> I know who you are and I want to help you. Can
> we talk?

As she hits send, her phone starts ringing. For one crazy moment, she thinks it's Lydia calling. Even though that's impossible because, apart from anything else, Lydia doesn't have Nuala's phone number. When she sees Sarah Fagan's name on her phone, Nuala is almost as surprised as if the caller actually was Lydia.

'Sarah? Talk about a blast from the past. How are you?'

She tries not to make herself sound too hopeful. She always got on well with Sarah, but they were never friends exactly. Nuala knows Sarah wouldn't be calling her about anything except work. Sarah Fagan was Head of Production at Scorpio Media, the company Nuala had worked at for six years until its CEO, Adrian Addenshaw, fired her. Since then, Nuala's had no contact with any of the people employed by Scorpio, including Sarah Fagan.

'I've been busy,' Sarah says. 'Too much on as always. I'm sure you know the feeling. You must be busy too, after that podcast. Which was brilliant, by the way. I kept meaning to contact you to tell you how much I loved it. Sorry I never got around to doing that.'

'Don't worry about it,' Nuala replies. 'You're not the only person I haven't heard from since I left Scorpio.'

'You didn't give us much choice,' Sarah says. 'After that stuff you said about Adrian, I think we all wanted to keep our distance.'

'I only said it because it was true.'

Nuala feels the old rage bubbling up. Everyone working at Scorpio knew that Adrian Addenshaw was a sexist, bigoted bully who treated people like shit and never thought twice about shafting someone if it helped further his own career. Despite knowing this, no one at Scorpio had the guts to stand

34

up to him. No one except Nuala, who had got tired of letting that horrible man walk all over her and had told him exactly what she thought of him.

'Well, water under the bridge now,' Sarah says brightly. 'As you probably know, Adrian's moved on. He's with Channel Four these days, where he's doing very well.'

Nuala wants to tell Sarah that, as far as she's concerned, her feelings about Adrian are as strong now as they've ever been. But she keeps quiet, because she can't risk upsetting Sarah who, just maybe, is calling to offer Nuala some work.

'I've got a slightly strange request,' Sarah says.

'I'm listening.'

'Does the name Andrea Leach mean anything to you?'

'Politician?' Nuala says, scanning the slim bits of knowledge she has about Andrea Leach. 'Isn't she part of some right-wing, anti-immigration party?'

'Not part of it,' Sarah says. 'She *is* it. They're a new party, not high profile yet. Although if Andrea has her way, that's going to change. They call themselves the Progress Party. Andrea's their figurehead. The money and brains behind it is her partner, a man called Roger Constantin.

'The party's got some pretty shocking policies. If Leach and Constantin had their way, we'd send back every single refugee who came into this country. Unfortunately, Scorpio has been given the unpalatable task of helping to raise the profile of Andrea and the Progress Party.'

While Sarah's speaking, Nuala is typing the name Andrea Leach into her computer. She gets millions of results, but the first one is what she needs. It's a link to the Progress Party's website. There, she finds a head and shoulders shot of Andrea. As the image loads, Nuala sees a striking woman in her late forties, possibly a few well-maintained years older. Blonde hair pulled back into a complicated bun. Elaborate gold earrings with a red stone in them and a matching necklace. The jewellery looks expensive, if a little old-fashioned.

'Andrea's approached us about doing a documentary,' Sarah says. 'An in-depth look at her background, her early life and how she became interested in politics. The thing is, Nuala, I think it could be pretty amazing. Say what you like about the woman, she's got huge charisma and will make for a great subject.'

'Fascinating, I'm sure,' Nuala says. 'But what's Andrea Leach got to do with me?'

'Quite a lot, as it happens. You see, she's very keen for us to make the documentary – but on one condition.'

'Which is?'

'She wants you to present it. She insists. She's said if we can't get you, then we can't make the documentary. That's why I'm calling – to ask if you'd like to work on a film about Andrea Leach.'

Chapter 8

The first thing I hear when I step into the house is the rumble of a man's voice, followed by Kath's laughter. Arnie's here. Again. I close the door quietly, hoping to sneak upstairs without either of them noticing I'm home. But apparently it's not my lucky day, because I'm halfway through taking my shoes off when Kath calls my name.

'Clare? Is that you?'

Who else would it be? I don't say that, of course. I shout out a hello and cross to the kitchen where the voices are coming from. It smells of garlic and spices and roast chicken, a delicious combination that makes my tummy rumble so loud I'm sure they can both hear it.

Kath is sitting at the table, sipping from a glass of red wine. Arnie is standing by the oven. He's wearing Kath's navy apron and it makes him look silly because it's far too small for him.

'Come and sit down,' Kath says, beaming at me like it's just great that we're all here together. 'Arnie's cooking dinner for us. Moroccan roast chicken with couscous.'

I'm starving, but I'd rather eat my own arm than have to sit here with them. But when I tell Kath I'm going to make myself a sandwich and eat in my room, she won't have it.

'Your diet is atrocious, Clare. A home-cooked meal is what you need after a busy day. Come on, have some dinner and a glass of wine. I won't take no for an answer.'

I bite the inside of my cheek, hard enough to make it bleed. I want to scream at Kath to leave me in peace, but I don't because I know she means well and also because I don't want to annoy her. This is her house, after all, and she can kick me out any time she wants to. So I force myself to smile and I sit down beside her and take the glass of wine that she pours for me. It looks like blood but smells like fresh cherries. I don't like the taste of wine but I like the way it makes me feel, softening the hard edges of the anxiety that never leaves me.

'A Moroccan Syrah,' Kath says, like I'm supposed to understand what that means. 'To go with our chicken. Arnie bought me a case of it, so drink up. There's plenty more where that came from.'

As it turns out, the dinner isn't as bad as I'd thought it would be. The food is proper delicious and, after a few glasses of the Moroccan Syrah, I feel looser, more relaxed than I've done in ages. There are only two things that stop me enjoying the meal more. The first is Arnie, who keeps firing questions at me like I'm a contestant in a game show. The second is the amount of effort it takes to not eat the food too quickly.

Soon after I moved in with Jasper, he told me that I didn't eat like a normal person. I ate too fast, he said, like I was scared someone else would eat my food if I didn't clear my plate as quickly as possible. According to Jasper, the way I ate was disgusting, more like a pig than a human. I never told him that this was because, when we lived on the farm, we only had fifteen minutes to eat our one meal of the day. If you didn't finish your food within that time, it was your own hard luck.

Ever since Jasper pointed it out to me, I've tried to change the way I eat. When I'm with other people, I try to match my eating with theirs. Kath eats really slowly, so I do the same – making sure I'm the last person to finish, not the first.

'How did you end up in Sheffield?' Arnie asks, as I'm scooping the last forkful of couscous and chicken into my mouth.

'Dunno,' I say, once I've swallowed the food down. 'Just sort of drifted here, I suppose.'

'But your accent,' he says, waving his fork at me. 'You sound like a southerner.'

'Clare grew up in Hereford,' Kath says.

'Really?' Arnie frowns. 'Funny, I wouldn't have said that's a Hereford accent.'

'When did you become an expert on accents?' Kath asks, smiling.

'I worked with a bloke from Hereford a few years back,' Arnie says. 'When he spoke, you'd swear he hailed from the West Country. But I can't hear any trace of that when Clare speaks.'

I don't know what to say to that so I stay quiet.

'Well, I'm from Wales and most people wouldn't guess from the way I speak,' Kath says.

'Fair point,' Arnie says, after a pause where I think he's going to disagree with her. 'So tell me, Clare. What's Hereford like?'

'It's okay.'

I've never actually been to Hereford, but I've read about it on the internet just so I'm able to answer questions like this. I give Arnie a load of information about the town until his eyes start to glaze over.

'How about you?' I ask him then. 'Where are you from?'

'Me?' He raises his eyebrows, like the question has surprised him. 'I'm a Mancunian, born and bred. Lived in and around Manchester most of my life until I retired last year. Thirty-five years with the police. I didn't know what to do with myself when I left the job. You need a focus after you retire. I found it almost impossible to fill my days when I first stopped working.'

'It's hard, isn't it?' Kath smiles at him with such fondness I feel something cold and hard wrap itself around my heart. I don't want her to like him the way she seems to. I wonder how she can't see what I do: that this man is dangerous.

'Especially at the beginning,' Arnie says. 'Over time you adjust and things get easier. I'll tell you something, Clare. If it wasn't for podcasts, I really don't know how I'd have got through those first few months. I live alone, and there were days that went by when I had no one to speak to. I listened to so many podcasts you wouldn't believe it. True crime ones, in particular. Something to do with my background as a copper, I guess, but I couldn't get enough of those true crime podcasts.'

Somehow, I manage to push my chair back, stand up and tell them both I'm not feeling well so I'm going to lie down. Kath says something as I leave, but I can't hear the words because Arnie's voice is repeating, over and over in my head, getting louder and louder until it's all I can hear.

As I leave the room, I imagine his eyes boring into my back, and by the time I'm upstairs lying on my bed, all the noise inside my head has narrowed down to a single thought that I cannot shift: *he knows who I am.*

Chapter 9

The meeting with Andrea takes place a week later in a hotel near Tower Bridge. It's one of those characterless chain hotels that have cropped up all over the country in recent years. At eleven o'clock on a Wednesday morning, there is only a handful of people in the bar. A couple of businessmen in dark suits sit opposite each other at a large table. They each have a laptop open in front of them, and are engrossed in whatever is on their screens. It's impossible to judge if the men are actually together, or just two strangers who happen to be sitting at the same table.

The only other person in the room is a woman sitting near the back of the bar. Nuala recognises her immediately from the pictures she's seen on the internet. Andrea Leach, leader of the nascent right-wing Progress Party.

Nuala has spent hours looking up everything she could find about Andrea. Which, given the woman's status, is surprisingly little. Another surprise is how much the real woman resembles the photos Nuala has seen online. Until this morning, she has assumed those glossy images have been airbrushed. Now, as she crosses the bar to where Andrea is sitting, she doubts that assessment.

At fifty-three, Andrea Leach is still a beautiful woman. Tall and elegant, with blonde hair scooped into a complicated knot at the back of her neck, she is dressed in a silk blouse and a fitted navy skirt that ends just below the top of her knee-high black boots. Nuala is pretty sure she recognises the boots from the Style section of the *Guardian*. If she's right, they're Christian

Louboutin and retail at around £1,200. She makes a note to look for the distinctive red sole later.

Nuala took a long time choosing her own outfit for this meeting. Black skinny jeans with white ankle boots and a slouchy turtleneck jumper that had seemed a good choice at the time but now makes her feel bulky and awkward in comparison to this woman's feline sleekness.

'Nuala,' Andrea purrs, smiling as she stands up and extends her hand. 'I'm so very glad you agreed to meet me.'

'The pleasure's all mine,' Nuala says, shoving up the sleeve of her jumper before reaching out to shake Andrea's hand.

'Very kind of you to say so. Shall we get started?'

They sit down, Nuala spotting the red sole of the boot when Andrea elegantly crosses her legs.

'Drink?' Andrea asks, waving the waiter over with a flick of her wrist.

'Sparkling water,' Nuala says. 'Thanks.'

Andrea orders their drinks, water for Nuala and a green tea for her.

'So,' she says as the waiter walks away, 'you know why I want to meet you?'

'You're interested in working with me on your documentary,' Nuala says.

'But do you know why?'

'Sarah told me it was because you liked my podcast.'

Andrea frowns. 'Like is such a lazy word. No, Nuala. I didn't *like* your podcast. I thought it was a shining example of investigative journalism at its best. I don't listen to many podcasts, but I was having problems sleeping towards the end of last year and a friend recommended *Black Valley Farm*. I listened to the first episode and was instantly hooked. I can't say it helped with my insomnia, because it was impossible to fall asleep while I was listening. How very clever of you to solve the crime the way you did.'

It wasn't clever, although Nuala can hardly tell her that. So she smiles instead and mumbles a thank you.

'As you know,' Andrea says, 'I didn't grow up in this country, so I wasn't familiar with the story. But that didn't take away from my enjoyment. Not one bit.'

'You're Australian, right?' Nuala asks, although she already knows the answer. Andrea grew up in the remote Australian outback. No neighbours for miles around, she was homeschooled and rarely saw other people apart from her parents.

'Yes, although I left when I was seventeen and never returned. England has been my home for longer than Australia ever was.'

That explains the accent, Nuala thinks. So far, she hasn't picked up even the slightest trace of an Australian twang.

'Ah, here are our drinks,' Andrea says, nodding at the waiter walking towards them. 'Excellent.'

The two women fall silent while the waiter places their drinks on the table. As soon as he's gone, Andrea leans forward and looks at Nuala intently.

'How did you do it, Nuala?'

'What do you mean?' Nuala feels uncomfortable, even though she should have expected Andrea to ask about the podcast. It's why she's here, after all.

'How did you find that woman when the police had no luck tracing anyone who'd lived on the farm?'

'I got lucky, I guess.' Nuala scoops the slice of lemon out of her glass and places it on a paper napkin, taking as long as she can to avoid making eye contact with the other woman. 'Plus, you know, a lot of time had passed since the original investigation. That made it easier for her to talk to me.'

'Yet she disappeared again so soon after speaking to you,' Andrea says. 'I suspect you kept in touch, but you're protecting her. Am I right?'

'No.' Nuala shakes her head. 'I really don't know what happened to her.'

'It's all right.' Andrea laughs. 'I get it. You're doing what any good journalist would do. You're protecting your source, and

I admire that. To hell with the police, anyway. If they'd done their job properly first time around, there wouldn't have been any need for your podcast. Although I do hope that maybe one day you'll trust me enough to tell me everything.'

'I didn't realise I was here to talk about the podcast,' Nuala says, doing her best not to sound too defensive. Briefly, it crosses her mind that Andrea Leach might be *truthfinder* before she realises how ridiculous that is. Her paranoia is making her distrust everyone she's encountered since getting those strange messages.

'But the podcast is the reason I'm so keen to work with you,' Andrea says. 'After listening to it, I knew you were the ideal person for the documentary. The level of investigation you applied is exactly what I'm looking for. You see, Nuala, many of my detractors believe there are dark secrets lurking in my past. They're wrong about that, but the more I deny it the more convinced they are that I'm hiding something. Which is why I thought of you when my team proposed the idea of a documentary. With you involved, no one can accuse me of covering anything up.'

Nuala nods, like she understands, although she isn't sure she does. She doesn't know much about politics, but she knows enough to understand that no politician in their right mind would be comfortable with every aspect of their past being made public. It makes Nuala wonder if Andrea has some other motivation for making this documentary.

'I'm going to give you carte blanche, Nuala. Full access to every area of my life, and full editorial control of the end product. We'll spend as much time together as you think you'll need, and I will answer any questions you want to ask me. I will never lie to you, or try to hide the truth in any way. How does that sound?'

'It sounds great,' Nuala says. 'Although, I have to say, as much as I'd love to work with you, are you sure you've thought through the implications of making a documentary like this?'

Andrea frowns. 'What do you mean?'

'We live in a world of cancel culture,' Nuala says. 'You might think there's nothing in your past you're ashamed about, or you want to hide. But what if I decide to include something you don't like?'

'I've told you,' Andrea says, 'you'll have full editorial control.'

Bullshit, Nuala thinks. She's only been here a short while but it's long enough to know that this is an intelligent woman she's dealing with. If Nuala finds something dark in Andrea Leach's past, there is no way on God's earth it will make it into the final documentary. On the other hand, a job is a job and right now Nuala's in no position to turn down work. Especially work that has the potential to lead to more work. Because if she makes the documentary and it's a success, who knows what doors that will open for her?

'Don't you see?' Andrea continues. 'This documentary is the only way of proving that there's nothing in my life I don't want people to know about.'

'What if I don't believe you?'

Andrea laughs. She has a good laugh, Nuala thinks. She throws her head back and lets rip a big peal of uninhibited joy that's infectious. Nuala feels the corners of her lips twitch and, before she can stop herself, her face breaks into a big, goofy grin that completely kills the cool, professional demeanour she'd been aiming for at the start of the meeting.

'This is the famous Nuala Fox honesty I've read about,' Andrea says, when she finally stops laughing. 'Oh come on, Nuala. Don't look so surprised. You're not the only one who's done her research. You lost your job at Scorpio because you weren't afraid to speak the truth.'

'I lost my job,' Nuala says, 'because my boss was a Grade A arsehole and I made the mistake of telling him what I thought of him.'

'What was it about him that made him an arsehole?'

'Where to begin? He was a bully, who treated people appallingly. He took credit for other people's work all the time. He was lazy, self-centred, opinionated. And a total sleaze.'

She stops speaking, aware too late that she's probably said too much. But to her relief, Andrea looks delighted at this outburst.

'Men are the inferior to women in every way,' she tells Nuala. 'Most of them don't realise this, of course. But it's the truth. I would never trust a man to work with me on the documentary. Even before I found you, I knew that only a woman could do this the way I wanted it to be done.'

'What way is that?'

'With intelligence and integrity.'

She has the most amazing blue eyes, Nuala thinks. Dark blue, almost indigo. It's difficult not to feel mesmerised when they're looking deep into your own eyes.

After reading about Andrea and her politics, Nuala hadn't expected to like the woman. The Progress Party stands for everything Nuala thinks is wrong with this country that's become her adopted home. It's right-wing, inward-looking, painfully patriotic. And disgustingly racist. Although if you weren't paying attention, it would be easy enough to miss the underlying ethos of the party from the information on their website. The language there is warm and inclusive. A mission statement on the party's homepage speaks about 'creating a Britain for everyone'. There are plenty of images of diverse faces, men and women of all races and ethnicities, including a few token photos of people in wheelchairs.

Yet when Nuala dug down into interviews with its founders, Andrea Leach and her partner Roger Constantin, their agenda became clearer. The Progress Party, it turns out, believes in 'old-fashioned values'. Its members are 'pro-marriage', 'pro-life' and are united in their desire to 'create a Britain with equal opportunities for British people, in a country where everyone can thrive'.

In Nuala's opinion, 'pro-marriage' is a euphemism for a range of prejudices, including sexism, homophobia, and the outdated idea of a woman's place being firmly in the home instead of the workplace. 'Pro-life' means anti-abortion and 'a Britain with equal opportunities for British people' is another way of saying 'a Britain that blocks immigration so that British jobs can be done by British people'.

Despite knowing all of this, here she is smiling while the memory of Andrea's laugh tinkles in her ears, and wanting nothing more than to get to the heart of this complex and compelling woman.

'After meeting you, I'm even more certain than I was before,' Andrea says. 'You're exactly who I need to work with me on this.'

She leans across the table and takes one of Nuala's hands in both of hers.

'So what do you say, Nuala? Will you take the job?'

She rubs the top of Nuala's hand with a thumb, in a way that feels weirdly – and uncomfortably – seductive. A lump appears in Nuala's throat and she can feel the hot flush of heat on her cheeks. Resisting the urge to fan her face with her free hand, she forces herself to smile instead.

'Of course,' she says.

'Good.' Andrea smiles and a tiny bird flutters inside Nuala's chest. 'We're going to make history, you and I. Just you wait and see.'

Chapter 10

Nuala Fox has a sing-songy voice that makes her sound super happy, even when she's describing what happened at the farm. *Black Valley Farm* is the first podcast she's made. According to the information on her website, she currently has several other ideas 'in development', whatever that means.

Episode one begins, like all the episodes, with a beautiful piece of music – a haunting combination of lonesome voices and a piano keyboard. From reading the credits, I know it's the opening chords to a song called '29' by Run River North, an American/Korean folk rock band.

As the music fades out, Nuala starts speaking.

> Hello and welcome to Black Valley Farm, a podcast that takes a fresh look at the murders of nine people at a remote Lincolnshire farmhouse. My name is Nuala Fox and, over the course of these eight episodes, I'll explore the lives of the victims and why they were killed. I discover a new witness in the case, and I re-examine the evidence against the main suspect, a woman known only as Lydia.

It's still strange, even now, to think of myself like that – as a suspect, or a fugitive. But that's who I've become. A woman who has spent the last ten years hiding, because I'm terrified of what will happen if anyone realises who I really am.

I imagine most people listening to this podcast are familiar with what happened at Black Valley Farm. For those of you that might not know, here's a brief recap:

Nine years ago, a hiker called George Fisher came across a remote farmhouse situated midway up a hill in the beautiful, rolling countryside of the Lincolnshire Wolds. Earlier that day, George had run out of water. When he saw the farm in the distance, he decided to drop in and ask if they'd refill his flask.

Later, George would tell police he had a premonition that something was wrong as he approached the farmhouse. He described an eerie stillness in the air, and he couldn't shake off a feeling of dread. The closer he got to the farmhouse, the stronger the feeling grew.

Should he have turned back? Maybe. But if he had, who knows how many more weeks would have passed before the bodies of those poor souls were discovered? Because instead of finding someone who could refill his flask, George Fisher discovered bodies. Nine of them, to be precise. Four women, one man and four children – a girl and boy in their early teens, and a younger boy and girl. Eight of the victims were killed in the fire that destroyed the building. The ninth victim, a woman, had been stabbed.

Nuala stops speaking, her voice replaced by George Fisher's, who describes in great detail how he found the bodies. When he's finished speaking, Nuala picks up the story again.

The subsequent forensic fire investigation concluded the fire had been started deliberately. It was a crime that shook the nation. Yet, somehow,

> the police have never charged anyone for these
> brutal murders.

I hit pause, giving myself a moment to let the memories roll in. I see them as they were back then, especially the younger children, Robert and Daisy. He had a mop of black curly hair and a freckled face. Daisy had turned seven a week earlier. She had wispy blonde hair and spoke with a lisp. She followed me everywhere. In the weeks after the killings, I remember the shock. The gradual realisation that they were dead, and it was all my fault.

I've listened to the podcast so often I know most of it off by heart. Yet I keep listening to it, again and again, hoping I'll find something I've missed. I'm not even sure, exactly, what I'm listening for, but the nagging need to know more never leaves me.

The next part of this episode is an interview with Colin Burke, the detective who led the investigation into the deaths at the farm. But I don't want to listen to any more. Not tonight. So I shut down the podcast and start playing around with my make-up, listening to Taylor Swift, who is a legend and I won't ever like anyone who doesn't love her music the way I do.

After forty minutes, I'm bored of looking at myself in the mirror. My mind drifts back to Nuala's podcast and, suddenly, I get an idea. Arnie told me he was a police detective. He said he worked in Manchester but he didn't say he'd never worked anywhere else too. What if he spent some time in Lincolnshire? Or maybe he was called in to help with the investigation. There are loads of possibilities and, if Arnie was involved in that investigation, then maybe that's why he's here in Sheffield. He saw the video, remembered me from his time as a detective and, somehow, he's managed to track me down. It's not a perfect explanation for why he's so interested in me, but it's the only one I can think of that makes any sense.

I grab my phone and open the internet, searching for 'Colin Burke' and 'Black Valley Farm'. The first result is a news story a few days after the discovery of the bodies. The story has three photos with it: the familiar one of me; a photo of the burnt-out remains of the farm; and one of Detective Inspector Colin Burke standing outside a flat-fronted building speaking to a group of journalists.

It's not the first time I've seen this photo. I saw it when the story was first published, and I've looked at it dozens of times since on Nuala Fox's website. But I've never looked at it to search for a likeness between Colin Burke and Kath's new friend. Looking at the photo now, it's clear that Arnie and Colin aren't the same person. Colin Burke is shorter than Arnie, and broader. And he's got a kind face with brown eyes that look sort of sad.

I spend the next hour searching through every single photo of the police investigation. Arnie isn't in any of them, but that doesn't mean he wasn't there. I know, because I've already looked him up, that Arnie isn't lying about his past. There are several news stories about different police investigations in Manchester where his name is mentioned. A few of them have photos of him too, and the man in those photos is definitely him, even though he's lost a bit of weight since then and he's not bald in the photos like he is now. But there's nothing about him working on any case in Lincolnshire.

When I'm finished, I look him up on social media. I can find plenty of people called Arnie Cummins, but only one who might be him. It's a Facebook account, private so I can't see any posts, but with a profile photo that looks a bit like Arnie, although it was clearly taken a few years ago. Unless I'm willing to create an account and send him a friend request, I won't know for sure if it's him or not. But I'm not going to risk that, so there's not much more I can do for now.

I'm tired, but I know I won't sleep yet. My mind is too busy with too many thoughts bouncing around inside my head. So I do what I do every evening since Kath showed me that video, I scroll through Nuala Fox's social media accounts. She's on

Facebook, LinkedIn, Twitter and Instagram. I check all of these several times a day, because even though it's been a year since the podcast first came out, Nuala is still promoting it. And I know for sure that if Nuala gets to see the video or the story in the *Sheffield Herald*, she'll jump on it as the perfect excuse to post another tweet about how brilliant her podcast is and why everyone should listen to it.

At first, I don't see anything interesting. I'm about to log off when a tweet from earlier catches my attention:

> Exciting news today. Can't breathe a word about it yet until it's confirmed but I'm about to start working on something VERY BIG INDEED. Watch this space, peeps!

Fingers of ice down trickle down my spine. Maybe it's nothing to do with me, but how could it be anything else? This is exactly what I've been so scared would happen. Nuala Fox has seen the video. She's seen it and she knows where I am, and she's coming to find me.

Chapter 11

The next day, Nuala Fox's big news is all I can think about. In my mind, it's got all mixed up with Arnie Cummins and the video of me on the *Sheffield Herald*'s website. I exhaust myself trying to see how it's all connected. By the time I get home from work that evening, my anxiety levels are spiking and there's a tightness in my chest that won't go away no matter how many deep breaths I take. Thankfully, the house is empty. Which means I can go into the kitchen and make myself a toasted cheese sandwich, instead of hiding away upstairs.

While I eat, I scroll through Nuala's Instagram and listen to music. I've got my earphones in, volume up loud, Lana Del Rey singing about chemtrails and waitressing in a white dress. There's still nothing on Nuala's social media feeds about her 'exciting news'. It feels like she's dragging it out on purpose, and I hate her for it. Frustrated with the lack of anything new on Instagram or Twitter, I go to Nuala's website.

She's got photos of me here, including a few Jasper gave her when she interviewed him. Of course, he only showed Nuala some of the photos he took of me. If she'd seen the rest, she might have realised the sort of man he really is. It makes my stomach twist until it hurts when I think that he probably still has those photos. Which is why I try not to think about Jasper or the photos. It's easier that way.

If it wasn't for Nuala's podcast, I might have been able to push my memories of Jasper to the back of my mind. But it's impossible to do that because Jasper is one of the people Nuala interviewed when she was making the podcast. In the interview, he made out that all he'd done was help me. That's a lie, because Jasper has never wanted to help anyone except himself.

He found me the day after I left the farm. I was sitting in the doorway of an empty building, confused and scared, when a man came over and started speaking to me. He asked me if I was okay and, when I didn't answer, he said if I spoke to him he'd buy me something to eat.

At the time, I thought he was being kind. I didn't realise that he'd already seen there was something wrong with me. He'd spotted it immediately. It was why he started speaking to me. Men like Jasper are only interested in women who are broken. Because it's easier to control a broken woman.

I remember how terrified I was that day. The disorientation and the confusion, the absolute terror. My senses were in overdrive as I tried to navigate this new and alien world. Jasper asked me my name and, without even thinking about it, I told him I was called Lydia.

He took me back to his flat. A dirty, cramped space with unfamiliar smells that, over time, I started to recognise as a mix of the 'doobies' he smoked and the takeaway meals he ate. Soon after I moved in, he ordered pizza. I remember that first bite, the explosion of textures and flavours, and wondering if I loved Jasper. This man who'd given me a home and introduced me to music and pizza with double cheese and pepperoni slices,, he seemed like my saviour.

The first time he tried to kiss me, I pulled back. But when he explained that I was being ungrateful, I believed him. I was scared if I didn't do what he wanted he'd tell me to leave. I had nowhere else to go, so I let him kiss me and do everything else he wanted to as well. I didn't like it, but each time it happened I told myself it wasn't too bad. And in a way, it wasn't. Definitely better than the times I'd been with Peter. Jasper could be scary, but living with him was still better than anything I'd known before.

Nuala's website also has a scanned image of the photo that was circulated in the days and weeks after the bodies were discovered. These days, my hair is cut short and dyed brown. I'm older now too, different to the scared teenager in Jasper's photos and the confused girl from the farm. Maybe I look so different that if you put a photo of me as I am now, alongside these ones, you wouldn't automatically think it's the same person.

I open YouTube, find the video and fast-forward to the final frame. I definitely look different here, but is it enough? Possibly, although the birthmark is impossible to miss. What I really need is to see all the photos side by side, so I can compare how I look now to how I did then. I can't do this on my phone, but I could do it on Kath's laptop – which is on the small table by the back door.

The laptop is password protected but Kath's got all her passwords and passcodes written onto Post-it notes she sticks onto the fridge. I get the laptop password off the fridge and type it in.

Within a few seconds, I have three different photos of myself open on Kath's screen. It only takes a few seconds more for me to see that, even in the most recent one, I don't look different enough. Anyone looking at these three photos would be in no doubt it's the same person in each of them.

Depressed, I go into the browser's history settings to delete the searches I've just done. As I'm scanning the list of recently visited sites, I see something that shouldn't be there.

Lana is singing a sad song about blue bannisters and a hole in her heart. The words on the screen blur and merge into each other. I have to blink several times before they come into focus.

Black Valley Farm: search for key witness continues.

It's the headline from an article in the *Guardian*, the only newspaper Kath reads. I remember when that article first came out, five weeks after I ran away. I was living with Jasper and he'd shown me how to use the internet. I spent most of my days sitting in his flat, reading about myself on the iPad he'd stolen soon after I moved in with him.

I click on the link now, and the story fills the screen. There's my face again, half-hidden behind the curtain of blonde hair. The site was visited at 9:35 p.m. yesterday evening. It must have been Arnie. I thought he'd stopped coming around, but it's possible he was here last night and I simply didn't know. I'd gone up to my room early and didn't come back down again. Maybe he's been here more than I've realised.

'Good evening, Clare.'

The voice, too close to my ear, makes me jump and shout out in fright. It's Arnie. He's here in the room, standing behind me. I slam the laptop shut and stand up, moving away from him.

'What are you doing here?'

He doesn't answer. Instead, his hand reaches out and I flinch, thinking he's going to hit me.

'You should be more careful,' he says, touching the earphone in my right ear. 'You'll damage your hearing.'

He steps back from me, just as Kath walks into the room.

'Everything okay?' she asks.

'Fine,' I tell her. 'I was just on my way to bed.'

At the door, I nod goodnight to both of them and get out of there. As I hurry up the stairs, I try to push down the panic that's rising through me but it won't go away. Everything has gone wrong and I don't know how to fix any of it.

Chapter 12

Ten days later, Nuala starts her new job. After dropping Josh at school, she takes the DLR to Lewisham. She's only on the train a few minutes when she receives another message from *truthfinder*.

> If you don't tell the truth, I'll do it for you.

Why now? Nuala wonders. It's been over a week since their last exchange of messages. She's been checking Instagram every day for a reply. Until now, there's been nothing. She types a reply: *Lydia? Is this you?*

She watches the screen for a while, waiting for a reply. When none comes, she puts her phone away. She can't worry about this today. She needs to be calm and focused. She's already stressed because she set off later than she intended. Josh was tired and grumpy and it took an age to get him ready for school. He kept telling her, again and again, about a man he'd seen on the street outside their flat. Three times, he made Nuala go to the window to see if the man was still there. He never was, and it took all of Nuala's powers of persuasion to convince Josh the man had been in his dreams, not really outside the flat.

She closes her eyes, takes some deep breaths and tries to clear her mind. But the Instagram message refuses to budge, *truthfinder*'s words playing on repeat.

What she'd done was stupid, she is well aware of that. She should have listened when Liz tried to talk her out of it, but

Nuala never listened when Liz offered sensible advice. Foolishly, she'd believed that Liz would love her, no matter what. Turned out she was wrong about that and, by the time she realised it, Liz was gone.

It's occurred to Nuala, more than once, that *truthfinder* might be Liz. Except Liz would never stoop to something so underhand. Besides, unlike Nuala, Liz has moved on. These days, she's happily engaged to Trish and living in a converted fisherman's hut on the beach at Dungeness. If it wasn't for Josh, who Liz adores as much as if he was her own child, Nuala and Liz would have lost contact the day Liz moved out.

But even though the rational part of Nuala's brain tells her *truthfinder* has nothing to do with her ex-girlfriend, the stubborn, pig-headed part of her needs to make sure. She takes her phone out again, finds Liz's Instagram profile and sends a quick message, with a link to *truthfinder*'s account. *Is this anything to do with you?* Three seconds later, she regrets sending the message. But when she tries to unsend it, she's too late. Liz has already read it and replied:

WtAf?

Nuala sends another message, apologising. By the time the train is pulling into Lewisham, Liz still hasn't replied. Nuala can hardly blame her.

It's a brisk thirty-minute walk from the station to the Regency house in Blackheath where the Progress Party have their headquarters. Enough time for Nuala to put thoughts of *truthfinder* to the back of her mind, for now at least.

She had assumed she'd be spending the morning with Andrea but, when she arrives at the house, the man who answers the door takes her to see Roger Constantin instead. Nuala recognises Andrea's partner from the photos she's looked at as part of her research, although in real life Roger is taller and wider than he seems in the photos. He's tanned too, a deep orange colour that can only have come from a bottle. His hair – black and, Nuala suspects, also from a bottle – is swept across the crown of his head to hide where he's started to go bald.

'Nuala Fox. Good to meet you, finally.'

As he walks towards her, Nuala's surprised by the strength of her reaction. He's an ugly brute, no doubt about it. But that's not why every cell in her body is recoiling from him. There's a sense of menace about him that's sent the animal part of her brain straight to fight-or-flight mode. With flight winning out. If she didn't need this job as much as she does, she'd turn around and walk out of this room right now.

When she shakes his outstretched hand, his grip is firm and he keeps her hand in his for longer than feels comfortable. Resisting the urge to wipe her palm on her trousers when he finally lets her go, she offers him a smile and manages to tell him she's pleased to meet him.

'Andrea speaks very highly of you,' Roger says, his eyes running up and down the length of her body before finally settling on her face.

'That's good to hear,' Nuala says.

'I prefer to hold judgement until I see what you can do for us.'

'Of course.'

The man's an arse of the highest order. Nuala realises she's going to have to give herself a good talking to several times a day if she's to avoid pissing him off. Because, as Liz liked to point out with irritating frequency, pissing people off is something Nuala excels at. Never more so than when she's doing it on purpose to get under the skin of someone she doesn't like.

'I'm sure as part of your preparation for the documentary you've done your research on both of us,' Roger says. 'So you'll have a clear idea of what the Progress Party stands for.'

Bigotry, racism, sexism.

'I think so, yes.'

'So you'll know that while Andrea is the face of the party, I'm the brains behind the operation.'

Nuala doesn't know that, but smiles and says in that case she looks forward to getting to know Roger as well as Andrea.

'You ought to know I've done my research too.' His eyes drop down, for a fraction of a second, to her breasts before he looks up at her face again.

Nuala clenches her hands into fists, digging her freshly painted fingernails into her palms until she trusts herself to say something other than 'go fuck yourself'.

'I'd expect nothing less,' she says through gritted teeth.

Roger takes a step closer, invading her personal space. As the stink of him clogs her nostrils, cologne and nicotine and an undertone of sweat, it takes all of Nuala's self-control not to spit into his orange face.

'Your politics are not aligned with the goals of our party,' Roger says. 'I've seen some of the crap you've posted on Twitter. If you want to stick this out, you'll need to become a lot more measured about what you say in the public domain.'

'My politics are none of your business,' Nuala says.

He smiles then, for the first time since she's been here. Seeing it is a deeply unsettling experience.

'They are if you want to continue working for me. You're only here because of Andrea. She wanted you for the job and, as you'll discover soon enough, what my beloved wants she tends to get. But don't fool yourself into thinking just because you're her first choice, that gives you some sort of power. Andrea's the subject of your documentary, but I'm funding it. If I decide I don't like you, then I will kick you off this film. From what I know about your career to date, I doubt you'll find it easy to get work anywhere else, will you?'

Before Nuala can tell this over-tanned piece of shit that she'd rather spend the rest of her life sticking pins in her eyes than stay another moment in this room with him, the door opens behind her and Andrea appears.

'Nuala, you're here! How wonderful. And I see you two have already introduced yourselves.'

Roger jumps back from Nuala, like he's been caught doing something he shouldn't. If Andrea notices, she doesn't react. She floats towards them, smiling delightedly at them both.

'Darling.' Roger puts his hands on Andrea's shoulders and kisses her on the cheek. 'Nuala was just telling me how thrilled she is to be working with us.'

'I hope you were being kind to her.' Andrea rolls her eyes at Nuala. 'He can be a bit of a grump sometimes, but don't take it personally. He's like that with everyone. Except me, of course.'

'I was being perfectly charming,' Roger says. 'Isn't that right, Nuala?'

He gives Nuala a big shit-eating grin, daring her to contradict him. But she's had enough time to compose herself, and she stays quiet. At least she has the measure of him, although she's not sure how helpful it is to know he's an utter piece of shit.

He's made it clear he doesn't want her here, and she is in no doubt he'll do all he can to get rid of her. Unless she finds a way of convincing him otherwise. Nuala's never been one to avoid a challenge, but the idea of having to ingratiate herself with a creep like Roger Constantin might be a challenge too far. Even for her.

Chapter 13

Nuala Fox has a new job. That's her exciting news, not the video. She hasn't said what her new job is. I think she's trying to get people to guess. She's posted a few images on Instagram, like little clues, but I haven't been able to work out what they mean. Today, her Instagram story is a photo of her walking down a pretty street with big houses on either side. According to the location tag, the photo was taken in Blackheath in south London. The photo's taken from behind, so I can't see her face. She's wearing a yellow coat, the colour of fresh buttercups. It's beautiful, and I think how special it would make you feel to walk around with that on.

I should be relieved that Nuala's news has nothing to do with me. But I can't shake off the feeling that something bad is about to happen. I keep going back over what I saw on Kath's laptop. Someone was looking up an old article about the farm. When I first saw it, I assumed it was Arnie. But what if it was Kath? The idea that she knows who I am, that she's been lying to me all along, just as I've been lying to her, makes me want to throw up.

More than once, I've almost asked Kath straight out about it. But I never do in case she tells me something I don't want to hear. Because the simple truth is, I love living with Kath and I'd be sad to leave. I can barely remember my father, but I know he was the reason I moved to the farm with my mother and brother. After the farm, there was Jasper's flat in Skegness and then the room I rented in London. When I left those places, all I felt was relief.

Tonight, after eating my dinner, I feel restless so I tell Kath I'm going for a walk. There's no moon, and the grey mist that hung over the city all day has been replaced by a murky blackness.

I like walking at night-time, looking through the windows of houses and imagining the people who live in them. Families with a mother who bakes cakes and a father who works in an office and takes his tie off as soon as he comes home, before lifting up one of his children and tickling them under their chin as he asks how their day has been. In the kitchen, his wife is cooking dinner and she has already poured him a glass of red wine which she hands to him as he kisses her on the cheek and tells her that the food smells delicious.

I have no idea if this is how people really live. For all I know, everyone else has lives that are as grey and lonely as mine. But it makes me sad to think of a whole world full of lonely people all hiding secrets and not trusting anyone they meet. So I let myself believe in these other lives instead.

When I've had enough of looking at other people, I put my earphones in and play an episode of Nuala's podcast. Weirdly, this is the only thing that distracts me from all the noise inside my head at the moment. It's like the podcast is the only real thing in my life and everything else is fake. I know that sounds stupid, but it's the only way to explain how I feel.

Welcome back to the second episode of Black Valley Farm, the podcast that sets out to explore the deaths of nine people in a remote Lincolnshire farmhouse eight years ago.

In the previous episode, I spoke with Detective Inspector Colin Burke, who gave me some background information on the farm and the people living there. He told me that Black Valley Farm was owned by a man called Peter Foster, later identified as one of the victims. Four of the victims, including forty-year-old Peter, were identified in the weeks following the discovery of the bodies. The other five victims have never been identified.

Peter Foster's ex-wife told the police that her husband had walked out on his family six years earlier. He'd left her for a woman called Rosemary who he'd fallen madly in love with. Mrs Foster wasn't able to provide any other information about this woman and, despite the police's best efforts, very little is still known about her.

However, we know that several of the women who were living on the farm had been reported missing by their families. Before they disappeared, these women had all been in abusive relationships. The police think the women were lured to the farm by Rosemary and Peter, who promised them a safe place to live.

Over the years, various stories have circulated about the people on the farm. The most common one is that they were involved in some sort of cult or religious sect, with Peter Foster as its leader. As you'll hear, during the following episodes, the truth is something very different.

Were we a cult? I don't think so. If we were, it certainly wasn't one with Peter leading it. There was only one person who controlled things on the farm, and that was Mother – the woman Nuala Fox calls Rosemary. She was in charge of everything: how we lived, what we did every day, what we ate and when we ate, where we were allowed to go and who we were allowed to talk to. She said we were a family, although I know now that other families are nothing like that.

Chapter 14

Nuala slides into the car beside Andrea and pulls the door closed. The car is plush and air-conditioned, a welcome relief after the mugginess outside.

'Where are we going?' she asks Andrea.

She'd been in Lewisham, buying food for dinner, when Andrea had called.

'I'll pick you up by the station in five minutes,' Andrea said, when Nuala told her where she was. 'Don't be late.'

Nuala had picked up the icy tone in Andrea's voice. It's only her fourth day on the job and she's already managed to piss off her new boss. Nuala was late for work this morning, although it hadn't been by choice. Josh had woken up with a fever, too ill to go to school. Nuala had had to arrange emergency childcare in the form of an agency nanny she couldn't really afford before coming to work. When she'd called to explain why she was running late, Andrea had made it clear she didn't approve of mothers who struggled to balance the conflicting demands of family and work.

'It's why I never had children of my own,' Andrea says now, as the car pulls away from the kerb. 'I've always felt it's not possible to be a good mother and be my best self at work. I really don't know how women like you do it.'

Nuala wants to tell Andrea that it takes two people to have a baby and it shouldn't be a given that it's always the woman who's expected to give up work once the child is born. She manages to keep her mouth shut, but knows there's a limit to how many times she'll be able to do this.

'If you're not able to keep your home life separate from your working life, perhaps we need to review things.' Andrea's voice is laced with irritation. 'I don't want to work with someone who can't put their heart and soul into this documentary.'

Resisting the urge to tell Andrea to go fuck herself, Nuala puts on her best smile and says there's really nothing to worry about.

'I'm every bit as committed to this as you are, Andrea. I promise you.'

'Good.'

'So,' Nuala says, after a moment. 'Where are we off to?'

'A meeting with a local community group,' Andrea replies. 'They're keen to hear our plans for tackling poverty, unemployment and rising crime. Problems faced by communities around the country, which conventional politics simply are not addressing.'

Nuala knows that the Progress Party has clear views on how to address issues like this. She's spent hours watching videos on an alt-tech video-sharing platform called YourTruth, which brands itself as a 'free speech' alternative to other, more conventional platforms.

The Progress Party has its own YourTruth channel and a shockingly high number of followers. Nuala has watched every one of the videos, most of them hate-laced speeches from Andrea, claiming her party is going to 'reclaim Britain for the British'. The way to do this, apparently, is by embracing traditional values such as marriage and family. Basically, Nuala reflects as the car crawls through south London's suburban streets, the party wants to recreate the country as it used to be a hundred years ago. A time when women didn't work, there was no contraception, and there were few non-white, non-Christian people living here.

Given their stance on the nuclear family, Nuala's amazed Andrea hasn't had more to say about her own status as a single mother. She suspects Andrea wouldn't be so reticent with her views if she knew about Nuala's fluid sexuality, a topic Nuala sincerely hopes will never come up for discussion.

Andrea has fallen quiet, and Nuala grabs the opportunity to check Instagram. Still nothing back from *truthfinder*. She doesn't know what's worse: getting another threatening message, or waiting for one. The last message she sent is marked as 'Seen' but, so far, *truthfinder* hasn't deigned to reply. Nuala taps her screen, contemplating sending another message, when she's interrupted by Andrea.

'You spend far too much time looking at your phone, Nuala. What on earth could be so important you have to check it every few seconds?'

'Sorry.' Nuala shuts down Instagram and puts the phone back in her bag.

'It's not good for your brain,' Andrea says. 'This obsession with screen time is why so many young people suffer from attention disorders these days. I sincerely hope you don't do that in front of your child. It's a terrible example to be setting him.'

'I'm sure you're right,' Nuala says brightly. 'Thanks for that, Andrea.'

Andrea looks at her as if she's trying to work out whether Nuala's being a smart-arse, because she must realise that Nuala's not interested in getting parenting advice from someone with no children of her own. In the end, she simply nods before turning her head so she's looking out the window instead of at Nuala.

Thankfully, Andrea loses interest in talking after that and the rest of the journey passes in peaceful silence. Fifteen minutes later, the car turns into an estate of flat-roofed, prefabricated bungalows and stops in front of a run-down brick building. A sign outside proclaims this dilapidated structure to be Craggy Vale Community Hall. Nuala climbs out of the car and looks around, intrigued. She had no idea estates like this existed.

'Cheap, post-war housing,' Andrea says, walking around the car to stand beside Nuala. 'Built for families who lost their homes due to bombing. Most of these estates have been erased, the land sold to private contractors. But this one has managed to avoid that fate. The buildings might look ugly, but there's a sense of community in a place like this that you won't find in many other parts of the city.'

There's a noticeboard beside the door, with a poster pinned to it announcing *An Audience with Andrea Leach*. The poster shows a photo of Andrea standing at a podium, her arm raised in a gesture that looks – to Nuala – uncomfortably like a Hitler salute. Beneath the photo is the Progress Party's logo, the words 'Britain for the British' in bold red text.

Another car, identical to the one Andrea and Nuala had been in, pulls to a halt beside them. As the doors open, Nuala recognises the two men inside. Dressed in dark suits that stretch across their overly muscled bodies, these men are Andrea's bodyguards. Nuala has never spoken to them. She doesn't even know their names, but wherever Andrea goes, her two goons are never far behind.

A sense of menace emanates from them. They're tall, well over six foot, with broad chests and thick shoulders. They both have completely shaved heads. To Nuala's eye, they're grotesque stereotypes.

'Where's Roger?' Andrea asks them.

'Right behind us,' one of them replies.

They hear him before they see him, the deep-throated growl of a motorbike roaring towards them. A Harley-Davidson, Nuala realises, as the bike appears in the distance, clouds of dust trailing behind it. As the machine screeches to a halt inches from where they're standing, Nuala's stomach constricts. She hasn't seen Roger since her first day. If today's encounter is anything like that, it's not going to be much fun.

Dismounting the bike, Roger pulls his helmet off and hands it to one of the bodyguards.

'These are the first things to go when we get into power,' he says. 'Takes most of the pleasure away from having a ride if you can't feel the wind in your hair when you're on it.'

He looks at Nuala.

'You like bikes?'

'I don't know,' she says. 'I've never been on one.'

'You hear that, Andrea?' Roger sounds appalled. 'The girl hasn't lived. Why'd you let her come in the car with you when I could have given her a lift?'

'You don't have a spare helmet,' Andrea says.

'So?'

'So, I'm not going to risk letting my assistant get arrested and have her face splashed all over the news, thank you.'

'She's your assistant now?'

Normally, the fact he's speaking about Nuala as if she isn't here would annoy her. But she's curious enough to hear Andrea's answer to his question that she barely notices.

'Not yet.' Andrea beams at Nuala. 'But I'm hoping after she's made her documentary, we might be able to persuade her to stick around. I've rather enjoyed her company these last few days.'

An unexpected rush of warmth fills Nuala's chest. She's pathetic. She should abhor Andrea and everything she stands for, yet here she is blushing like some stupid schoolgirl with a crush just because Andrea has paid her a compliment.

'Let's get inside.' Roger pulls up the sleeve of his leather biker jacket and makes a show of checking the time on his oversized Rolex. 'Should have a good turnout this afternoon. We've been canvassing hard in this area, lots of support for the party in a place like this.'

Entering the hall, they're greeted by a roar of applause. A sea of white faces turns to look at them. Andrea squeezes Nuala's arm, whispers that she'll see her afterwards, and moves along the aisle towards the small stage at the top of the hall. Nuala looks around, unsure what she's meant to do. The hall is crowded and she can't see anywhere to sit down. Eventually, she sidles towards the back and leans against the wall behind the rows of chairs.

She watches Andrea walk onto the stage, her arms raised above her head as she beams out at the adoring crowd. She's mesmerising. They're not due to start filming the documentary for another few weeks, but Nuala knows what she's witnessing is TV gold.

In her mind, the documentary's already taking shape. The ninety-minute programme will start and end with a scene exactly like this. Andrea Leach, glorious and impossible not to look at, standing on a stage in front of an adoring crowd. After the opening scene, they'll cut to the bleak and dusty Australian outback where Andrea lived until the age of seventeen, when her parents were killed in a freak accident and she found herself alone in the world. The rest of the programme will chart Andrea's rise, from those inauspicious beginnings to moments like this.

The applause gradually fades and people start sitting down. Andrea crosses the stage to the podium. She straightens her back, gazes out at the crowd, smiling. Nuala waits for the speech to begin. But something's wrong because the smile has gone and Andrea's staring down the hall towards Nuala. Her face has turned white and her lips have tightened into a narrow, straight line. She looks very, very angry.

At first Nuala thinks it must be because she isn't sitting down. Then she sees there's someone else still standing too. A man two rows in front of Nuala. It's him Andrea is looking at, not Nuala. There's a tension in the room now, a fizzing like electricity that only these two people seem to understand.

Abruptly, Andrea looks away from the man and gives the slightest – almost imperceptible – nod of her head. It's an instruction that's acted on immediately. The two bodyguards start moving down the hall towards the man. They move fast, but the man is faster. He pushes his way past the people sitting alongside him and races down the aisle.

He passes Nuala, then pauses. His head turns and he looks directly at her. Something flashes across his face – surprise, or anger; it's so brief she has no time to work out which it is – and he's gone, disappearing out the door at the back of the hall.

Nuala chases after him, needing to know who he is and where he fits into Andrea's story. But when she pushes open the door of the community hall and steps outside, there's nothing to see except rows of flat-roofed bungalows either side of a dust track road.

Chapter 15

There's an atmosphere in this place. Excitement mixed with something that intensifies Leo's underlying sense of unease. The people in this room are angry. He can feel it, in the overheated air and the low rumble of voices. Every single person in here is white. Leo knows, because understanding demographics is a key part of his business, that less than 40 per cent of London's population identify as White British. You wouldn't think that if you looked around this community hall.

The place is rammed, every available seat taken. Presumably by people who believe in Andrea Leach's populist bullshit. It makes sense, of course, for her to target communities like this one. Here, in this deprived part of south London, surrounded on all sides by streets where the houses sell for well over a million pounds, it's no wonder these people feel life has treated them unfairly.

In the social circles Leo moves in, it's easy to believe London is a liberal, cosmopolitan bubble entirely disconnected from the petty racism and populist politics that seem to be on the rise in so many other parts of the country. But sitting here today, he sees how wrong he and his friends are about that.

He's chosen a seat near the back, close enough so he'll have a clear view when Andrea comes onto the platform that's masquerading as a stage. Far enough from the front to make a quick exit if he has to. After the Brexit vote, Leo's friends and colleagues consoled themselves with the fact that the majority of Londoners had voted to remain. Only five of the city's thirty-three boroughs voted to leave – a tiny minority that in no way reflected voting patterns in other parts of the country.

The problem with this complacency, Leo reflects as he looks around him, is that it entirely ignores the views of those Londoners who actually voted to leave the EU. And when those people are ignored – by those with all the money and all the power – their sense of isolation and exclusion increases. Leaving them ripe for monsters like Andrea Leach to sweep in and exploit their vulnerabilities and weaknesses and petty-minded bigotry to her own ends.

Finding her was a stroke of luck. After he saw her that day at the hotel, Leo finally remembered the name of the man she was with. Roger Constantin. Leo had met him, briefly, at a business lunch last summer. He'd got the distinct impression then that the guy was an asshole and, when Leo did an internet search on Roger, this was confirmed in spades. Because only an utter piece of crap could be behind a political party as odious as this one. When he read about Andrea Leach, he realised he would probably have found her eventually. As it was, her connection to Roger Constantin made Leo's job easier than it might otherwise have been.

There's a hugely overweight woman sitting on his left side, her face shiny with sweat. Leo can smell her when he breathes in, a bitter stench of body odour and stale cigarettes. When she turns to speak to him, he sees that both her top front teeth are missing, giving her a lisp that makes it difficult to understand what she's saying.

'You live on the estate?'

Her tone is friendly enough, but Leo picks up an underlying threat in the question. He doesn't know if that's his own unconscious bias coming out, or if this woman is actually challenging him.

'I don't actually, no.'

'Where you from, then?'

'Barking,' Leo says, picking the name of a deprived borough in east London.

'My sister lives out that way,' the woman says. 'Becontree. You know it?'

'Yeah, of course. Great place.'

'You want a bun?' The woman holds up a plastic box containing a selection of sticky doughnuts.

'No thanks.' Leo smiles, hoping she won't be offended by his refusal to take one.

In the end, he never finds out whether he's annoyed her or not because a subtle shift in atmosphere makes it clear the show's about to start. People around him sit up straighter in their chairs, look at each other with faces full of anticipation and excitement. Like children at Christmastime, Leo thinks. Even though he finds the politics of every single person in this room abhorrent, he feels a sudden rush of sympathy towards them. These people are victims, after all.

The real enemy is Andrea Leach, and politicians like her. Narcissists who exploit the poor and the downtrodden and use their trampled hopes and dreams to further their own self-ambitions. Behind him, he hears the doors swing open. There's a collective intake of breath as heads turn to watch Andrea enter the hall.

As she walks up the central aisle, head high, looking straight ahead like a bride on her wedding day, Leo's stomach clenches with a fear he hasn't felt in a long time. He sees her face in profile as she passes. The straight nose and high cheekbones, the hint of a smile playing at the corner of her mouth.

Her hair is different, dyed platinum blonde and gathered in some sort of bun at the base of her neck. But apart from that, and the barely perceptible pattern of tiny lines at the corners of her eyes, she hasn't changed at all. A fact that does nothing to calm the fluttery fear crawling up his throat.

She's on the stage now and the crowd are going mental. The room feels as if it's going to lift off the ground with the roaring and the clapping and the wild sense of something longed for finally happening. It's almost tempting to get swept up in it all, and maybe he would have if it wasn't for the wave of memories that are rushing towards him too fast and too powerful. Suddenly, he's no longer here in the hall with all these people. He's back there and he's a child again and he's scared and lonely and helpless to change what's happening to him.

No. He cannot let it happen. Not here, not now. He pinches the soft flesh of his inner arm, using the pain to bring him back to the present. Gradually, the feelings fade and he's here in the hall again. He becomes aware of two things at the same time. First, that everyone else has sat back down and there are only two people left standing – him and her. Second, she is staring straight at him and it's clear from the expression on her face that she's recognised him.

In that moment, his fear disappears completely. Replaced with a wild exhilaration. This is what he wanted. It's why he's come to this shitty part of south east London. To show her that he's found her, he's not scared of her, and he's not about to let her get away with this charade.

She looks away, signalling to the two bulked up bodyguards Leo spotted earlier. Time to go. He pushes his way along the row, ignoring the protests as he steps on toes and jostles against bodies too big for the chairs they're sitting in.

As he races towards the door at the back of the hall, he sees something out of the corner of his eye. Not something. Someone. He slows down, looks to his left and sees Nuala Fox staring at him.

Behind him, he hears the bodyguards shouting at him to stop, and the thud of their footsteps getting closer. No time to think about Nuala Fox now, or wonder what she's doing here. He throws himself at the doors. They swing open and he's outside, racing along the dusty road, swerving right and ducking into the narrow alleys that run along the backs of the single-storey, flat-roofed prefabs.

He races through the network of cheap housing, fly-tipping and burnt-out cars until he's out of the estate and onto a main road. There's a bus stop up ahead, a bus indicating to pull out. He runs faster, shouts at the driver to wait.

As he reaches the bus, the doors are already closed. When he bangs on them, nothing happens and Leo thinks the bus will drive off, leaving him here. But at the last moment, the driver rolls his eyes and the doors slide open. Leo jumps in. The bus pulls away from the kerb. Through the back windows, he sees one of the bodyguards running out from the estate then stopping and looking up and down the road.

When there's enough distance between them, and Leo is certain that no one is going to come after him, he takes his phone out and types Nuala Fox's name into his internet browser.

Chapter 16

It's been another bad day and, by the time evening comes around, the chaos of crazy thoughts and the pressure building in my chest has become unbearable. I feel like I'm going to explode and I know there's only one thing that's going to fix this. I get home as quickly as I can, anticipating the sensation of the sharp blade against my skin.

But when I get inside, Kath is in the hall and she says she wants to talk to me. I tell her I need the loo, speaking too fast as I race up the stairs without stopping to take my shoes off first.

Later, I don't know how much time has passed but the worst of the panic is over and I'm so exhausted all I can do is lie on the bed with my eyes closed and listen to Taylor Swift. If I could, I'd lie here forever and never leave this room again. Two sharp knocks on my bedroom door is all it takes to jolt me right back out of the stillness.

'Clare? Is now a good time to talk?'

I'm about to tell her to go away when I remember the search history on her laptop. If I don't speak to her now, I'll spend the rest of the night wondering what she wants.

'Arnie's asked me to have a word,' she says, when I open my bedroom door.

A chill runs through my body. This is it. He's told her who I am and she's here to tell me the police are on the way over.

'Let's go downstairs,' she says. 'We can talk over a cup of tea.'

My brain has stopped working and all I can do is follow her down the stairs into the kitchen. I sit at the table, waiting, while Kath puts the kettle on and prepares two mugs of tea.

'Arnie's friend wants to meet you,' she says, when the tea is finally made and she's sitting across the table from me.

It's so different to what I was expecting, the words don't make any sense.

'What friend?'

'Mick Dunn. I told you about him before, remember? He owns a pub on West Street, a live music venue. Arnie's had a word with him and he's keen to hear you sing. He's always on the lookout for new talent, apparently.'

It takes a moment for me to remember who she's talking about. When I do, I shake my head. 'No.'

'Clare, listen to me.' Kath reaches across the table and takes my hand in hers. 'You can't keep running forever. There's so much else you should be doing with your life instead of cleaning other people's houses. You have a beautiful singing voice. This could be a real opportunity for you.'

Her face blurs as my eyes fill with hot tears. I hate her for making me believe – even for a moment – that my life could be something else. I pull my hand away and stand up.

'You don't know anything about me,' I tell her.

'I know you're not happy.'

I can't listen to any more. There's a red rage burning through me and I want to hurt someone. A long-ago memory flashes through my mind. The knife in my hand, the moonlight reflecting off the blade as I lifted it high above my head; the sudden, shocking feeling of power that surged through me in that moment. Suddenly, I'm scared of what I might do if I stay here in a kitchen full of knives with a woman who's trying to make me do something I don't want to.

'Think about it, at least,' Kath says. 'The pub's called McCool's. It's on West Street and Mick is expecting you at six o'clock Monday evening.'

I back away from her, into the hall and out the front door. It's dark and cold, but I barely notice. I've got my phone in the back pocket of my jeans, earphones still connected. I choose a playlist at random, not caring what song comes on first, just needing the noise to block out everything that's whirling inside me like a tornado.

Alice In Chains, 'Man in the Box'. The music starts slow, but gets faster and louder. It makes me want to run to the very edge of the world and jump off, howling my rage into the empty nothingness all around me until my voice is hoarse and my throat is raw.

I don't want this life. I want to stop being Clare and become the person I'm meant to be. Someone who wears make-up and has boyfriends and sings in bars late at night with people listening and cheering.

I walk faster, as if I can somehow run away from thinking about what that other life might be like. But no matter how fast I walk, or how loud Layne Staley sings his sad and beautiful songs, I can't block out Kath's voice, telling me the name of the pub and the time I'm meant to be there.

Chapter 17

It's the end of her first week in the new job. So far, Nuala doesn't feel she's any closer to getting to know Andrea. It's clear that there's more to her than the side of herself she presents to the world. But it's also becoming clear that this is the only side she's going to show Nuala or anyone else.

Take that guy who turned up at the community centre, for instance. Nuala's certain Andrea recognised him. But when she asked Andrea about him, Andrea claimed she'd never seen him before. As someone who would get an A-grade in bullshitting if there was an exam on it, Nuala knew Andrea wasn't being straight with her. Which means that ever since that day, Nuala's become a little obsessed with trying to find out who he is. So far, all her investigations have hit a dead end but she's going to keep trying.

She'd hoped to get some work done this evening, but Josh is playing up, refusing to eat his pasta. He's been in a mood ever since Nuala picked him up from the childminder's earlier. She knows what the problem is. He's angry with her because she's working again, so she isn't there to pick him up at the school gates anymore. Instead he's met by Susan, the childminder, and spends two hours at her house before he sees his mummy. Nuala knows that Josh enjoys his time at Susan's. There are other kids to play with, something he doesn't have when he's here in the flat and it's just the two of them. But, as Nuala also knows, it's possible to enjoy one thing while you're missing something else. One doesn't cancel out the other. So even though she's tired and it's driving her slightly nuts the way he's pushing the food around on his plate instead of eating the damn stuff, she doesn't say anything.

The whole way home, she'd been thinking about how soon she could get him to bed. It's not that she doesn't want to spend time with him, but she's keen to get on with her work. Each evening this week, after Josh was in bed, she'd written up her notes from the conversations she'd had with Andrea and her team that day. Watching Josh now, Nuala decides work will have to wait. Her son is more important.

'Let's go to the park,' she says.

She can see from the expression on his face that he's not sure whether it's a genuine suggestion or something she's said so he'll finish his food. Six years old and already he knows she's full of shit.

'Come on.' Nuala stands up and holds out her hand.

He hesitates, just for a moment, before his perfect little face breaks into a huge smile and he reaches for her hand. Ten minutes later, they're in the playground. Nuala is pushing Josh on a swing as he squeals with delight and tells her he wants to go higher.

It's a cool evening, and Nuala's glad she made Josh put on his coat before coming out. The sun has already set and dusk has settled over the city. In another half an hour, it will be dark. For now, though, there's enough light for her to see her son soaring up towards the pale grey sky.

She was surprised, when they arrived, how many other parents and kids were here. Week nights with Josh follow a strict schedule that doesn't include coming out after tea to have a play in the park. Now they're here, Nuala wonders why she doesn't do this more often. Before she remembers how much effort she's put into creating a fixed routine for Josh, so he'll have a safe and secure childhood that's as far removed as possible from the one she had.

When she first became pregnant, after she'd decided she wasn't going to have a termination, Nuala read every parenting book she could lay her hands on. Through these, she learned the importance of creating a routine early on in your child's life. Until recently, she attributed much of Josh's easy-going nature to the military-level schedule of feeds, sleeps and playtime. By three months, he was sleeping through the night – the first of any of the babies from Nuala's antenatal group to achieve this crucial milestone. Looking back, it seemed that all the stages after that were just as easy. Part of the reason for this was Josh's nature. But it was also, Nuala was certain, because she had thrown herself wholeheartedly into the business of motherhood, with a zeal that had pissed off the other new mothers she knew to the point they'd stopped inviting her to their regular get-togethers.

At the time, Nuala hadn't cared about being ostracised from a group of women she had nothing in common with apart from the fact they'd all recently given birth. Lately, however, she's started to regret the absence of other parents in her life. Because where she'd once believed she had nailed parenting, these days she was constantly questioning herself.

School was the catalyst for this change. Now Josh was at school, there was a huge chunk of her son's life that was outside Nuala's control. And she hated it. If she didn't need to work, she would never have sent him to school. She would have home educated him, continuing to control every aspect of his childhood because that was the only way to make sure nothing bad ever happened to him.

When Josh grows bored with the swings, he runs over to the climbing frame. The whole time he's on it, Nuala has to clench her jaw shut to stop herself telling him every few seconds to be careful. The longer she watches him, imagining all sorts of terrible accidents that might happen, the more she regrets coming here. They could be at home now, tucked up beside each other on the sofa, reading a story. He would be safe, instead of putting his life at risk on a contraption that has no place in a playground meant for small children.

Fortunately, it's getting properly dark now and she has a perfectly valid reason for giving him a five-minute warning. Most of the other people who were here when they arrived have left. In their place, a group of teenagers have taken over. They're too big and loud to be here, but Nuala remembers what it was like at that age. When being at home is hell and the only other option is the local park where, if you're lucky, some of your friends will be too.

On the walk home, Josh is giddy from the surprise adventure. He's holding her hand one minute, then skipping ahead of her the next, before turning and running back to give her a hug. It's delightful and worth the climbing frame angst. Already, Nuala knows this won't be their last post-dinner trip to the park.

'Look.' Josh stops suddenly and points at a man walking towards them on the other side of the street. 'It's the bad man.'

'Who do you mean?' Nuala looks over but, in the dark, she can't see his features properly.

'The one who's watching us.'

Her heart shudders and, for a moment, she's sure it stops beating altogether.

'What do you mean, Josh?'

'I told you, Mummy. The man outside my window. The bad man. That's him.'

Josh has always had an active imagination, seeing people who weren't there and inventing stories about things that had never happened. Even so, Nuala's not going to let some random stranger stand outside her son's bedroom window watching him while he sleeps.

'Hey!' She shouts across at the man, but he doesn't react. Instead, he keeps walking, looking straight ahead, as if he hasn't heard her. Which is impossible, because she's got a loud voice and he's literally just on the other side of the street.

'Hey, you!'

Louder this time, no way he could have missed that. Yet he doesn't turn around or slow his pace.

'Josh.' She kneels down and looks into his blue eyes. 'I'm going to go and have a talk with the man. But I need you to stay here while I do that. Do you understand, Josh? Stay here and don't move.'

'Don't go, Mummy.' He shakes his head and she's about to tell him it's okay, she'll only be a few seconds, a minute at the most. But his bottom lip starts to wobble and she knows he's on the verge of tears. She can't leave him alone if he's upset.

'Okay,' she says. 'Come on. Let's go home.'

As they continue towards the flat, she turns and scans the street but it's empty. The man is gone and now it's just her and Josh and the silver slice of a crescent moon in the dark night sky.

Chapter 18

Nuala spent the weekend on high alert, repeatedly looking out the windows of the flat for Josh's 'bad man'. But there's been no sign of him since that night, and she's starting to think he's another figment of Josh's overactive imagination. The messages from *truthfinder* have dried up too, and after all the stomach-churning anxiety they caused, Nuala feels calmer and more in control again. She's starting to feel a little foolish that she let herself get so easily spooked by some freak who probably spends all their time sending threatening messages to people they've never met.

Monday morning, she's finally managed to get some time in with Roger. They're in his office, a light-filled room at the back of the house with French doors leading to a well-tended garden. It's a large space, but nowhere near big enough for the monstrous desk he's sitting behind. The desk is made out of a dark wood that's been polished until it shines, with six green leather panels across the front that do nothing to improve the overall effect.

'Got it shipped over from the States,' Roger says, clearly mistaking Nuala's fascination with the desk for admiration. 'Five grand's worth of walnut and leather. A lot of money for a desk you might think, but worth every penny. I've had this baby for over ten years and I've no plans to replace it any time soon.'

He folds his fingers behind the back of his head and leans back in his chair, beaming at Nuala. Like the rest of him, the smile is fake and, even though she wants this interview to go well, Nuala can't bring herself to smile back at him.

'Everything we talk about today is off the record, right?' he asks.

'Absolutely,' Nuala says. 'Obviously, once we start filming we'll need to get some footage with you. And I'd love an interview as part of that. But today is really about making sure that, when we do start to film, we're getting the balance right.'

Roger frowns. 'I'm not sure I understand.'

Of course you don't, Nuala thinks. It took days for him to even agree to this initial meeting. When he finally said he'd do it, he kept cancelling at short notice. Turning up for work this morning, she'd half expected him to cancel again. Instead, when she'd knocked on his door, he'd invited her in and told her how much he'd been looking forward to their 'little chat'.

'Well,' Nuala says, choosing her words carefully because despite her visceral dislike of the man, she needs to keep him on side. At least until this documentary is finished. After that, she sincerely hopes she'll find an opportunity to tell Roger Constantin exactly what she thinks of him. 'Andrea is the leader of the Progress Party, but I know you're just as key to the party's success as she is.'

She can see he likes that, so she keeps going. 'As you said yourself the first time we met, Andrea is the face of the party, but you're the brains. Ideally, I'd like you to have a central role in this documentary we're making.'

She smiles now, pleased with herself for hitting all the right notes. Roger smiles back, and this time she knows it's the real thing.

'Maybe I was wrong about you, Nuala Fox.'

She tilts her head, acknowledging both the truth of his words and the compliment that underlines them.

'So,' Roger's arms drop back down and he sits up straighter. 'Where do you want to start?'

Nuala takes her phone out of her bag, hits record on her voice recording app and puts the phone on the ugly desk.

'Hey, I thought this was off the record,' Roger says.

'It is,' Nuala assures him. 'But it would help enormously if I could record the conversation. My memory's not the greatest, you see. This means I won't miss anything important.'

While she waits for him to give his permission, she takes another look around the room. None of her other encounters with Roger have taken place in here. Until today, his office has been strictly off limits and she's always been curious to see what it's like. Apart from the desk, there's nothing offensive about the rest of the room. There's even one whole wall lined, floor-to-ceiling, with books. They're too far away for Nuala to read the spines, but she's going to make sure she finds a way to ask him about them during their conversation.

'Okay,' Roger says eventually. 'But on the clear under-standing that you don't use the recording for anything else. And you promise me you'll delete it as soon as you've got what you need from it.'

'Of course.'

'I've only got an hour,' Roger says. 'So let's get cracking.'

Nuala starts with some basic stuff, asking Roger questions she already knows the answers to, like where he's from and about his early career. It's clear from the get-go that he likes talking about himself, which makes this easier than she'd anticipated.

'Tell me about how you and Andrea met,' she says, when he finally stops talking about the multiple start-ups he's turned into successful businesses and the number of boards he's sat on as his wealth and business interests have grown over the years. In The World According to Roger Constantin, he's a hugely gifted businessman with an astonishing intelligence.

'We met at a bar in Greece,' Roger says. 'Santorini, to be precise. I was on holiday with a few of the lads. She was living there at the time. The night in question, she was having a drink by herself. I saw her, and I liked what I saw, so I went over and asked if I could buy her a drink. She said yes and we got talking. The rest, you could say, is history. Or destiny, whatever you want to call it.'

'So you got together that very first night?' Nuala asks, properly interested now.

'Nuala Fox!' Roger pretends to be shocked but she's pretty sure he's kidding around. 'What are you implying? Of course we didn't. You clearly don't know my darling Andrea as well as you think you do. She's not the sort of woman to make things easy. I had to do a lot of chasing at the start, believe me.'

Nuala's impressed. Letting someone else do the chasing isn't something she's ever been very good at, but she admires anyone who's got that particular talent nailed.

'She was a nobody back then,' Roger says. 'But if you mention that to anyone else, I'll make sure you regret it.'

'So why are you telling me?'

'Because it's important you understand.' Roger leans forward, elbows on the desk. 'Andrea is a formidable woman. She was forty-five years old when I met her, but she could have passed for a woman ten years younger. From the moment I saw her, I knew there was something special about her. People are drawn to her, they want to be around her. But back then, she wasn't interested in becoming a public figure. That transformation is all down to me.'

Roger pushes his chair back, stands up and walks across to the wall of books.

'Here.' He takes a book from one of the higher shelves and hands it to Nuala. '*Pygmalion*, by George Bernard Shaw. Most people know it because of the film that's based on it, *My Fair Lady*. But really that's not a patch on the play.'

Nuala takes the book because it's clear that's what she's meant to do, and flicks through it.

'You could say I was Professor Higgins and Andrea was my Eliza. Of course, Andrea wasn't really an Eliza. She was sophisticated, even back then. But she lacked a purpose. That's what I gave her. I made Andrea who she is today. I've had many successes in my life but she's my greatest one to date. And the best is yet to come. One day, Andrea Leach will be prime minister. When that happens, Nuala Fox, wherever you are in the world, you'll remember this conversation and you'll know that I'm the reason she made it to the top.'

Chapter 19

Monday comes around quickly. I race through the day, cleaning every house better and faster than I've done before. Mrs Farnshaw is my last job. Normally, she likes me to have a cup of coffee with her before I start cleaning. Today, I know if I have to slow down and talk to her about the weather and her garden and her plans for the weekend, I will scream at the top of my voice and I might never be able to stop. So when she asks if I'd like a coffee, I tell her I don't have time today and push away the twinge of guilt when I see how disappointed she looks.

I'm hot and sweating when I've finished, but outside there's a cold wind that whips through me as I race down the hill from Mrs Farnshaw's house. I run fast and don't stop until my chest is aching and my stomach is heaving and I have to lean over and puke up the runny vomit that's risen up the back of my throat.

But it's still not enough to get rid of the restless itchiness just beneath my skin. If I go home now and have to spend another night alone in the attic room watching my face in the mirror and eating cheese toasties and pretending, I'll burst wide open.

The appointment with Mick Dunn is at six o'clock. It's five o'clock now, and the pub is about half an hour's walk from here. Which gives me plenty of time to get there, take a quick look inside and see what it's like. After that, if I don't want to stay, I don't have to. But the closer I get to West Street, the more I want this. So I make my decision. I'm going to meet Mick Dunn and sing for him. I'll sing better than I've ever sung before, and if he offers me a job, I'll take it.

I walk fast and reach West Street within twenty minutes. Up ahead, on the right-hand side of the street, I can see the sign for McCool's pub. There's a tram coming towards me, along the line that runs down the middle of the street. When it stops, near the pub, only one person gets off. A man I instantly recognise.

It's Arnie, jumping down from the tram and walking towards the pub. I step back, the breath catching in my throat. I can't do this if he's going to be there, watching me with his beady grey eyes and whispering into Mick Dunn's ear, talking about me.

There are other pubs on West Street, and I walk into the one that's closest. When I push open the door and step inside, everyone who's already in there turns to stare at me. I almost turn around and go back out, but the woman behind the bar smiles at me. So I walk towards the bar instead of away from it.

The woman is about my age. She's got blonde hair, piled up on top of her head, and she's wearing bright red lipstick, the colour of fresh strawberries. She's smiling, like she's actually happy to see me.

'What can I get you, my love?' she asks.

Jasper used to take me to a pub called The Star. It was a horrible place with a sticky carpet that smelled of stale bodies and beer. He liked getting me to drink alcohol because he said I was funny when I was drunk.

'A bottle of WKD, please.'

'Any particular flavour?'

I didn't know there were different flavours. When I was with Jasper, I only ever drank the blue one.

'Um, blue please.'

'Ooh, Blue Lagoon.' She smiles again, and the tightness across my neck and shoulders eases a little. 'That's my favourite, too.'

She gets one of the bottles from the fridge behind her and pours some of the blue drink into a glass that she has already added ice to. After I pay, I want to stay at the bar talking to her but she's already moved away to serve someone else.

I find an empty table and start drinking. When the bottle is empty, I go back to the bar to order another one. I do this three more times and, when I go back a fourth time, the woman isn't smiling any longer.

'You sure you need another one?' she asks.

'Yes, I'm sure,' I tell her, and she frowns like I've said something wrong. When she fills my glass, she doesn't put any ice into it. I want to ask for some, but she's looking so cross I don't bother.

Stupid cow, I think, as I make my way back to my seat. The floor feels like it's moving beneath me but, apart from that, I'm super relaxed now. I don't even care that I've missed the meeting with Mick Dunn. I don't care about anything except staying here and holding on to this relaxed, happy feeling for as long as I can.

There are two guys a little older than me sitting a few tables away. When one of them catches my eye and winks at me, I giggle and wink back. Then I wink again, my insides fizzing at what I'm doing. Drinking WKD is brilliant. It's like magic, because earlier I was feeling so trapped inside my body that I wanted to explode or fly off a high cliff or do anything that would make me stop being me. But look at me now! I'm in a pub, winking at some random guy while I sip my blue drink.

A bit later, I go to the toilet. When I see my face in the mirror, my lips are blue. I stick my tongue out and that's blue too. I take out my phone and start taking photos of my tongue. It looks like a blue snake, but when I bite down it hurts so I know it really is my tongue.

On the way back to my seat, I'm wobbling a little bit. I bump into a table and knock over someone's drink. A man calls me a dozy bitch. It's not nice to call someone a bitch but I don't tell him this because I'm at my table now and there's a new bottle of WKD waiting for me.

I look around the pub, confused. There wasn't a bottle there before I went to the toilet. I remember draining the last one and leaving it on the bar on my way to the loo, thinking I'd get another one when I came out of the toilet. Except I'd forgotten, hadn't I?

'A little present.' It's the man I was winking at earlier. He's standing beside me, a bit too close but I don't tell him this because he's just bought me a drink.

'Thanks,' I say.

I sit down, and so does he, and soon we're chatting like we've known each other for ages. His name is Dave, and he works in the Tesco Express near here.

'Today's pay day,' he says. 'So I'm out on the town tonight. How about you? You got a name, then?'

I'm so relaxed, I nearly tell him my real name, but I remember just in time.

'Clare.'

'Pretty name for a pretty girl,' Dave says.

He puts a hand on my leg and squeezes my thigh.

'You fancy coming out to play this evening?' he says.

'Maybe.'

I've finished my drink and I want another one, but Dave's hand is on my leg and I don't know how to ask him to move it without seeming rude. When his hand moves higher up my leg, I try to shift away. He squeezes harder, hurting me. I make a little yelping sound and he laughs.

'You like this, don't you, Clare?'

I don't like it. Not one bit. The room is swaying. Dave's voice sounds far away, even though he's right beside me, his fingers pushing and squeezing. He has big teeth, like a wolf, and he looks as if he's going to eat me all up. My stomach heaves and, before I can stop myself, a burst of blue vomit spews out of my mouth and splashes over Dave's face and clothes.

'Fucking hell,' he roars, letting me go as he stands up.

I puke again, making a puddle on the floor beneath my feet. The bitter smell fills my nose and I retch once more, but there's nothing left inside me except a few watery bits that I spit out.

Things blur together after that. The blonde woman appears, dragging me by the arm, up and out of my chair and across the pub. I clatter into tables and chairs and people, before a whack of cold air hits my face as the door is pulled open and I'm shoved outside.

I fall on the ground, landing hard on my hands and knees. Too drunk to move. Best thing to do is stay here until the world stops swaying. A pair of brown shoes appear in front of me. Then a face, as he crouches down to look at me. A jolt of recognition rocks through me. I close my eyes, shake my head.

'I thought it was you,' Arnie says. 'Looks like you've got yourself into a bit of a state. You'd better let me help get you home.'

I try to stand up, to get away from him, but he's grabbed hold of my arm and is pulling me up.

'Let me go,' I say, flapping my hands in front of his face.

'You're slurring, Clare. I can't understand a word you're saying.'

I try again, but can't get my tongue to work. Then I remember. My tongue is gone, replaced by a blue snake that's growing inside me and is going to keep growing until there's nothing left of me except a huge, writhing blue snake that not even Arnie will be able to hold on to.

Chapter 20

Leo pulls open the door and steps inside the cool, dark space. Here, in a converted arch beneath one of the Victorian rail bridges behind London Bridge station, is where Bermondsey Beer began. Ten years since he brewed the first batch. One year and two months exactly before the fire that destroyed Black Valley Farm, killing the people locked inside.

The news had almost destroyed him. There'd been a time, when he first heard what had happened, that he had thought about giving up. But he hadn't. Somehow, he'd kept going. Thanks, mainly, to his remarkable knack of compartmentalising the different bits of his life. A skill that seems, on the whole, to have deserted him recently. Because now he's allowed himself to unlock the box that contains the memories of the first sixteen years of his life, he isn't able to get the box shut again.

These days, Bermondsey Beer is a nationwide operation with bars and breweries in twenty different locations across the country as well as a head office on the top floor of a modern building on the waterfront in St Katherines Dock. But Leo still pays the rent on this place. He comes here whenever he's had a bad day, to remind himself of how much he's achieved since he first started brewing beer.

Back then, it had been just him. Making batch after batch of beer that never lived up to what Leo was looking for. He'd been on the verge of giving up when, suddenly, he nailed the recipe and the process. Bermondsey Beer has often been described as an overnight success, but there's no truth in it. It took years of hard graft, and there were plenty of moments – especially in the early days – when Leo thought he might never succeed.

He scans the rows of bottles on the shelves that run along the far wall. Eventually, he chooses one of their early brews – Waterloo Sunset, a red ale that's won the CAMRA Champion Bottled Beer of Britain Award three times so far. Cracking open the bottle, he allows himself a moment to breathe in the rich, malty smell before taking a long, glorious slug. As the beer slides down his throat, his mouth fills with flavours of butterscotch and caramel.

He sits down in his old office chair, swivelling round and round while he drinks and tries to get his thoughts into some sort of order. A train rumbles, the sound soothing and reassuring. Despite the turmoil inside his head, the rest of the world continues as normal. Trains keep running, people commute in and out to work, babies are born and people die. Life, in all its glorious confusion, will carry on long after Leo has gone.

When the bottle is finished, he opens another one. A pale ale this time, called Blonde on Blonde. If Leo was to name one beer in the collection to take with him to a desert island, it would be this one, along with a copy of the album it's named after.

He finishes the second bottle. So far, the beer hasn't given him what he was hoping for. The tension in his shoulders and the back of his neck hasn't eased and his mind is no closer to slowing down.

It wasn't meant to be like this. All the hard work, the years he spent travelling from bar to bar trying to flog bottles of beer that no one had ever heard of, the endless begging to the banks for loans so he could pay the handful of people he'd employed, the long nights when he couldn't sleep because of the stress of trying to keep everything going. All this so he could prove to himself he was more – so much more – than the boy he'd once been.

These days, he's a successful, respected businessman at the top of his game with his whole life in front of him. At a dinner party recently, someone who knows someone who works in TV suggested that there might be a slot coming up on *Make Me a Millionaire*, the reality show where budding entrepreneurs pitch their business ideas to a panel of millionaires in the hope they might invest in them. If it happens, Leo would be the youngest millionaire to take part.

This life he has now is what matters, not everything that went before. The past is the past, and if he wishes he could have done some things differently, it's too late for that. He can't go back and change what's already happened. Which is why he's done everything in his power to put it behind him, move on with his life. Always looking forward, never back.

Yet here he is, sitting in a hollowed-out railway arch, dwelling on the past he's worked so hard to forget. *Why?* He shakes his head. The question is pointless. He already knows the answer. Atonement. Some twisted belief that if he does something, if he stands up and tells the truth, that it will somehow absolve him. As if it could ever be that easy. What he did was unforgivable. He's carried the guilt of that single mistake with him ever since. He's learned to live with it, using work as the distraction he needs so he never has to stop for long enough to consider how very different things might have been if only he'd been braver.

He takes his phone out, opens up Facebook and does a search for Arnie Cummins. As the photo of the old bastard loads, Leo's gut tightens. He remembers the day, four years ago, when his PA came into his office to tell him he had a visitor.

Arnie had looked different to how Leo remembered him. If it hadn't been for his eyes, hard and mean like they'd always been, he might have even thought it was a different man. But it was him all right. Telling Leo some bullshit about how much he'd missed him and how many years he'd spent looking for him.

With every word that spewed out of Arnie's mouth, anger spread through Leo's body until he felt as if there was fire running through his veins. Later, he could barely remember lunging across the space that separated them, throwing Arnie to the ground and punching him, over and over and over.

Leo had wanted to kill him, would have killed him too if Harry hadn't intervened, grabbing Leo and dragging him up and away, then holding onto him while he struggled and screamed at the piece of shit lying bleeding on the ground that he hated him and he never wanted to see his face ever again.

Leo hasn't seen Arnie since that day, except when he looks him up online like he's doing now. He'd created a fake Facebook account, which he used to become online friends with Arnie. Like most of the people Arnie is friends with, Leo's fake account is that of a retired police detective.

Logging into Facebook now, Leo scrolls through Arnie's feed. There are several new posts, including a link to a video shared by one of Arnie's friends. Leo's seen some of the shit Arnie's friends have shared in the past and he's inclined to scroll past the link when something stops him. There's an image with the link, a close-up of a woman's face. Her features are blurred, as if she'd been moving when the shot was taken. Even so, she looks familiar, and when Leo clicks on the link that opens the video his fingers are shaking.

The link takes him to the website of a paper called the *Sheffield Herald*. There's a caption above the video: 'Woman throws herself in front of bus to save child.' Leo pauses. He doesn't have to watch it. He can shut it down now, finish up his beer and go back to his riverfront apartment and the life he's worked so hard to build for himself. But if he does that, he'll never know. So he hits play and watches the clip. When it's finished, he rewinds to the beginning and watches it again. This time, he pauses at the final shot – a close-up of a face he hasn't seen in many years but is instantly recognisable.

He reaches out with his index finger, tracing the tear-shaped birthmark beneath her left eye. In that moment, his past comes racing out of the dark corners where he's hidden it away for so long. And as he looks into the woman's blue eyes, he knows he will stop at nothing until he finds her.

He calls Danny Robb, a private detective he's used a few times before. Danny answers on the second ring, like he always does. Leo thinks Danny must spend his life waiting for his phone to ring.

'I need your help finding someone,' Leo says, once they've got the usual greetings out of the way. 'I don't have much information, except that she's in Sheffield. And I've got a video I can send you, so you can see what she looks like.'

After agreeing a price with Danny, Leo ends the call, forwards the video to Danny and cracks open another beer. There's a niggling sensation at the back of his mind, like he's missed something. He opens the video, watches it again but that doesn't help. It's only when he goes back to Arnie's Facebook profile and scrolls through his posts again, that Leo finds what's been bothering him.

The most recent post from Arnie is about a Thai restaurant he's been to. There's a photo with the post, showing a plate of noodles, but it's not this that has snagged Leo's attention. It's the caption beneath the photo, giving the name of the restaurant and its location: Sheffield.

As he looks at the photo, Leo feels the old rage unfurling inside him. *You bastard*, he thinks. *You fucking bastard*. There's only one reason Arnie Cummins has gone to Sheffield, and it's sure as hell not to check out the quality of the city's restaurants. He's gone there for her.

Chapter 21

The smell is the first thing I notice when I wake up. Followed by the uneasy sense that something is wrong. I open my eyes and, as I wait for them to adjust to the darkness, the sense of dread grows inside me. Gradually, the familiar shapes of my bedroom come into focus and the pressure on my chest eases. It's okay. I'm safe.

The relief doesn't last, because now I'm more awake, I recognise the smell. Cologne. The same pungent stink that hangs around the house whenever Arnie is here. I sit up, heart pounding as I scan the room. But there's no one else here.

I lean across to flick the switch on my bedside lamp. Blinking in the sudden brightness, I realise I don't remember coming to bed. I have a pounding headache. My throat is sandpaper dry and there's a bitter, unfamiliar taste in my mouth. As I try to work out why I'm feeling so dreadful, it all comes rushing back. The pub and the drinks and the man called Dave with the wandering hand. And Arnie. Vaguely, like a half-forgotten dream, I remember sitting with him in the back of a taxi. And later, here at the house, trying to tell him I didn't want him to come inside but he insisted. Said he had to make sure I was okay.

But he didn't come up here. He stood at the bottom of the stairs, watching me while I clawed my way up the three flights. Once I was inside my room, I shut the door and fell straight asleep. Which means he came up after that.

The thought makes my skin go cold. I look down at my body, relieved to see I'm still fully dressed. Jeans, jumper, even my handbag wrapped around my shoulder. When I check the time, it's eleven thirty. I have no idea what time I got home, or how long I've been asleep.

I stand up, slowly because the room starts to spin, and cross to the chest of drawers. I open the bottom drawer where I keep the pretty clothes I've managed to collect over the years. I never wear these clothes outside my room, but I like having them. This is also the drawer where I keep my money. One hundred and eighty-five pounds saved up since I moved in with Kath.

It's obvious right away that someone has been looking through this drawer. I make sure the clothes are always neatly folded and in order – tops on the left, skirts and trousers in the middle, scarves and hats on the right. Tonight, they're all jumbled up in a big mess.

I dig beneath the mess, breathing a sigh of relief when my fingers touch the envelope at the bottom. And when I check inside it, the newspaper clippings and the necklace are there too. But if Arnie's been looking through this drawer, which I'm sure he has been, he couldn't have missed the envelope. I keep my money in there too and I count it quickly, checking it's all there, even though I know that's not what Arnie was looking for.

I start to tidy my clothes back into their neatly ordered piles. As I think of Arnie's fat fingers messing through my stuff, I can feel the fury fizzing up inside me. I hope he's still here, so I can ask him what the hell he was doing coming into my room and looking through my things.

When everything is back the way I like it, I open the bedroom door and hear their voices downstairs. Arnie and Kath. I picture the two of them, huddled together in the kitchen, drinking red wine and talking about me.

I run down the stairs, almost falling over in my rush to get to the kitchen and confront him. The stink of his cologne is worse down here and I wonder how Kath can bear it. If love is blind, it's not just her eyes that have a problem. It's her nose too.

'Clare.' Kath jumps up as I push open the door and walks over to me.

She puts her arms out, like she's about to give me a hug. But she must see something in my face, because her arms drop back down again without touching me.

'I'm so glad you're okay,' she says. 'Arnie told me what happened, but neither of us can understand why you got into that state in the first place. Do you want to talk about it?'

He's watching me, but he doesn't say a word. The anger fizzes and spits inside me.

'You were in my room,' I say, staring right back at him. 'What were you doing there?'

'I was checking you hadn't choked on your own puke.'

'Bullshit.' I step past Kath, my hands curling into fists. 'You were looking through my things. And before that, earlier this evening, why were you there outside the pub when I came out? Were you following me, Arnie?'

'Clare!' Kath's voice is sharp and angry.

'It's okay,' Arnie says. 'Clare's had a bad experience this evening. It's no wonder she's feeling a bit confused.'

'I'm not confused,' I shout. 'Tell me who you are and why you're here. What do you want from me? Who are you and why are you so interested in me?'

'That's enough,' Kath says. 'Arnie did you a huge favour tonight, Clare. You were damn lucky he turned up when he did or God only knows what might have happened to you. I'm very grateful to him, and you should be too. Arnie is my friend and I won't allow you to speak to him like this when he's done absolutely nothing wrong.'

I barely hear her. All my attention is focused on Arnie and the way he's looking at me, like I'm a stupid little girl he can do whatever he wants to.

'Did you find what you were looking for?' I ask him.

He drains his glass and stands up.

'I should probably leave,' he says to Kath. 'It's late and Clare clearly doesn't want me here.'

'It's my house, not Clare's.' She looks from him to me. 'Go back to bed, Clare. I've had a long day and I don't want to have to deal with you right now. We'll talk tomorrow.'

She starts to turn away from me, but I reach out and grab her shoulder.

'Don't you dare touch me.' She swings back to look at me, her face cold and angry. 'Get out, Clare. Go and sleep off your hangover. If you stay here a moment longer, I can't guarantee things won't end very badly for you.'

I want to grab her again and shake her until she listens to me. Make her see that I'm not the person she should be angry with. It's Arnie. But I know there's no point. She's already crossed the kitchen and is sitting down beside him, her head turned away from me like she can't bear to look at me.

The last thing I see, before I step out of the kitchen and close the door, is Arnie wrapping his arm around Kath's shoulders and whispering something I can't hear.

Chapter 22

Alan Wilson is a legend in the world of investigative journalism. He's an old-school hack, with a dogged reputation. Over the last few years, his career has taken something of a nosedive. He's fallen out with the new proprietor of the broadsheet newspaper that had been his primary employer for the last twenty-plus years. Since then, he's apparently struggled to find regular work. With one exception, Nuala hasn't seen a decent piece by Alan Wilson in recent years. That exception is why she's here this evening, sitting across a table in a not very pleasant London pub with Wilson, instead of being at home with Josh.

'You're the only journalist I can find who's writing about the Progress Party,' she tells Alan. 'Why is that? Andrea Leach makes for a great story. She's charismatic, she's attractive, and she's leading a political party that doesn't believe in the concept of feminism. The piece you wrote about her is excellent but, from what I can see, you're a lone voice. Why do you think no one else is interested in her?'

Alan lifts his pint of Guinness and takes a deep drink before replying.

'Three reasons. One: Roger Constantin's an influential man. He's put a lot of work into making sure nobody's going to write negative pieces about his beloved Andrea. Two: for now, the so-called "party" is a small-scale affair. They haven't registered with the Electoral Commission, which means they're not able to stand in elections yet.'

'But they're planning to register next year,' Nuala says. 'As soon as that happens, surely they'll come under more scrutiny?'

'Definitely. Although that won't change the third reason why no one's interested in them at the moment, and that's Andrea herself.'

'What do you mean?'

While she waits as Alan drinks more Guinness, Nuala takes a sip of her wine and tries not to wince. She should have known the wine in a place like this wouldn't be up to much. It was Alan who suggested they meet here; a tatty pub on the ground floor of a concrete block of council flats behind King's Cross station. The sort of place Nuala normally wouldn't be seen dead in. Although it's clear from the way the barman greeted Alan earlier that he's something of a regular. In fact, Alan has the unhealthy aura of a man who spends too many hours a day drinking pints of Guinness in places like this.

'Most of my colleagues think there's absolutely nothing interesting about the woman,' Alan says.

'Well that's bullshit.' Nuala thinks of the moment in the community hall, the way all those people in the room seemed to adore Andrea as she stood before them. Remembering that now, Nuala suddenly feels scared.

'What about you?' she asks, when Alan doesn't speak. 'What do you think of her?'

Again, she has to wait for his answer until he's had a drink. When he's finished, the glass is empty.

'Let me order another one of these first,' he says.

'That's okay,' Nuala says, as Alan makes a half-hearted attempt to heave himself out of his chair. 'I'll go. You stay there.'

Unsurprisingly, Alan doesn't protest. Instead, handing Nuala his empty glass, he says she might as well order some crisps at the same time.

'Cheese and onion, mind. I can't stand salt and vinegar. And you'd better make it two packs. I skipped lunch today and I'm bloody starving.'

Nuala refrains from saying that with a stomach as big as his, skipping lunch is no bad thing. She takes the glass and hurries to the bar, keen to get back to hear what else Alan's got to say.

As an Irish person living in London, Nuala knows it's almost impossible to find a pub that can serve a decent pint of Guinness. It turns out this dump is the exception, and she has to wait for what feels like forever for the pint to settle before the barman tops it up and finally hands it over.

'Look at that,' Alan says, as Nuala returns with the fresh pint. 'Liquid of the gods. Martin there, the guy behind the bar, is second-generation Irish. His dad used to run this place and Martin's been pulling pints of Guinness since he was a kid.'

'You were about to tell me what you think of Andrea,' Nuala reminds him.

'I think she's a fraud.'

'How so?'

Alan frowns. 'I'm not sure. Haven't worked it out yet. There's something off about her. You sense it too, don't you? It's why you wanted to see me.'

He's right. The more time Nuala has spent with Andrea, the more convinced she's become that Andrea is hiding something.

'I took this job,' she says, 'because I needed the money. I wouldn't have gone near it otherwise. Everything about the Progress Party is abhorrent, in my opinion. They're a bunch of racists and homophobes, and when I first met Andrea I expected to hate her.'

'But you didn't?'

Nuala shakes her head, remembering that first meeting in the hotel bar.

'She charmed the shit out of me. And I'm someone who finds ninety per cent of people annoying as hell. But there was something about her that had me acting like a lovesick teenager. I found myself really wanting her to like me.'

'It's how people like her work,' Alan says. 'They use their charisma to get people to do what they want.'

'When you say "people like her", what do you mean exactly?'

'I've spent the last year investigating Andrea Leach,' Alan says. 'I've seen her giving speeches, so I've witnessed her charisma first hand. I'm pretty sure she's got some sort of personality disorder. She's a sociopath or a narcissist, maybe. Or some combination of both. Who knows?'

'She's a politician,' Nuala points out. 'Aren't most of them sociopaths or narcissists?'

'True,' Alan says. 'But you know what makes Andrea different? Becoming leader of the Progress Party seems to be the single most interesting thing she's done. You know her better than I do, Nuala. Do you really believe a woman like that has led such an utterly uneventful life until now?'

'It hasn't been entirely uneventful,' Nuala says.

'Come on,' Alan says. 'Her parents died when she was still a teenager, and she left Australia to go travelling. She's lived abroad ever since. Before she met Roger she was living a hermit-like existence in Santorini. She doesn't appear to have had any previous relationships, or done anything significant. Do you really believe a woman like that was single her entire life until she met Constantin?

'I went to Santorini a few months ago, you know. Spoke to some of her neighbours. None of them had anything to say about her – good or bad. She kept to herself, apparently. Why do you think that was, Nuala?'

'She was hiding from something,' Nuala says. 'Or someone. An abusive ex-partner, maybe.'

She thinks of the man who showed up at the community centre that day. The man Andrea claimed she'd never met before, even though Nuala's certain that's a lie. Is he the person Andrea's hiding from? He seems too young to be an ex-partner but it's not beyond the realms of possibility. A woman as attractive as Andrea would surely have her choice of men, young and old.

'It's possible,' Alan says, 'but I don't think that's it.'

'What do you think, then?' Nuala asks.

Alan drinks some Guinness, shrugs.

'I don't know, Nuala. But if I was to bet on it, I'd say it's linked to this documentary she's got you working on.'

'I'm not sure I understand,' Nuala says.

'She's told you she wants you to make a warts and all documentary, right? Well we both know that's bullshit. Andrea Leach is a politician, and there's not a politician out there who would pay a journalist to dig into every aspect of their private life.'

He's right, of course. It's exactly what Nuala had thought the first time she met Andrea.

'You think I should quit?' she asks.

'Hell no. I think you should stick with it. She'll try to drive the narrative, make sure you only cover areas of her life she's comfortable with you looking into. Your job is to ignore that, keep digging into her past until you find the truth. Whatever that turns out to be.'

Alan drains his glass and looks hopefully at Nuala.

'I've got to go,' she says. 'I promised the babysitter I'd be home in time to put my son to bed.'

She thanks Alan for his time, orders him a final pint at the bar and walks out into the crisp October evening. The conversation has left her with a sense of unease she's unable to shake off. She's more certain than ever now that Andrea's hiding something. It's also clear that Andrea thinks she's clever enough to conceal her past from Nuala. But if Andrea believes that, then she has seriously underestimated Nuala. The documentary is meant to be a thorough investigation into the life of Andrea Leach. And that's exactly what it's going to be.

Chapter 23

It's early morning, grey light trickling into my room through the open curtains. I've been awake all night, packing my bags and listening again to every episode of *Black Valley Farm*. Each time I listen to it, there's a niggle at the back of my mind that's like an itch I can't reach so it never goes away.

There were eleven of us living on the farm the night I left. By the following morning, nine of us were dead. Which means two of us are still alive. Me, and the woman Nuala interviewed in the final episode of the podcast.

Last week, something extraordinary happened. I got an email from a woman calling herself Marianne, who claimed she had important information for me. As you can imagine, it's not that unusual for me to get emails of this nature. Ninety per cent of the time, those emails turn out to be a hoax. Not this one, though. I contacted Marianne and we arranged to meet. After several meetings and conversations, she eventually agreed to be interviewed for this podcast. Here is a recording of that interview.

Nuala and Marianne get their introductions out of the way and Marianne begins speaking about her time at the farm. She starts by explaining how we all ended up living together.

> 'People called it a cult, but that's not what we were.
> It was a haven for women who needed to escape.
> Rosemary saved us, and we loved her for it. Those
> years I spent living on the farm were the happiest
> I've ever been. Trying to rebuild my life after that
> terrible night hasn't been easy.'

'Can you tell me about the night of the fire?' Nuala asks in a soft voice when Marianne stops speaking.

'I hadn't been able to sleep, so I'd got out of bed and gone for a walk. That's the only reason I didn't die too. The farm was located in the middle of beautiful countryside with rolling hills in every direction. It was a clear, cloudless night. Out there, in the middle of nowhere, I could see so many stars. Thousands of them twinkling in the dark sky. I remember thinking how beautiful it all was, how peaceful.

'I was walking through the empty fields when I heard a scream. A few seconds later, there was a loud explosion. The sounds came from the farm and, when I turned around, I could see an orange light in the distance.

'I ran back as fast as I could, but I wasn't fast enough. By the time I'd got there, the whole house was on fire. It was obvious whoever was in there had no chance of surviving.'

She stops speaking and Nuala waits a moment before asking her next question.

'What about the woman who wasn't inside the house? The woman who'd been stabbed. Did you see her?'

'Yes, I saw her. It was dear Rosemary, who had saved so many of us. She'd been stabbed in the stomach. I tried to save her. I gave her CPR and mouth to mouth, but nothing worked. She was already dead.'

In my mind, I see her like I'm back there. Rosemary, or Mother as we called her, falling to the ground. The look of shock on her face when she realised what had happened. A shiver runs down my spine and I press pause, not wanting to listen to anymore.

I check the time. Five minutes past six. The first coach to London leaves at six forty-five. I stand up, take a final look around the room. My body feels heavy, weighed down with exhaustion and sadness. Each time I think about never seeing Kath again, no more chats at the end of the day or eating dinner together in her lovely kitchen, I get a hard lump in my chest that won't go away.

I'm almost at the front door when I notice Kath's handbag on the hall table. It's open, with her wallet sticking out. Before I can stop myself, I reach out and take the wallet. There's cash in there. Twenty-five pounds. And a plastic card like the ones people use to pay in shops and take money out of cash machines. You need a code to take the money out but, like everything else, the numbers for Kath's card is on a Post-it note stuck to the fridge.

I slip the card and the cash into the back pocket of my jeans, and I take a photo of the Post-it note with the code on it. I feel sick, even though I know I'll pay back every penny as soon as I'm working again. But there's no getting away from the fact that I'm stealing from one of the kindest people I've ever met. It's more proof of what I already know about myself: I'm a bad person.

Outside, I close the front door as quietly as I can and walk away from the house. I think of Kath, lying in bed upstairs with no idea she's going to wake up and find I'm gone and I've taken her money with me.

As I walk down the hill, away from the house, the city is spread out before me. Behind it, the curved head of a pink sun is slowly edging its way over the horizon. I stop walking, overwhelmed by the sudden, shocking beauty as the sun turns from pink to orange to a deep, dark red that spreads across the sky and the city and reaches all the way up to where I'm standing on the hill, warming my face and my hands while my chest aches with sadness.

It's not too late to turn back, but my mind is made up. I'm going to London. I want to find Marianne, the woman on the podcast. There was no one called Marianne living on the farm, which means she lied about her name. But that's not all she lied about. I need to find her, so I can look her in the eye and make her tell me why she lied about the other things too.

Chapter 24

Nuala is late for work. By the time she arrives at Andrea's house, she's sweating and out of breath. She had to run most of the way from the train station. Josh was difficult this morning, pretending he wasn't feeling well even though he didn't have a temperature and scoffed down two bowls of Weetabix. On the fifteen-minute walk to school, he was grumpy and uncommunicative. Nuala had wanted a word with his teacher, but class had already started by the time they arrived.

She spent the entire train journey worrying about him, and she's still worrying about him as she rings the doorbell and waits to be let into Andrea's house. On the train, she googled 'How do you know if your child is being bullied?' and has convinced herself that's why Josh has been so reluctant to go to school this week. She's a terrible parent, clearly, because if she wasn't, surely he would have told her what's going on. The fact he hasn't is all the proof she needs that she's failed him.

Normally, the front door is opened by one of the goons. So it's a surprise when today Nuala finds herself face to face with Andrea. She braces herself for a dressing down, because she's ten minutes late and Andrea's already made her feelings about tardiness crystal clear. But Andrea surprises her by smiling and telling Nuala she looks particularly lovely today.

'I was thinking we could walk into the village and have a coffee,' she says, stepping outside and pulling the door closed. Making it clear the decision's already made, whether Nuala likes it or not. 'My treat.' Andrea links her arm in Nuala's and guides her back out of the front garden and onto the street.

As they stroll towards Blackheath village and Nuala listens to Andrea telling her what a great job Nuala's doing, she thinks how difficult it is to be immune when Andrea switches on the charm. Nuala knows it's all fake, that Alan Wilson is right and Andrea's most likely some sort of sociopath. But there's still a pathetic part of Nuala that likes being flattered in this way.

'We haven't spoken much about your podcast,' Andrea says, once they're settled in one of the chi-chi coffee shops that are scattered throughout Blackheath. 'It struck me this morning how odd that is.'

'Odd, why?' Nuala asks.

'Because the podcast is the reason I was so keen to work with you. I've already told you how brilliant I think it is. But I haven't asked you why you decided to make it in the first place, or how you managed to track down all those people. It must have taken so much work. Tell me, what inspired you to make it?'

She sits back in her chair and beams at Nuala, clearly waiting for her to start talking.

'Well,' Nuala says, 'when I was growing up, a woman was murdered in my home town. The murder became part of our town's folklore. Everyone who lived there knew about it. The killer has never been caught, and I guess I grew up intrigued by the whole idea of unsolved crimes. When I started working in broadcasting, I'd always had it at the back of my mind that I might one day do a true crime podcast. Then one night I was in a pub and I got speaking to this guy who told me about the killings at Black Valley Farm. I knew, right there and then, that this was what I wanted my podcast to be about.'

'Why not the murder in Ireland?' Andrea asks. 'If that's the one you grew up hearing about, wouldn't it have made more sense for you to investigate that instead?'

Over the years, Nuala has learned not to let her face show any emotion when she's asked this question. As she always does, she gives an answer that is part truth and part total bullshit.

'I already knew too much about the Irish murder. I mean, I grew up hearing all these different rumours about who had killed the woman, and why. With the murders at the farm, I felt like I was approaching the story completely fresh.'

Andrea raises her right eyebrow, but doesn't say anything.

'What?' Nuala says.

'You already knew too much?' There's a hint of a smile at the edges of Andrea's lips. 'Surely that's a good reason to pursue your own investigation?'

'When I left Ireland,' Nuala says, deciding it wouldn't do any harm to give Andrea a little more, 'I never wanted to go back. I didn't have a particularly happy childhood –' understatement of the century – 'and going back to make the podcast in Ireland would have meant having to see people I didn't want to.'

'That makes sense.' Andrea reaches across the table and puts her hand over Nuala's. 'I'm sorry. I shouldn't have pushed you to tell me that. It's your private business, after all.'

'It's okay.'

'No.' Andrea gives Nuala's hand a quick squeeze. 'It's not okay. Besides, it doesn't matter why you chose the farm as your subject. You did a great job, that's what's important. I would really love to know more about how you made it and how you managed to find all those people, especially that woman in the final episode. What was her name again? Mary, Margaret?'

'Marianne.'

'Yes.' Andrea beams delightedly. 'Marianne. Of course. But then she disappeared again, didn't she? That must have been so frustrating.'

Marianne is the last thing Nuala wants to talk about, now or any other time. She forces herself to smile, and pushes her chair back.

'Excuse me,' she says. 'I just need to pop to the loo.'

She grabs her bag and heads to the toilet before Andrea can say anything. Inside the ladies she splashes cold water on her face and looks at her reflection in the mirror. The face of a liar, she thinks, before grabbing a handful of paper towels and padding the drops of water off her face before her make-up starts to run.

This whole conversation has made her uncomfortable, and it's not only because of the memories it's stirred up. Her sister's murder is always with her, a dark presence lurking beneath all the good moments in Nuala's life. Lovely Marion, who was bludgeoned to death on her way home from the pub one night and whose killer has never been found. Mostly, Nuala tries not to think about Marion or what happened to her. But right now, thanks to Andrea's questions, it's difficult to think of anything else.

It's not the first time Andrea has asked Nuala about Marianne and the podcast. Of course, there might be nothing behind Andrea's questions, but Nuala knows there must be a reason Andrea's so interested. As she stares at her reflection in the mirror, Nuala suddenly works it out. When she does, it's so obvious she doesn't know why she hasn't thought of it before now. Because it's clear as day that Andrea must have a personal connection to one of the victims. And Nuala's going to go out there right now and ask Andrea which one of them it is.

She picks up her bag, already planning what she's going to say, when her phone pings with a notification. It's a new Instagram message. She holds her breath as she opens the app, half afraid to see who it's from. When she reads the message, she knows her fear was justified. It's from *truthfinder*.

There's no text, just a photo that seems to take an age to load onto her screen. When it finally appears, she wishes it hadn't. More than anything, she wants to unsee it, make it go away. Her stomach contracts, vomit bursts up her throat. She leans over the sink, retching until her eyes water. When she's finished, she lifts her head and looks in the mirror again.

But this time, she doesn't see her own face staring back at her. She sees the picture on her phone. Her son, hanging off the high rails of the climbing frame in the little park down the road from their apartment. In the photo, Josh is smiling. His little face lit up, bright and happy, without a care in the world.

Chapter 25

Nuala tells Andrea she isn't feeling well. It's a crap excuse, but she doesn't care whether Andrea believes her or not. The only thing on her mind right now is her son. Someone has been following him, watching him, taking photos of him.

A combination of fear and anger gives Nuala the fuel she needs to get through the next few hours. On the train, she calls ahead to the school and tells them she has a family emergency back in Ireland which means she'll need to take Josh out of school today. The woman she speaks to says something about unauthorised absence, but Nuala cuts her off mid-sentence. Half term starts in a few days, and Josh is only six. At that age, Nuala's pretty sure most of the school day is spent playing rather than learning.

The next phone call is going to be a bit trickier, but she has thought through all her options and this is the only one that feels right. Even so, after she scrolls through her list of contacts and finds the name she wants, she hesitates before making the call. The train is pulling into Limehouse station before she presses her thumb on the screen. She puts the phone to her ear as she gets off the train, hears it ring out twice and then her ex-girlfriend's familiar voice:

'Nuala? Is everything okay?'

She stops walking and closes her eyes, soaking up the sound of Liz's voice. A man walks into her, muttering something rude as he pushes past. She opens her eyes, flicks him the finger and realises she doesn't know how to tell Liz why she's called her out of the blue like this.

'What's going on?' Liz says. 'Is Josh okay? You'd better not be calling to tell me he's not coming to stay next week. Three whole days with my wee man. I'm ridiculously excited.'

Wee man. The phrase triggers a rush of memories. Happy times when Liz, Nuala and Josh were a family. Before Nuala messed everything up to the point Liz decided Nuala wasn't the person she wanted to spend the rest of her life with.

'He's fine.' Nuala starts walking, the heels of her shoes clicking on the tiled platform. 'But something's come up at work. I was wondering if you'd be able to take him a little sooner than planned.'

'How soon?'

She uses her Oyster card to push through the ticket barrier and walks down the steps to street level.

'Today?' Then, when Liz doesn't reply, 'There's no one else I can ask. Please, Liz?'

When they were still together, they'd spoken about Liz adopting Josh so they would both be his official parents. Even though that never happened, Nuala knows Liz loves her son every bit as much as she does. As for Josh, he adores Liz. There were many things Nuala and Liz didn't see eye to eye on, but they've always been united when it comes to Josh. Liz and Nuala might not be a couple any longer, but Liz will always be part of Josh's life.

'It's not very convenient,' Liz says after a long pause. 'Is there really no one else who could help you out?'

Nuala doesn't bother replying, because they both know the answer to that one. Of course there isn't anyone else. Nuala is brilliant at pissing people off, not nearly as good at making friends. The handful of friends she managed to accumulate have mostly drifted away in recent years. At first, Nuala was so caught up caring for Josh and trying to pick up the broken pieces of her career, she barely noticed. By the time she did, it was too late.

'You're the only one I trust.'

Liz sighs. 'Tell me why. Because if you want me to babysit your child at such short notice, then I need to know what sort of shit you've got yourself into this time.'

'I'm not in any shit,' Nuala retorts, angry at Liz for assuming the worst – even if she happens to have hit the nail right on the head. 'It's a work thing, that's all.'

'What sort of temping job is so important you have to find someone else to look after your son?'

'I'm not temping at the moment. In fact, I've started something really exciting. I'm working on a documentary.'

'What's it about?'

'I'm not allowed to say,' Nuala says. 'It's all very hush, hush. If I tell you, I'll have to kill you.'

Obviously, she means this as a joke but Liz doesn't laugh.

'You haven't changed, Nuala. Then again, I don't know why I ever thought you would.'

'What's that supposed to mean?' Nuala asks, pissed off now. She'd forgotten this side of Liz – the holier-than-thou attitude and the ridiculously high standards that no normal human could ever have any chance of living up to. Just because Liz would rather die than ever tell a white lie or bend the rules, she expects everyone else to be the same.

'It doesn't matter,' Liz says. 'Tell me what time you'll be coming down.'

'I'm on my way to pick him up now,' Nuala says. 'We'll need to go home and pack up his stuff. I reckon we could be with you by mid-afternoon.'

'Fine. But you'd better understand, I'm doing this for Josh, not for you.'

'I know.' Nuala's eyes pricked with unexpected tears. 'Thanks, Liz.'

Three hours later, she's pulling up outside a pale blue, weatherboard cottage on the windswept Dungeness coast. Stepping out of the car, Nuala looks around, her chest aching with the pain of past mistakes that she can never undo. This place is exactly the sort of home they'd spoken about living in together one day. Now, Liz is living their dream with a woman Nuala has never met, while Nuala is still in London, still putting her career before everything else. Or, as Liz might say, at the cost of everything else.

The front door opens and the ache in Nuala's chest grows worse as Josh lets go of her hand and races towards the woman who'd been such an important part of the first four years of his life. Liz's face lights up with that big, wide smile of hers, as she swoops Josh off the ground and hugs him to her.

'Thanks for this,' Nuala says, when she's close enough to smell the familiar citrus and jasmine scent of Liz's favourite perfume.

'You want to come in for a coffee before you head off?' Liz asks.

Nuala wants nothing more than to step inside this pretty house, and spend the next few days hanging out on the beach with her son and the only woman she's ever loved.

'No thanks.'

'Suit yourself.'

'Is Trish okay about Josh being here?' she asks.

'Trish doesn't live here anymore,' Liz says. 'We split up.'

'Oh.' Nuala has to bite her lip to stop herself smiling. 'I'm sorry to hear that.'

'Are you in some sort of trouble?' Liz asks suddenly. 'Is that what this is about?'

'No.' Nuala lies, because it's always been easier to lie to Liz than tell the truth. One of the reasons, although not the only one, that Liz decided she'd had enough.

'So it's nothing to do with that weird message you asked me about?'

Nuala has an overwhelming urge to tell her then. In fact, there's a whole load of things she wants to say right now. Starting with sorry and ending with a plea for Liz to give their relationship another chance. But it's too late for that. When she left, Liz made it perfectly clear there wouldn't be any second chances where Nuala was concerned.

'Absolutely not.' Nuala fixes a smile on her face, calls goodbye to Josh, who barely looks around, thanks Liz again and gets the hell out of there before she makes a complete tit of herself.

Chapter 26

I'm staying at a hostel in Deptford. It's the cheapest place I could find. I've got a bunk bed in a shared room. Compared to some other places I've stayed, this one isn't too bad. The bathrooms are clean, there's a common room on the ground floor and I have a curtain I can pull across my bed for privacy. The bed costs £20 a night, which includes access to the hostel's Wi-Fi. I had to use Kath's card to pay because they wouldn't accept cash when I checked in.

It's three days since I left Sheffield and I'm still missing Kath. I miss the conversations we had in the evenings, the meals Kath used to cook for me and all the different ways she tried to show me that my small life mattered.

After the farm, I taught myself to stop missing people. I found a way to push down the pain and ignore the aching sadness that was so bad it sometimes felt like I was drowning. It's easier – far easier – to not feel anything. It's the feelings that cause pain. No feelings means no pain.

On a TV programme I watched a while ago, the police were able to track down a suspect from his mobile phone signal. So one of the first things I did after I arrived in London was to buy a new, pay-as-you-go handset. It's cheap and clunky but it's fine for browsing the internet during the long evenings at the hostel.

My plan is to find Nuala and ask her about Marianne. I thought this would be easy. On Nuala's website, there's a link you can click on to send her a message. But when I tried to do this, on the coach from Sheffield to London, there was a box asking for my email address. I don't have an email or any social media accounts.

I could create a false email address, but I don't know if the police might be able to use that to find me and I don't want to risk that. So instead of contacting Nuala through her website, I've been using her social media posts to try to find her. I know from her Instagram account that she travels to work on the DLR. I don't know where her journey starts but it ends at Lewisham. From there, Nuala walks to Blackheath, where her new job is.

Like I've done the last two mornings, I get up early and arrive at Lewisham DLR station a few minutes before six. Over the next few hours, there must be hundreds of people going in and out of the station. But I can't seem to spot Nuala Fox and, by nine forty-five, I know I'm not going to see her. This is the third morning I've done this, and I'm starting to worry I'll never find her. The problem is, there are simply so many people it's too easy to miss her.

According to the map on my phone, it's a twenty-five-minute walk from Lewisham station up to Blackheath. I walk the route shown on my map, looking for the pretty street Nuala posted a photo of. There are plenty of lovely streets but none of them is the one on Nuala's Instagram. I know I've only been in London a few days, but I'm already feeling disheartened. This is going to be harder than I'd realised.

Blackheath is beautiful. It's a village with a few winding streets all leading to a massive open space lined with huge houses. I spend the next few hours walking around and looking at the people sitting in the bars and coffee shops. There are lots of women about my age, but they look so different to me it's like we live on different planets. Apart from my jacket, which I took from Mrs Heaton's house last summer because I knew she'd never miss it, and my underwear, everything I'm wearing has come from a charity shop. Nothing fits properly and when I catch my reflection in a window, I see someone fat and ugly with horrible hair and a white face. In contrast, these Blackheath women have shiny hair and skin that glows and they're wearing leggings that fit them like a second skin. They are all so skinny, they've clearly never eaten a cheese toastie in their entire lives. And I'd bet my last pound that none of them have arms so covered in scars they have to wear long sleeves all the time.

They move about in shiny packs, their voices loud and confident as they pass me on the street without noticing me. Something hard and unpleasant settles in my chest each time I have to step aside so they don't knock into me.

Later, I walk down to Greenwich and spend the afternoon wandering around aimlessly. As the sun starts to sink low in the sky, I head back to the hostel. I'm almost there when I get a sudden, overwhelming urge to hear Kath's voice. I still have her number because my contacts transferred across automatically when I set up my new phone. Before I can change my mind, I take out my phone and make the call.

'Hello?' Kath answers almost immediately.

'Hi,' I say, barely managing to speak above a whisper. 'It's me.'

'Clare? Oh thank goodness. I've been so worried about you. Where are you? Are you okay?'

'I'm fine.'

Before I can say anything else, someone grabs hold of me from behind. I open my mouth to scream, but a hand clamps across my face, blocking out the sound. An arm wraps around my middle and I'm dragged back, into the alley that I've just passed. The phone slips from my hand, crashes onto the ground.

I try to get out of his grip, arms and fists and legs and feet lashing out, my fingers scrabbling at the hand across my face. But nothing I do makes any difference. He's pulled me into the alley, long and narrow with tall buildings on either side that block out the sky.

Panic flares up inside me as he shoves me, face first, into the wall. His body is hot against my back. I can't breathe because he's holding me so tight and I know he's going to hurt me and I won't be able to stop him.

'Stop fighting, Clare. It's okay.'

No. It's not possible. But I'd recognise that voice anywhere. Fear gives me strength and I throw my head back, feel it connect with his face. He screams and lets me go and, as I swing around, I see him stagger back, hands over his face.

I almost make it, am nearly back on the street, when he grabs me by the hair. Again, I try to fight him off, but he's too strong. He pulls harder and suddenly I'm falling back and there's not a single thing I can do.

Chapter 27

I land on my back, hitting the ground hard. I can't see him, but I can hear him. Heavy breaths and the sound of a zip being opened. When I roll over and try to get up, he grabs my shoulder and I scream.

'Stop it.' Arnie crouches down in front of me, his face too close to mine, his hand covering my mouth. The stink of his cologne makes my stomach twist. 'Please. Stop making that racket.'

I want to ask him what he's doing here, how he found me and what's going to happen now, but I can't speak. Even when he takes his hand away, it's like my mouth has forgotten how to form words.

'Come on,' he says. 'Let's get you off the ground.'

He half-drags, half-pulls me until I'm standing up. I look around for my bag, which fell during the scuffle.

'Here.' He holds it up. I remember the sound I heard. The bastard was looking through my stuff. Again.

'I want to talk to you, that's all,' he says, as I grab the bag and swing it over my shoulder. 'If you knew how long I've been trying to find you…' His voice cracks, like he's about to cry. 'Sorry. This isn't easy for me. Listen, I don't want to do this here. Is there somewhere we can go where we can talk properly? How about the hostel where you're staying?'

'No. Not there.'

'Okay. That's okay. There's a pub at the end of the road. Let's go there.'

He puts his hand out, gesturing for me to walk ahead of him. I take a few steps forward, my body tense as I wait for him to grab me again. But nothing happens and before I know it, we're walking side by side towards the pub. At some point, day has become night. If it wasn't for the street lights and the welcoming glow from the pub, we'd be walking in pitch darkness.

'How did you find me?'

'You used Kath's card to pay for the hostel.'

As soon as he says it, I feel so stupid. I should have realised the banks could track where the card was being used. Any normal person would have known that. But I'm not normal and never will be.

'I shouldn't have taken her card,' I say. 'It was wrong of me, I know that. But I'm going to pay her back. Every single penny.'

'It *was* wrong,' he says, 'but I'm glad you did. If you hadn't, I'd never have found you. And you have no idea how long I've been looking for you.'

A chill runs down my spine. This is the second time he's said that.

'Who are you?'

He stops walking and looks at me.

'You really don't know?'

I search his face, trying to think where I've seen him before but it won't come to me. When I shake my head, he scowls.

'Try again.'

There's a memory then, distant and vague but strong enough to trigger a warning. This man is dangerous.

'Maybe when we sit down and talk, it will come back to me,' I say, forcing my voice to sound neutral so he doesn't know how scared I am.

'Let's hope so.'

In the pub, he holds onto my arm and insists we go together to the bar when he orders the drinks. It's because he doesn't want to let me out of his sight in case I run away. Which is exactly what I'm intending to do.

There's only one person behind the bar, a man about the same age as Arnie. As he serves drinks, I ask him where the toilets are.

'Ladies over there on the left.'

I thank him and pull my arm free as I tell Arnie, in a loud voice so the barman can hear me, that I need to use the toilet. He looks angry, but there's not much he can do to stop me with the barman right beside us.

'I won't be long,' I say, 'and when I come back we can chat properly. I can't wait.'

I feel his eyes boring into my back as I cross the bar. I know I only have a minute, two at most, before he comes looking for me. Inside the ladies, there are two cubicles and one window. It's high on the wall, and narrow, but if I can find a way to climb up there I might be able to squeeze through it.

A toilet flushes, the door to one of the cubicles opens. A woman a few years older than me comes out. She nods hello at me and goes to wash her hands in the sink. I see her face in the mirror, watching me. Probably wondering why I'm standing out here instead of going into one of the cubicles.

'Clare?' Arnie's voice, on the other side of the door. 'Everything okay in there?'

'Fine,' I call back. 'Almost ready.'

The woman dries her hands on a paper towel and whispers across to me, asking if I'm okay.

'I need to get away from that man,' I whisper back.

She nods. 'Stay here. Go into one of the cubicles and lock it. Don't come out until I'm back.'

I do exactly as she says, and wait for what feels like forever. Outside, I can hear raised voices and the scuffle of feet. Arnie shouts something, but he's further away from the toilets now and I don't catch what he's shouting about.

Then the woman's back, knocking on the cubicle door and telling me it's okay, I can come out.

'Is he gone?' I ask, opening the door.

'I told Bob he was a problem and he got a few of the lads to throw him out. But I can't promise he won't be out there waiting for you.'

'So what do I do?' I ask, because right now I have no idea. 'I'm staying in the hostel down the road, but he knows that. Even if he's not outside the pub, he'll be waiting for me at the hostel.'

'Listen to me.' The woman puts her hands on my shoulders. She's got blonde hair and a hard face but, when she speaks, her voice is soft and her eyes are kind. 'I don't know who that bloke is or why you're scared of him, but I know what it's like to be scared. My first husband was a violent pig. He's dead now, but that doesn't stop me sometimes being frightened that he's going to turn up one day and punish me for having the guts to leave him when I finally did.

'This is my pub and I'm not going to let a young woman like you walk out of here if it means putting you in danger. I've got a spare room upstairs. You can stay here tonight. I'll call my sister, get her to come over and pick up your things from the hostel. Because you know you can't go back there, don't you?'

'Yes.'

'Good.' The woman smiled. 'I'm Jess, by the way. What's your name, love?'

'Clare Brown.'

'Well then, Clare Brown, I'm very pleased to meet you. Now don't you worry about that fella of yours. Whatever he wants from you, he's not going to get it tonight. And tomorrow, after you've had a good night's sleep, you and I will take a trip to the local police station and you can get them to make sure he can't ever hurt you again. How does that sound?'

'Fine.' I smile, because what else can I do? It's not like I can tell this woman, who's shown me such kindness, that a trip to the police station is the very last thing I'm going to do.

Chapter 28

I spend the night in Jess's spare bedroom and leave early the following morning before she's up. Her sister brought my things across from the hostel last night, which means I don't need to go back there.

Like the other mornings, I walk to Lewisham train station. The only difference today is that I'm carrying my big rucksack with all my things in it, as well as my handbag. By the time I reach the station, I'm hot and out of breath.

I keep thinking I see Arnie, catching glimpses of him in every café I pass and seeing his face on the buses that move at snail's speed in the early rush-hour traffic. He's everywhere and nowhere, because each time I see him, it's never really him. Just my stupid brain trying to scare me because it knows I'm safer when I'm scared. Being scared is what's kept me hidden all these years.

Lewisham station is as busy as ever. I wonder how many people pass through it each morning. Hundreds, maybe thousands. It's difficult to imagine that many people all doing the same journey, together, each day. It's a little after eight thirty when I see a sudden flash of yellow in the crowd. It can't be, surely? But then I see her face and it really is her. Nuala Fox in her yellow coat, moving like she's got something bouncy in the heels of her shoes.

I'm standing on the opposite side of the road, and Nuala doesn't so much as glance across as she glides past. She doesn't walk in the direction I'd expected. Instead of going towards the hill that leads up to Blackheath, she goes in the opposite direction – into the centre of Lewisham. I count to thirty in my head and go after her.

I follow her through the back streets of Lewisham that wind gradually up to a part of Blackheath I haven't been to before. After about twenty-five minutes, Nuala swings right into a tree-lined street that I immediately recognise from her Instagram photos. The houses here are all huge and beautiful.

I hang far enough back so that Nuala won't see my face if she turns around. Now I've finally found her, I'm suddenly scared of actually talking to her. Nuala walks fast, her heels click-clacking on the pavement, only slowing down to push open the gate of one of the houses midway along the street. This time, I count to sixty before I move forward.

The house is double-fronted and detached, with floor-to-ceiling windows on either side of a shiny black front door. The garden is plenty big enough for the three cars that are parked in the driveway. Two black SUVs with tinted windows sit alongside a red convertible. There's a small sign on the pillar by the gate with the words 'Progress Party' written on it in black and, in red text beneath, 'Britain for the British'. Above the sign, there's a security camera facing the street.

I cross the road to get a better look at the entire house. I catch a flash of movement behind one of the upstairs windows, and see the outline of a person standing there. The sun is behind me; its reflection bouncing off the window means I can't see the person in any detail, not even to make out if they're a man or a woman. But whoever they are, they'll be able to see me clearly.

I'm shivering, and it's got nothing to do with the October weather. Some animal instinct, warning me. Crossing back over, I read the sign outside the house again. *Britain for the British*. What does that even mean?

I take out my phone, type 'Progress Party' into the internet search engine. The signal's rubbish, and the information takes a while to load. Eventually, I get a list of newspaper articles and a Wikipedia entry. I click on this and wait, again, for the inform-ation to appear. When it finally does, I scan the text. Words jump out at me: 'far right' and 'fascism' and 'xenophobia'. I'm not sure what they mean exactly, but I think they're describing something bad.

The Wikipedia page says the party was founded by people called Roger Constantin and Andrea Leach. There's a link for each of their names. I click on the link for Roger first. When the photo loads, I see a man in his forties or fifties with tanned skin and dark hair swept back from his face. Nothing about him is familiar. I shut the photo down and click the link for Andrea Leach.

It takes another age for the photo to appear. When it does, I stop breathing. There's a screeching sound inside my head, pounding against the sides of my skull and behind my eyes. A cascade of memories rushes towards me, too fast and too furious and far, far more than I can cope with.

On the street, a woman is walking towards me. There's a young girl with her, and they're holding hands. The woman smiles but, as she gets closer, the smile disappears and she crosses the road, hurrying the girl along with her.

I squeeze my eyes shut. It's a mistake. It has to be. Because this cannot be happening. She's dead. I killed her and my memory of that moment is seared onto my brain. But when I open my eyes and look at my phone, her face is still there. The same indigo blue eyes, the same smile that seems charming until you know she only smiles like that when she's about to hurt you.

Chapter 29

Roger is standing at the window, looking out towards the street. As Nuala watches, he takes his phone out and dials a number.

'There's a woman outside,' he says to whoever he's called. 'She looks a bit dodgy. Can one of you go check her out?'

He hangs up, puts his phone in his jeans pocket and turns his attention to Nuala. 'We get a lot of people turning up here, looking to cause trouble. Not everyone understands what we're about.'

It's not that people don't understand, Nuala thinks, it's that they don't like your politics. But she doesn't say this. Partly because her mind is preoccupied with *truthfinder*, still trying to work out who they are and when they'll make their next move. And partly because, despite a slight easing in his attitude towards her, she's still trying to keep her interactions with Roger to a bare minimum.

The other day, she overheard him once again telling Andrea his reservations about hiring Nuala. Turns out she wasn't his first – or even last – choice to make the film. He'd wanted someone with a much bigger profile than Nuala has. Someone like Emily Maitlis or Fiona Bruce, instead of 'some jumped-up mick with an attitude'.

'Everything okay?' Andrea asks, coming into the room.

She smiles at Nuala, who makes herself smile back. Since yesterday at the coffee shop, she doesn't know whether she can trust Andrea. She's gone back over that moment repeatedly, and there's something about the timing that unnerves her. It seems an odd coincidence that, two minutes after Andrea was asking difficult questions about Marianne, Nuala received the message on Instagram. Plus, when Nuala left the toilets and went back to the table, she could swear she'd seen Andrea quickly slipping her phone into her bag as if she didn't want Nuala to see it. Nuala's starting to think Andrea and *truthfinder* might be the same person.

At least Josh is safe, which is more important than anything else. He called last night, full of stories about his first day at Dungeness and asking how long he could stay because 'it's much more fun here than at home, Mummy'.

'We're fine,' Roger says, answering Andrea's question, 'aren't we, Nuala?'

'Roger was telling me you sometimes get people turning up here looking to cause trouble,' Nuala says.

'It doesn't happen very often.' Andrea frowns as she looks across the room to Roger, still standing by the window. 'Is there someone out there now?'

'I've sent the boys to check her out,' Roger says, 'nothing for you to worry about.'

But that doesn't stop Andrea crossing the room to see for herself.

'I can't see her properly,' she says. 'She's too far away for me to make out her face.'

'The cameras will have captured her,' Roger says, referring to the security cameras dotted around the perimeter of the house.

Nuala zones out as Andrea and Roger start talking about some dinner they're going to later this evening. Today is meant to be the first day of filming. They're due to record an interview, an intimate conversation between Nuala and Andrea, focusing almost completely on the first seventeen years of Andrea's life. The camera crew have set up in the room next door, and Nuala's arrived early to make sure everything is ready to go. But so far, Andrea hasn't shown any interest in the interview. Instead, she's thrown Nuala an endless list of excuses for delaying it.

Nuala can't sit around all day waiting for Andrea. She needs to do something. As she runs through her list of options, she gets an idea.

'Excuse me,' she says. Then, when they both turn to look at her, 'The woman outside. Why don't I go and speak to her? It might be good for the documentary to get some footage of people who don't agree with your politics.'

'That's a terrible idea,' Roger says quickly.

'Is it?' Andrea says. 'We want to be as open as possible, remember? There's no point doing this if we don't respond to the views of our detractors.' She turns to Nuala. 'Do it. Go now before the boys scare her off. Get the conversation on camera so I can watch it and respond to whatever puerile allegations she throws at me.'

Before she goes down the stairs, Nuala pops her head into the room they've set up for the recording and tells Gary, the cameraman, there's been a change of plan.

'I'll speak to her by myself first,' she says. 'Hopefully I can persuade her to give us an interview. As soon as she gives the go ahead, I'll call you.'

But when she gets outside, there's no woman to be seen. Just Goon Number One who's speaking on his phone. When he sees Nuala, he ends the call and slips the phone into the front pocket of his too-tight jeans.

'The woman who was here a few minutes ago,' Nuala says, 'where is she?'

'What's it to you?' he asks.

'I want to speak to her.'

As she brushes past him, he grabs her by the arm.

'Be careful. Something's not right with that one.'

Nuala looks down at his hand on her arm.

'Let go of me.'

'We know all about you,' he says. 'The allegations you made, and the reason you lost your job. Women like you, who go around trying to ruin men's reputations, don't deserve to be working.'

'I don't have to explain myself to you,' Nuala says, trying to keep the tremor out of her voice. 'Now you've got exactly two seconds to let me go before I scream as loudly as I can.'

He leans his face close to hers. His breath smells of meat and boiled vegetables.

'You've got a little boy,' he says. 'Josh, isn't it? A good name, that. Shame he hasn't got a dad. Young men need good role models. Maybe you should start bringing him to work. We could take care of him, show him a thing or two about what it means to be a man.'

Nuala's stomach spasms and bile rises up in her throat.

'Fuck off,' she hisses.

He laughs and lets her go, stepping back with his hands in the air, as if he's harmless. She feels dirty, like he's defiled her. She wants to hit him, punch his ugly face and flatten his nose. But he's already turned away and is walking back to the house, clearly bored with her now he's had his say.

'Wanker,' Nuala mutters, before running away from him. She runs fast, needing to put space between herself and what's just happened. The street ends in a T-junction. If Nuala turns left, the road will take her up the hill towards Blackheath. If she goes the other way, she'll end up in Lewisham. After a moment's hesitation, she swings right and runs down the hill.

She swerves past several people – an elderly couple, a gang of teenage girls, a man weaving left and right as if he's had too much to drink. And then, up ahead, she sees a woman bent double like she's trying to catch her breath, an oversized rucksack on the ground beside her.

'Hello?' Nuala calls. 'Excuse me, can I speak to you?'

The woman looks up and Nuala waves.

'Hello,' she repeats. 'A quick word, if that's okay?'

She's close enough to see the expression on the woman's face. And recognises it for what it is: fear. For some reason, this woman is terrified.

'It's okay.' Nuala stops running and puts her hands in the air, unconsciously imitating Goon One's gesture from a few moments earlier. 'I just want to talk to you.'

It's obviously the wrong thing to say. The woman picks up the rucksack and starts running. And she's fast, very fast. Nuala chases after her, down the hill towards the main road at the end. But by the time she reaches the bottom, the woman is gone. Nuala stands on the street, hands on her hips while she waits for her breathing to return to normal, trying to work out where she's seen the woman before.

The question bugs her for the rest of the afternoon, and later, when she's at home that evening. But it seems like the harder she tries to remember, the more elusive the memory becomes until, eventually, she has no choice but to give up trying.

Chapter 30

My head is spinning with too many thoughts. I'd forgotten what real fear feels like. This dizzying, spiralling, out of control panic. I need to get away from here, but I can't move. Someone touches my shoulder, and I scream. I'm too scared to look around because I know it's her. But then I hear a man's voice, asking me what I'm doing. I twist my head a fraction. See big shoulders bulging through the fabric of a white shirt. Not her, then.

I duck sideways, away from him, and suddenly I'm moving. He shouts after me, telling me to stop, but I keep going. I run until I can't run any further. Throwing my rucksack to the ground, I lean forward, hands on my thighs, waiting for my breathing to slow down.

'Hello? Excuse me, can I speak to you?'

It's Nuala Fox. She's running towards me, waving. When she sees me looking at her, she stops running and tries to tell me it's okay, she just wants to talk to me.

I grab the rucksack and run away. I can hear her shouting after me, but I don't stop. People's faces flash past me. A man is in front of me with a black dog on a long lead. I swerve to the left, narrowly avoiding the dog, and keep running until I've reached the bottom of the hill and I'm standing on a busy road with cars roaring past in both directions. When I risk looking back, there's no one following me.

It's not the first time something like this has happened. I've seen her before, countless times. Except, of course, it's never actually her. This is different. Because all the other times, I saw someone who looked like she did back at the farm. The woman in the photo is older. Her hair is a different colour and she has lines around her eyes that were never there when I knew her. She looks like she's aged, which is exactly what she would have done if she was still alive.

But she's not alive. This is the one thing I know with absolute certainty. I start laughing, and can't stop, relief making me hysterical. I laugh until tears are pouring down my face and my chest aches. When the laughing eases off, I get my phone out and open the internet again. As I wait for the photo to load, I tell myself – over and over – that as soon as I see it I'll realise I've made a stupid mistake. But that's not what happens. If anything, when I see her this time I'm even more convinced. It's Mother.

'No. No, no, no, no, no.'

I close my eyes shut, forcing my mind to go back to that night. It was cold. I remember shivering as I pulled open the front door and saw the two women outside. There was a full moon and that made them seem ghostly, like two silver spirits. After that, the memories blur and get confused. Someone was screaming, I think it was me but I can't be sure. The knife was in my hand, although I don't know at what point I went to get it or what I'd been planning to do with it. The one clear memory I have is the rush of blood, warm and wet against my skin and smelling of the coins we kept in the big glass jar in the kitchen.

I stabbed her with that knife. I felt her blood and I watched her fall. I didn't stay to see her die but I knew I'd killed her because hers was the first body George Fisher saw when he arrived at the farm that afternoon ten years ago. And on Nuala's podcast, Marianne said she saw Rosemary's body too. So who is this woman I'm looking at?

Her blue eyes bore into me from the screen, and it's like she's really looking at me. I stuff the phone back into the pocket of my jeans and I start running again, faster this time, trying to escape the sound and the memories and the rage and the fear. I run until my lungs won't let me go any further, and my legs are so heavy I can't go another step, and my heart is beating so hard and fast it feels as if it's about to burst through my chest. And I wish it would. I wish my whole body would explode into thousands of tiny pieces until there's nothing left of me at all.

Part Two

Chapter 1

Before

Lydia's new home was called Black Valley Farm. She didn't know where, exactly, the farm was – but it was a long way from her old home in Cambridge, where she had lived for the first thirteen years of her life. They'd moved here to get away from her dad, because of his drinking and his anger issues. Mum had told Lydia the farm would be a new start for them both, somewhere they'd be safe.

At first, Lydia had been excited about the move. She loved her dad but she was scared of him too. He was mostly drunk, and always angry. Three weeks before they left, Mum had ended up in hospital. If it wasn't for Mum's friend Rosemary, they'd have had nowhere to go. But Rosemary owned the farm and she wanted it to be a sanctuary for women like Mum, who had husbands that beat them so badly they had to go to hospital.

There were fourteen people living on the farm, ten adults and four children – Lydia, and her brothers and sister, Leo, Billy and Martha. They weren't her actual brothers and sister, but she had to pretend they were. You had to pretend a lot of things on the farm. You weren't allowed to call Rosemary by her name. Instead, you had to call her Mother because she was the mother of all the children who lived here. Which was confusing and unfair, because Lydia's real mother lived here too, except now she was called Aunt Elizabeth and she mostly acted as if she didn't remember she had actually once been Lydia's mum.

They didn't have a TV on the farm, or a radio. There wasn't even a telephone, so Lydia couldn't dial 999 and ask someone to come and rescue her. Worse than all of this, though, were the clothes. When she'd arrived, Rosemary had taken her suitcase and told her she wouldn't be needing any of those clothes anymore. On the farm, all the girls wore the same clothes – a long white skirt and a blouse that you had to wear buttoned up right to your neck, even if it was too tight and made you feel like you were choking.

The farm was a two-storey, grey-brick building in the middle of nowhere. Apart from Mother and Peter, who lived in the annex which was a narrow building attached to the side of the farmhouse, everyone else lived together in the main house. Upstairs, there were three bedrooms and one bathroom. The girls all slept together in one room, the 'aunts' in the big room at the front. The smallest bedroom was for the boys, Leo and Billy.

Outside the farmhouse, all you could see were fields and hills and, far away in the distance, shimmering like it was a dream, was the sea. Lydia liked to imagine what it would be like to race across the green fields and not stop until she reached the water. This was something she could only imagine, not do in real life, because the children who lived on the farm weren't ever allowed to leave.

A high metal fence surrounded the farm, and the entrance was blocked off by massive iron gates that were kept locked. The fence and the gates were electric, which meant if you touched them you got a shock. Even if someone managed to climb the fence or the gates, there was barbed wire running along the top that would cut through their clothes and skin.

Living on the farm was like being in prison, and Lydia hated it. She wished, more than anything, she could go back to her old life. Even at home with Dad, with his drinking and his shouting and his big fists, was better than this place. Plus, Rosemary-who-she-had-to-call-Mother-even-though-she-wasn't-her-mother was every bit as mean and scary as Dad. The only difference was that Mother wasn't always mean, which meant that Lydia could never work out if she loved Mother or hated her.

Take this week, for example, when Lydia's bleeding had started. She'd gone to the toilet after morning prayers and seen the blood on her pants. At first, she'd thought it was a Punishment for the bad things she'd done, and the bad thoughts she still had every single day about hating Mother and Peter and the other adults in this stupid place.

She had stuffed her pants with toilet paper and done everything she could to hide the bleeding from the others. But the blood had soaked through the paper, staining her white skirt. She'd been terrified when little Martha asked her what the stain was. You weren't allowed to get your clothes dirty, and when Aunt Leila came over to her after the evening meal and said Mother wanted to see her, Lydia had expected the worst.

But Mother had been pleased, not angry. She'd explained what the bleeding was and told Lydia this would happen to her every month. The bleeding was a gift, a sign that Lydia was growing up. In a few years, Mother said, Lydia could start her training to become an aunt. And even though Lydia didn't want to be an aunt because no way was she going to be living in this terrible place when she was older, she couldn't help the warm glow in her stomach when Mother stroked her face and her shoulders and told Lydia how special she was.

'Our bodies belong to the Lord and we worship him by creating life in his image,' Mother whispered, her voice soft and soothing like a half-remembered song from when Lydia was a little girl. 'It's a blessing, dear Lydia.'

That had been four days ago and, ever since, Mother had treated Lydia differently. Today, before evening prayers, she'd called Lydia into the kitchen of the annex where Mother lived with Peter, and offered her a whole slice of chocolate cake. It had been, by some way, the most delicious thing Lydia had eaten since arriving on the farm.

But no amount of kindness or chocolate cake was going to change Lydia's mind. She hated the farm and, the first chance she got, she was getting out of here.

Chapter 2

I've come to Hastings, a seaside town on the south coast.

I'm staying in a room over a pub, on a cobbled street in the Old Town. The room is small, but it's got its own bathroom. More important, the landlord didn't seem bothered when I asked if I could pay with cash. I've been here for hours now, too scared to leave my room. If I could, I'd stay here for the rest of my life, hidden away from the world and all the dangerous things that are out there.

I've spent the time reading everything I can find about Andrea Leach. My eyes are gritty from staring at the screen on my phone. Here are the things I've learned about her. She grew up in a remote part of Australia, hundreds of miles away from anywhere. She didn't go to a proper school, all her lessons were done through something called School of the Air. Her parents owned a huge farm, called an outback station, with thousands of acres of land.

The farm was so big they needed a small plane to get from one end of the property to the other. When Andrea was seventeen, her parents flew off in the plane one morning to check some sheep at the far end of the farm and never came back. The plane crashed, killing both her parents. Soon after that, Andrea sold the farm and left Australia. After years spent travelling and living off her inheritance, she settled on the Greek island of Santorini where she eventually met a man called Roger Constantin.

Eighteen months ago, Roger and Andrea started a new political party. In one article I read, the Progress Party was described as a 'minor political party which, more than likely, will die a death over the next year'. But not everyone agrees. One journalist in the *Guardian* says it's an abhorrent, far right party that should be shut down before it causes any real damage. I have no idea what 'far right' means and, after looking it up on the internet, all I really understand is that it's something to do with politics and it's the opposite of something called 'Communism'.

I've got a photo of Andrea Leach open on my phone. I keep zooming in and out, searching her face for differences from the face I remember. They must be twins, I've decided. Or doppelgangers, which is a new word I learned today when I was trying to make sense of this.

Part of me wishes I hadn't run. Because if I'd gone into the house and looked Andrea in the face, I'd know for sure. But I already know, don't I? My memories of that night are a confused jumble, but I remember that moment. The weight of the knife in my hand, and the blood. The look on her face as she fell, angry and confused and a little bit scared.

Is it possible none of that happened? No. Yes. Maybe. I don't know. Terrified that my confused brain has tricked me, that nothing I remember is actually true, I grab my rucksack and start looking through it. At first, I think the envelope isn't there and this makes me even more scared. I turn the rucksack upside down, emptying the contents onto the bed.

The envelope is the last thing to fall out. I lay the newspaper clippings on the bed side by side, in the order they were first published. It's all there, exactly as I remembered. I'm not going mad. The necklace has fallen out too. I pick this up now, fingering the heart-shaped locket with the first letter of my name – my real name – engraved on it. Most of the memories associated with this necklace are bad ones. I should have got rid of it years ago, but I've never been able to. It's the only thing

I've got from my previous life. Maybe I keep it to remind me that I wasn't always boring Clare Brown.

As I look at the first newspaper story, I remember Jasper showing it to me. He was angry, his skinny body shaking as he pointed at my face on the front page and asked me what the hell I'd done. When I didn't answer right away, he grabbed me by the throat and pushed me up against the wall of the sitting room. He said he'd kill me if I didn't tell him the truth. He kept his hand around my throat while I spoke, the words tumbling out of me because it was a relief to finally tell someone.

When I'd finished, he smiled and asked me what it had felt like to stick a knife into someone and watch them die. On the podcast, he said he'd been scared of me. That wasn't true. He'd never been scared, but I had. More or less the whole time we were together.

Pushing Jasper to the back of my mind, I scan the rest of the stories. My young face in every one of them, different words written about me depending on the newspaper. In some, I'm a 'witness', in others a 'suspected killer'. In all of them, there are details of nine victims, including the woman who was stabbed.

I killed her.

I killed all of them.

They were my family, and they're all dead because of me.

Chapter 3

They're in Andrea's office, the cameras rolling as Andrea tells Nuala about her decision to leave Australia.

'After my parents died, I thought about staying on the farm by myself. But it was so remote. We lived in the middle of the outback, you see. Our closest neighbour was over a hundred miles away. Once I'd got over the initial shock of losing my parents, I knew I needed to get away. I was desperate to travel and see the world I'd learned so much about. I wanted to visit Venice and Paris and come to England, where my mother was from. I wanted to live a bigger, more exciting life than I could ever have on the farm. Of course, it wasn't as easy as simply packing a bag and heading off. I had to sort out my parents' affairs first, sell the farm, apply for a passport.'

'And while all that was going on, you were alone on the farm?'

'Yes.'

Nuala waits for Andrea to say more, but it's clear that's as much as she's going to get out of her for now. Elinor, the director, obviously thinks the same because she suggests they should take a break.

'I'm stepping outside for a bit of fresh air,' Andrea says, standing up and opening one of the French windows that lead into the garden.

'How do you think it's going?' Elinor asks Nuala, as soon as Andrea's out of ear shot.

'Not great,' Nuala says. 'It feels like she's delivering a pre-prepared script.'

'Yeah.' Elinor nods. 'I've picked up on that too. I'm thinking maybe we change where we shoot the next bit. We could see if she'd like to do it outside? There's something about this room that's not working.'

Nuala doesn't think the room's the problem. It's Andrea. She's been distracted ever since yesterday, when that woman appeared. Watching Andrea in the garden now, Nuala decides to join her.

'Isn't it beautiful today?' she says, sitting down beside Andrea on the wrought iron bench. 'Difficult to believe it's almost the end of October.'

Andrea's eyes are closed, her face turned up to the sun.

'I love the warm weather,' she says. 'I can't understand those people who moan about climate change. The warmer the better, as far as I'm concerned.'

'I guess if you were still living in Australia you might feel differently,' Nuala says. 'Especially if you lost your home and family in one of those terrible fires they've been having.'

Andrea shrugs, as if she couldn't care less about the fires and loss of life and everything else related to climate change.

'Tell me something, Nuala,' she says after a moment, 'do you ever wonder where she is now?'

'Who?'

'Lydia. The girl from the farm who killed those people. Where did she go? How is it possible, in this day and age, for someone to remain hidden all this time? When I listened to the podcast, I thought it was such a shame you'd discovered so much but hadn't ever managed to track her down. It makes all your hard work feel a little unfinished, don't you think?'

'I agree,' Nuala says, wondering why Andrea's brought this up out of the blue. 'I wish, more than anything, I'd been able to find her. But I never did.'

'Yet with that distinctive birthmark,' Andrea says, 'surely someone must know where she is.'

At the back of Nuala's mind, an idea is forming. But each time she tries to focus on it, it slips out of reach.

'It's easy to hide a birthmark,' Nuala says. 'All you need is a bit of concealer, right?'

'If I'd been making that podcast, I wouldn't have given up until I'd found her. That's where you and I are different, Nuala. I'm not a quitter.' Abruptly, Andrea stands up. 'Excuse me for a moment, I need a word with Roger.'

Nuala watches her go back inside, wondering what the hell that was about. It's clear that Andrea's pissed off about something. And while Nuala knows she has an excellent track record of pissing people off, she honestly can't think of anything she's done to upset Andrea. But she's obviously done something and, unless she can fix it, this documentary is dead in the water. Which means Nuala needs to find Andrea and ask her, straight out, what she's done wrong.

But when she goes back inside, there's no sign of Andrea.

'She didn't tell me where she was going,' Elinor says 'She didn't speak to me at all, in fact. Has something happened, Nuala?'

'No, of course not.' Nuala gives Elinor what she hopes is a reassuring smile as she passes.

When she steps into the hallway, she hears their voices coming from the room Roger calls 'the security hub'. He showed it to Nuala soon after she started, when he was giving her 'the grand tour'. The room has four computer screens that are connected to the security cameras at various locations around the property.

'Can't be too careful,' Roger had told her. 'Plenty of nutters out there who have it in for us. These cameras make sure we can keep track of any unwanted intruders.'

From where she's standing, Nuala can't make out what Andrea or Roger are talking about. As quietly as possible, she moves along the corridor until she's close enough to hear them.

'You'd better find her,' Andrea says. 'She's a threat and we need to neutralise her.'

'How do you know her?' Roger asks.

'That's not important,' Andrea says. 'All you need to know is that she could destroy everything.'

'I'll need a bit more information than that,' Roger says. 'We're in this together, remember? If this woman has something on you, I want to know what that is.'

'She's someone I knew when I lived in Santorini,' Andrea says, after a long pause. 'She was fixated on me back then in a totally unhealthy and terrifying way. Both her parents were dead and she saw me as some sort of surrogate mother. I suppose these days her behaviour would be classed as stalking.

'She started following me. Everywhere I went, there she was. When I asked her to stop, she turned violent. She broke into my house and trashed it. In the end, I had to take out a restraining order against her. I thought she'd moved on but if she's turned up here, it's clear she hasn't.'

'You've never mentioned this to me before,' Roger says quietly.

'It was all very distressing,' Andrea says. 'I try my best not to think about it. Please, Roger. Will you fix this for me? I can't bear to live like that again, looking over my shoulder all the time, never knowing when she's going to be there.'

The door to the room is open just enough for Nuala to see inside. Andrea and Roger are standing with their backs to her, facing the row of computer screens. The same image is on all four screens. A still, taken from the security cameras, of a woman standing on the street outside looking directly at the house. The image is grainy, and the woman's features are blurred, but Nuala recognises her instantly as the woman she chased after yesterday. And in that moment of recognition, the idea that has been piecing together moves to the front of her mind, fully formed.

She knows exactly who this woman is, and where she's seen her before.

Chapter 4

Before

Two days after her sixteenth birthday, Mother took Lydia to her private rooms and told her she had a present for her. Lydia was excited, because in all the time she'd been living on the farm, no one had ever given her anything. Mother handed her a small, square box that was wrapped inside pink paper with a pattern of red and yellow balloons. Lydia held the box, too scared to open it in case that wasn't what she was meant to do. But then Mother smiled and told Lydia to go right ahead and rip that paper off.

Inside the box, there was a gold necklace with a heart-shaped locket, the letter 'L' engraved on it. Lydia had seen other necklaces like this. All the aunts wore them, each one with the first letter of their own name engraved onto the heart. As Mother placed the necklace around Lydia's neck, she said Lydia was a very lucky girl because she was about to embark on a special adventure. Tonight, she was going to start the important job of helping to create new life.

If Lydia had known then what she knew now, she would have thrown the necklace at Mother and told her to keep it. Because creating new life turned out to be a disgusting, horrible thing that you had to do again and again, month after month, with Peter, who was the only man on the farm and smelled of something bitter and evil. Each time Lydia did it with Peter, Mother was there too. Watching to make sure Lydia didn't mess it up. The first few times, Mother had to hold Lydia down.

Until Lydia realised it was easier not to fight. It hurt less if she lay there silently and let him do it to her, while Mother stood by the bed watching them.

The only good thing about it was that you got to eat different food when you were trying to make a baby. These days, Lydia was allowed to eat her dinner with Mother and Peter, and the food they ate was way better than the food the children and aunts were given.

Mother started treating Lydia differently too. Not just by letting her eat better food, but in other ways too. In the past, whenever Mother told Lydia that she loved her, Lydia hadn't believed her. Because if you loved someone, you didn't hurt them or make them scared of you. But after she started trying to make a baby, it was like Mother really did love her. She started giving her hugs and, whenever she saw Lydia, she'd smile like she was actually pleased to see her.

At least, that's how it had been to start with. Recently, Lydia could feel something was changing. Each month, when her bleeding came again, Mother seemed to withdraw a little more. The last time Lydia started bleeding, Mother had taken her into the prayer room and had made Lydia kneel for the whole day, praying to the Lord to bless her with a child.

More than anything, Lydia wanted the prayers to work. She wanted to make Mother happy. Plus, if she did it, if a baby started growing inside her, she wouldn't have to do that horrible thing with Peter anymore. Even before this, Lydia had hated Peter. He was a tall, evil pig with piggy eyes and long, black, greasy hair, and he spent his days trying to catch the children doing something bad so he could tell Mother about them. He'd told Lydia it was their duty to try to make a baby, but she knew he liked doing it with her and that made her feel sick and hate him more.

Two of the aunts were pregnant at the moment. Aunt Sarah's baby was due in three months, and Aunt Katherine's the month after that. The babies didn't belong to the aunts, they were

Mother's children. Aunt Sarah and Aunt Katherine's job was to make the babies for Mother. As soon as the children were born, they would be handed over to Mother, like Robert and Daisy had been after they were born. When Lydia got pregnant, her baby would also become Mother's child. Which was fine by Lydia because sixteen was way too young to become a mother.

Today, Lydia was meant to be working in the garden with Aunt Elizabeth. She had been looking forward to this for two reasons. Firstly, because working in the garden was better than any of the other jobs. Out there, with the sun on your back and the countryside stretching out all the way to the sea, you could pretend you were free. The second reason was Aunt Elizabeth who, although she pretended she wasn't Lydia's real mother anymore, was kinder to Lydia than any of the other aunts. Lydia always felt better after they'd spent some time together.

But instead of being out in the garden with her real mother, Lydia had been made to come to the prayer room with the others. Next to the Box, the prayer room was the second worst place on the farm. For starters, it wasn't even a proper room. It was a shed behind the farmhouse with a false roof to make it look like a church, that was always too cold in winter and too hot in summer. When you were in here, praying, you weren't allowed to speak or look around or do anything except kneel on the hard ground with your hands clasped to your chest.

Today's service was a special one to ask the Lord for his forgiveness for whatever sins Lydia had committed and to grant her the blessed gift of a child. Mother stood at the top of the room, leading the prayers, while everyone else knelt before her.

For a while, Lydia prayed as hard as she could, but it didn't take long for her mind to start wandering. Praying was so boring, and they hadn't even been allowed breakfast which meant her tummy was grumbling. She could hear similar noises coming from other people's bellies too. Now, instead of begging for forgiveness as she was meant to be doing, all Lydia could think of was food – particularly, the things she used to eat before she moved to the farm. Pizza with tangy tomato sauce and stringy melted cheese; salt and vinegar crisps, and dry roasted peanuts; chocolate ice cream.

She groaned, the sound too loud in the quiet room. To cover up the mistake, she squeezed her eyes shut and pressed her forehead against her folded hands. She held her breath, waiting for Mother to react, but nothing happened. When Lydia risked opening her eyes a few minutes later, Mother's head was bent, her lips moving as she prayed.

Lydia tried to focus, but it was impossible. Her knees hurt, her stomach was rumbling louder than ever and she needed the toilet. She glanced across the room at Leo, kneeling on the ground beside Peter. Since Billy had died last year, they were the only two men on the farm. Although you couldn't really call Leo a man because – at fifteen – he was actually a year younger than Lydia.

At the top of the room, Mother was standing now, her hands held out in front of her, palms facing up towards Heaven.

'Dear Lord, we are grateful for this family you have given us. We give thanks every day for the life we have here in this beautiful place. We beg you now, Lord, help us to grow our family. Grant Sister Lydia the blessed gift of a child created in your image.'

Lydia turned her head a fraction, saw Aunt Elizabeth staring right at her. Before she could stop herself, Lydia gave her real mother a tiny smile. When they first came to the farm, Lydia had missed her mum terribly and had refused to call her by her new name. Until Mother made it clear what happened to children who didn't obey the rules. Most of the time, Lydia hated Aunt Elizabeth for this, but sometimes, like when they're together in the fields, she sensed there was still something there between them.

She wanted Aunt Elizabeth to smile back, but her mother was looking scared. At first, Lydia didn't understand what she could be frightened of. Then she realised the praying had stopped and, in its absence, was a deathly silence.

Aunt Elizabeth lowered her eyes. A trickle of ice-cold fear ran down Lydia's back. Slowly, she turned her head until she was facing the right way again. But it was too late. She felt the weight of everyone staring at her as the silence was broken by the tapping of stiletto heels on the hard wooden floor.

'Sister Lydia.'

Mother's voice was soft as she held out her hand, but her face was hard and angry. Lydia didn't move.

'Sister Lydia, please rise and come with me.'

Lydia looked up at Mother, standing above her with her hand out, waiting. So close Lydia could smell the sickly sweet stink of her perfume. She stood up, put her hand in Mother's and allowed herself to be led out of the prayer room. When she passed Aunt Elizabeth, Lydia looked directly at her. Her mother, who had once told five-year-old Lydia that she was the most precious thing in the entire world, kept her eyes down. Refusing to look at her own daughter as she was led away for her Punishment.

Chapter 5

Present

There's a fat silver moon and the sky is twinkling with the lights of thousands of tiny stars as we race across the wide open fields. We're holding hands, and running so fast it feels like flying. There's a wild feeling in my chest, like my heart is getting bigger and soon it's going to explode and my insides will burst open and all the little bits of me will fly into the sky and I'll become part of this great big world that is so new to me.

A scream cuts through the dream and suddenly I'm wide awake. And scared. I look around, trying to work out where I am, but I don't recognise this room. I've never seen it before and, outside the window, there's more screaming. It sounds like someone is dying.

Fluttery fear rests in my stomach and my chest is too tight. Breathing is difficult. Memories of the dream are still with me. I see us, like we were that night, holding hands as we ran towards our future life. The giddy feeling of freedom, mixed with the shock of what I'd done. The loud noise and the burst of orange light. The slow realisation that she wasn't coming back, followed by the fear of suddenly being alone.

There's another scream. My heart leaps into my throat before I realise it's a seagull. The sound reminds me of the time I spent with Jasper. The seagulls would wake me in the morning there too. Screeching on the flat roof of the block of flats next door, demanding to be noticed.

Sure enough, when I pull back the curtains to check, I see two big white birds sitting on top of the building opposite. One of them looks over at me, before opening his mouth and letting out another scream.

'Stupid bird,' I mutter, dropping the curtain and walking back to the bed. My head is fuzzy, my arms and legs ache with exhaustion. I barely slept last night, but I know I won't be able to go back to sleep now. Outside, it's a bright, sunny day and I decide to get dressed and go to the beach.

Jasper's flat in Skegness was five minutes from the beach. There, the sea was wild and rough. Here in Hastings, it's not like that at all. It's calm and so still it's more like glass than water. At the edge of the horizon, where the sea meets the start of the sky, there is a row of ships.

Out of nowhere, I start crying. The sea blurs behind the tears that run down my face. I rub them away, angry at myself for being so weak. A breeze rustles along the surface of the water and brushes against my skin.

I close my eyes, listening to the crunching sound the waves make against the shingle as I slowly breathe in and out. Gradually, the chaos inside my head clears. As it does, I realise something so obvious I don't know why it's taken me so long to see it.

With my eyes still closed, I make a list of the things I know are true.

Number 1: Nine people died that night – four women, one man and four children.

Number 2: One man and one woman were later identified, and so were two of the children. The other victims were never identified.

Number 3: One of the women was stabbed.

I open my eyes and scan the beach, although I'm not sure what I'm looking for. Maybe a reason why she lied. Because I know now, that's what happened.

Number 4: The woman who was stabbed wasn't
Mother, which means Marianne lied when she
told Nuala Fox what she'd seen that night.

It's like I've been seeing everything through a fog that's suddenly
cleared. For the first time since leaving Sheffield, I know what
needs to happen next.

Back in my room, I use my phone to create a fake Instagram
account. Too angry to be cautious because I am one hundred
per cent certain now that the woman on Nuala's podcast who
called herself Marianne was Mother. Or Andrea Leach, as
she's calling herself these days. I thought I knew exactly what
happened that night, but I'd got it all wrong. I need to know
the truth, no matter how painful it will be.

When the account is created, I take a selfie and send it to
Nuala along with a short message.

> This is Lydia, from the farm. I'm ready to speak to
> you. Please call me.

I add my phone number, check the selfie one last time, take a
deep breath and hit 'send'. There. It's done.

Chapter 6

That afternoon, they're in the East End of London. Not the 'old' East End, Andrea explains, which was traditionally home to generations of immigrants but these days is mainly populated by affluent, left-wing hipsters who don't have any idea how difficult life is for those less well off than themselves. No, Andrea is taking Nuala to the 'real' East End, which, apparently, is Dagenham, where 44.9 per cent of the population identify as white and British.

They have another community hall booked and, as Nuala watches Andrea work her magic on the crowd, she's amazed at how easy it is to see through the charm once you know it's all a big act. Now that she sees Andrea for who she really is, Nuala's embarrassed she let herself be taken in so easily.

They're filming today and, after the event, Nuala spends some time speaking to anyone who'll give her the time of day.

'What is it about the Progress Party that appeals to you?' she asks a tiny woman who could be any age between thirty and sixty.

'It's the only party that gives a damn about people like us,' the woman says, gesturing to the other people who've come today to hear Andrea speak.

This sentiment is shared repeatedly with every person Nuala speaks to. The narrative here is simple but effective: immigrants are taking our jobs; because of this we struggle to make ends meet; get rid of the immigrants and our lives will be improved dramatically.

By the time they've finished, Nuala's jaw hurts from the effort of keeping her mouth shut and not telling these people that Andrea Leach doesn't give a damn about them, and all she's doing is using their deprivation to further her political career.

In the car, on the way back to Blackheath, Andrea is all smiles and lightness. Her mood has lifted significantly since this morning and Nuala decides to take advantage of this to ask Andrea the question she's been dying to ask all day.

'Do you remember that woman who was hanging around outside the house yesterday?'

Andrea frowns, as she pretends to think. 'Oh yes.' Her face clears, as if she's just remembered. 'What about her?'

'When I ran after her,' Nuala says, 'I thought there was something familiar about her. I couldn't work it out at first, but I have now. She's the spitting image of Lydia, the woman you were asking me about earlier today.'

'Is she?' Andrea's eyebrows shoot up.

Nuala takes her phone out, scrolls through her photos until she finds one of Lydia.

'See for yourself,' she says, holding out the phone.

But Andrea shakes her head and waves the phone away. 'I didn't even see the girl the other day. How on earth would I know who she does or doesn't resemble?'

'It's definitely her,' Nuala says.

'So what?' The lightness and charm is gone now as Andrea doesn't bother to hide her irritation. 'If you think I care about some nobody who has nothing better to do than turn up outside my house causing trouble, then you're very much mistaken, Nuala.'

Bullshit, Nuala thinks. *You're a liar and you don't fool me for a second.*

'Don't you think it's strange?' Nuala says, ignoring the way Andrea's staring at her as if she wants to kill her. She's not about to be intimidated by this right-wing phoney. 'First, I make a podcast about the killings on the farm. Then, because of that podcast, you decide to hire me. Shortly after that, Lydia herself turns up outside your house. Why?'

'How the hell would I know?' Something cold and hard flashes across Andrea's face. For a moment, Nuala thinks Andrea might hit her. But she doesn't. She laughs instead.

'You got me there for a second, Nuala. You know, I actually believed you really thought the woman yesterday was the same one the police have spent all these years looking for.'

'I'm not kidding around,' Nuala says. 'It was her. No doubt about it.'

'How could it be?' Andrea asks. 'Even if, by some outside chance, Lydia is still alive and she's listened to your podcast, wouldn't you be the one person she'd be doing her best to avoid?'

'What if she wasn't there for me?'

It's the wrong thing to say. Or the right thing, depending on what Nuala wants from this exchange.

Andrea leans forward and taps the driver on the shoulder.

'Pull over as soon as you can,' she says. Then, to Nuala: 'I don't know what game you're playing, lady. But we're done. Roger was right. We should never have hired you. We should have chosen a professional, someone who actually knows what they're doing.'

'I am a professional,' Nuala says. 'If I wasn't, I might have let this go. But I'm not going to do that. What's your connection with Lydia, and why are you so scared of her?'

'Get out.'

The car has pulled into the side of the road and Andrea waits for Nuala to do as she's been told.

'Now,' Andrea says, when Nuala doesn't move. 'And don't bother coming back to work. You're fired.'

'You didn't hire me because you loved the podcast,' Nuala says. 'You wanted information from me. Come on then, now's your chance. What is it you want to know? I'll tell you anything because, unlike you, I've got nothing to hide.'

Andrea's lips curl into something that, under other circumstances, might be classed as a smile.

'I think we both know that's not true.'

Nuala has her hand on the door, ready to open it. Part of her knows she should leave it there. But there's a bigger part of her that needs to hear Andrea say it.

'What do you mean?'

Andrea leans forward, her blue eyes boring right inside Nuala's head.

'Marianne,' she whispers, before sitting back in her seat and turning her face away from Nuala.

'Excuse me?'

But Andrea doesn't answer.

'It's you then,' Nuala says. 'You're *truthfinder*, aren't you?'

She doesn't expect a response and, when she doesn't get one, she opens the door and steps out into the cold autumn afternoon. As she watches the car drive off, she thinks how strange it will be to not travel to Blackheath tomorrow and continue with the documentary.

She should feel gutted; this job was the opportunity of a lifetime. But all she feels is a giddy excitement. There's a story here, possibly the biggest story of her life. Andrea might not realise it yet, but she made a big mistake this afternoon. Because now Nuala knows, beyond doubt, that Andrea Leach is connected to what happened at Black Valley Farm ten years ago.

Chapter 7

'You're sure it was her?' This is the second time Leo has asked the question, because he still can't believe what Harry has just told him.

'As sure as I can be,' Harry says. 'Besides, why else would Nuala Fox go chasing after her? Lucky I was able to stall her. By the time she got away from me, the girl was long gone.'

Leo can't help wondering if Harry had done the right thing. If Nuala had managed to catch the girl they'd know for sure who she was. Without that certainty, he has nothing.

'And this was yesterday.' Leo sighs, frustrated. 'You shouldn't have waited this long to tell me.'

He's been travelling for work, got back earlier today. Harry had sent him a message saying they needed to talk, but refused to speak to Leo until he could see him face to face. Leo tried to explain that they could do face to face over Zoom, but Harry's old-school. Told Leo that wasn't going to happen, and the conversation would have to wait until Leo was back in London.

'Would it have made any difference?' Harry says. 'She's gone, Leo. Trying to find her again is like trying to find a needle in a haystack.'

'You've really no idea where she went?' Leo asks.

'Sorry, mate. Like I said, when she showed up outside the house, Roger sent me outside to get rid of her. By the time I realised who she was, she'd already run off. I might have gone after her, tried to speak to her, but then Nuala appeared and I had to deal with her instead.'

Harry's the only person who knows about Leo's past. They've been friends for years, ever since Leo arrived in London. Back then, Leo had been homeless and utterly alone in the world. He'd seen a sign on the window of a pub in Bermondsey, looking for a barman. The landlord, Harry's old man, had taken pity on the scrawny teenager who'd come in asking about the job. He'd told Leo he could have the job on a trial basis and, while he was there, he could live with the family in their apartment above the pub.

It was Bill, Harry's father, who nurtured Leo's interest in beer and funded Leo's first ventures in brewing. As the business grew, no one could have been more proud or supportive of Leo's efforts. Now, Bill and his wife are both dead and the pub has been converted into apartments. But the bond between Leo and Harry remains.

Harry was the first person Leo employed, and he'll make sure Harry has a job with him for as long as he wants it. Whenever he's asked what, specifically, Harry's role is with the company, Leo always gives vague answers. Because the truth is, Harry's job entails a bit of everything. Including, for now, being Leo's eyes and ears inside the Progress Party's headquarters.

This evening, they're sitting on the terrace of Leo's riverfront apartment. It's dusk, the sun has set further west along the river and the sky is gradually darkening. Leo's drinking beer, using the alcohol to smooth away the worst edges of his anxiety. Harry, a teetotaller, is holding a mug of green tea that looks ridiculously tiny in his enormous hands. A wind is blowing, rippling the surface of the Thames and chilling Leo's face and hands. He doesn't mind the cold, would rather sit out here than go inside. His apartment is light, spacious and airy, but he knows the moment he's in there, he will feel trapped, claustrophobic, as if the walls are closing in on him. Better, for now, to be out here in the cold.

Leo drinks some more beer while he absorbs what Harry has told him this evening.

'Okay,' he says eventually. 'We know she's not in Sheffield any longer, which is good. It's more than that idiot Robb was able to tell me.'

Danny Robb was the private detective Leo had hired to track down both Arnie Cummins and the girl in the video. Earlier this week, Danny had contacted Leo to tell him he'd found Arnie. Apparently, he'd rented an apartment in Sheffield and was volunteering at a shelter for homeless people. The idea of Arnie doing anything to help anyone other than himself was so laughable, Leo had thought at first the detective was bullshitting him. It was only after Robb sent photos of Arnie at the shelter that Leo had believed him. So far, Robb's had no luck finding the girl from the video. Now, at least, Leo knows why.

'Why was she there?' he wonders aloud.

'Same reason you've got me working there,' Harry says. 'She's seen Andrea somewhere – maybe in a news article or something – and she's recognised her, exactly like you did.'

Leo frowns. 'Unless she was there for Nuala.'

Harry shrugs. 'It's possible, I guess. Either way, it doesn't matter, does it?'

'What if Nuala got to her somehow?' Leo asks.

'How?' Harry says. 'We both know how difficult it's been to find her. Why would Nuala Fox have more luck with that than you've had? She's a single mother, living in an ex-council flat in Wapping. No way does she have the resources to hire a PI like you've been able to.'

'She's a journalist,' Leo says. 'I'm sure she's got her own methods for finding people who don't want to be found.'

'Nah.' Harry shook his head. 'If the girl showed up for Nuala, why would she run away from her? It doesn't make any sense, mate.'

Leo thinks about this for a moment, and realises Harry is right.

'So what do I do now, Harry?'

'You wait,' Harry says. 'Andrea's rattled because of this. And people who are rattled make mistakes. Sooner or later, she's going to mess up.'

'And if she doesn't?'

'Listen to me, Leo. A few months from now, the Progress Party will register with the Electoral Commission. Once that happens, there'll be a lot more people digging into Andrea Leach's background. It's only a matter of time before someone works it all out.'

'You think?'

'Yes, I really do.'

Leo takes a sip of his beer, and refrains from telling Harry what he's really thinking. That he's not come this far to sit back and relinquish control to fate or some journalist with a bit more talent and integrity than Nuala Fox. He has never been a patient man and he's already waited far too long for the world to know the truth about Andrea Leach.

Chapter 8

I spend the afternoon on the seafront, walking to Bexhill and back again while I wait to hear from Nuala. By the evening, she still hasn't been in touch and I'm starting to worry I've done the wrong thing by contacting her. For all I know, the podcast wasn't even her idea. It could have been Mother, manipulating Nuala from the start, getting her to lie and say she was dead so no one would know she'd made it out of there. The more I think about it, the more sense it makes. In the podcast, Marianne described the farm as a haven. There can only be one person who really believed that's what it was.

As I turn the corner onto the road where the pub is, I freeze. There's a man coming out of the pub and, even though I'm quite far away, I recognise him straight away. It's Arnie, walking down the street towards me. I duck down the nearest side street, moving quickly, too scared to look behind me in case I see him coming after me.

Up ahead, I see another pub. I go inside and hurry towards the toilets. The barman shouts something at me as I pass, but I ignore him. The toilets stink, but they're empty and there's a sash window that lifts easily when I give it a shove.

I clamber through this, drop down and find myself in some sort of alley that runs along the back of the row of buildings. I move cautiously towards the end, pausing to check the street in both directions. I can't see Arnie, but that doesn't mean he's not there somewhere, waiting for me.

I pull my head back, so I can't be seen from the street, and lean against the wall while I try to make sense of what I've seen.

Arnie is here. In Hastings. This morning, I sent a message to Nuala Fox. Then this afternoon, Arnie turns up. That cannot be a coincidence. My stomach has twisted into a tight knot and there's a bitter taste in my mouth and throat that won't go away no matter how many times I swallow.

They're working together. Arnie. Nuala. Mother. I don't know why, what hold Mother has over the other two, and maybe that doesn't matter. What's important is I can't trust anyone. Contacting Nuala was a mistake.

I stick my head out again and, when I still don't see Arnie, I make my way slowly back to the pub, keeping a lookout for him the whole time.

'There was a fella in here just now,' Louis, the landlord, says as I enter the pub. 'He was asking about someone called Clare Brown but, from the description he gave me, I wondered if it was you he was looking for.'

Louis thinks my name is Susan. He doesn't know anything else about me, because he hasn't asked. Which, I think, suits both of us just fine.

'What did you tell him?' I ask.

'Said there was no one matching that description staying here,' Louis says. 'Don't think he believed me, though.'

'Thank you.'

'I should probably tell you to speak to the police,' Louis says, 'but I have a feeling you might be hiding from them too. For what it's worth, love, that bloke didn't give me the impression he was going to back off. Best thing you can do is pack your bags and move on somewhere else. My brother's got a B&B in Brighton. I could give him a call if you like. Persuade him to let you pay for your room with cash?'

It's a kind offer, but I can't do that. I need to go somewhere no one, not even Louis, knows where I am. He seems to understand this and doesn't push things. After I've packed my bag, he offers to drive me to the station and I say yes because there's less chance of Arnie seeing me if I'm in a car.

'Tell you what,' Louis says, once we're on our way. 'How about I drop you at Bexhill station? For all you know, that fella who's looking for you came down here by train today. Might be safer for you to take the train from a different station.'

'If you really don't mind?'

He leans over and pats my knee. With another man, the gesture could be sleazy. Not with Louis.

At Bexhill station, I thank Louis again and I'm about to get out of the car when he stops me.

'Listen, love. I spent too many years running away from people and situations that scared me. Took a long time to realise that sometimes you've got to stop running and face up to things. I'm not saying you're wrong to keep away from the bloke who came looking for you today. But I get the impression he's not the only thing you're running away from. You can't run forever. Sooner or later, you'll have to face up to whatever it is you're so scared of. The longer you leave it, the harder it's going to be.'

'What if you're running because you did something so terrible it means going to prison for the rest of your life?'

'You think prison would be any worse than how you're living now?'

I don't know how to answer this, so I stay quiet.

'Think about it,' Louis says. 'That's all I'm asking. Now go on. I've got a pub to run and you've got a train to catch.'

I say goodbye, get of the car and watch him drive away. Long after he's out of sight, I can still hear his question ringing in my ears. As I walk inside the station and check the departures screen, I'm no closer to coming up with an answer.

Chapter 9

This is Lydia, from the farm. I need to speak to you. Please call me.

It's Sunday night. Nuala is home alone, sitting in front of her laptop with Lydia's message open on the screen. She's called Lydia's phone countless times. So far, Lydia hasn't answered any of Nuala's calls. In fact, every phone call she's made since Friday has gone straight to voicemail. So, either Lydia has switched her phone off or she's blocked Nuala's number.

'Why aren't you picking up?' Nuala mutters, re-reading Lydia's message for the umpteenth time.

The message was sent on Friday, the day after Lydia showed up outside Andrea's house. Yet when Nuala had tried to talk to her, Lydia ran away. At some point she clearly changed her mind, which is why she got in touch. So what's happened to make her change it back again? As well as calling the phone number Lydia gave her, Nuala has tried replying to the original message. But the Instagram profile Lydia used has been deleted. Unless Lydia changes her mind and returns Nuala's calls, Nuala has zero hope of finding her.

Earlier, Nuala opened a bottle of wine. She rarely drinks, and never when she's at home with Josh because she doesn't want to set a bad example. But this evening, Josh is in Dungeness and Nuala needs something to take the edge off her irritation at coming so close to finding Lydia only to lose her again.

Shutting down Instagram, Nuala opens the Progress Party's website, zooming in on a photo of Andrea. Ever since she climbed out of Andrea's car on Friday, Nuala's felt nothing but relief. A feeling that intensifies now with each sip of wine she takes.

Andrea Leach is a liar. Nuala has spent the last two days making notes and collating all the information she has on Andrea and Lydia. It's clear the farm is what connects the two women, but how?

As she tries, once more, to find the answer to that question, Nuala takes another look at the notes she's made on Lydia. Around the time of the fire, a woman called Belinda Lowry was driving from her home in Hallington to her job in Skegness. When she saw a young woman, alone at the side of the road, Belinda stopped to check if she was okay. It was five o'clock on a summer's morning and Belinda was concerned to see a woman out alone in such a remote spot that early.

When she got out of the car, Belinda noticed two things. First, that the woman was, in fact, a teenager rather than someone older, as she'd first thought. The other thing she couldn't miss was the blood. The girl was covered in it. Brownish red streaks across her face, dried splatters on her hands and arms, and staining the front of her unusual white top. Somehow, Belinda persuaded the girl to get into her car and proceeded to drive her to the closest hospital, which was in Skegness. Along the way, the girl refused to speak, apart from telling Belinda that her name was Lydia. When Belinda eventually pulled up outside the hospital, Lydia wouldn't get out of the car. So Belinda went into the hospital to get help. When she came outside a few minutes later, Lydia was gone. Belinda Lowry never saw her again.

Later, when the police found some photos of the people who'd lived on the farm, Belinda identified Lydia as one of the children. She recognised the distinctive birthmark beneath Lydia's left eye. Until Nuala's podcast, this was as much as anyone knew about the mystery teenager.

While she was making the podcast, Nuala had spoken to Jasper Foyle, a man Lydia had lived with briefly. According to

Jasper, Lydia was a strange, secretive person who had threatened him when the stories of the farm first appeared. Nuala has always doubted Jasper's claims but, in the absence of any other information, she'd decided to include Jasper's interview in the final edits.

Nowhere has Nuala found a single thing that hints at a connection between Lydia and Andrea. Frustrated, she goes into the kitchen to get some more wine. When her glass is full, she goes back into the sitting room and settles on the sofa, letting her mind go in whatever direction it wants to.

The lack of control is the problem. Things are happening *to* her, instead of *because* of her. She takes another sip of wine as she contemplates this grim fact. For a woman who's spent years fighting to be in control of every aspect of her life, this is intolerable. She has to find a way of turning things around so she's back in the driving seat.

By the time she's emptied her glass, she's got an idea. It's kind of crazy and, even with the buzz from three glasses of wine, she's not entirely sure that what she's planning is sensible. But she can't see any other way out of this mess.

She goes into the bathroom and looks at the award on the shelf. If she goes ahead with this, she'll probably have to give the award back. So what? It's an ugly thing, anyway. The ugliest thing, by far, in her lovingly curated home. The evening she'd been presented with it should have been the proudest moment of her career. Instead, no matter how hard she tried to enjoy the moment, she couldn't shake off the underlying sense of shame. Because even then, she'd known that she didn't truly deserve this accolade.

The simple truth is she'd fucked up. She tried hard, at first, to convince herself that what she'd done wasn't that bad – a simple white lie in pursuit of a greater truth. When that didn't work, she consoled herself with the knowledge that it was too late by then to change things. What was done was done, and she would have to simply accept that and move on. But she hasn't been able to move on, so she's going to do what she should have done from the beginning. She's going to tell the truth. Because it's never too late to do the right thing.

Chapter 10

Before

Time had lost all meaning. The thick silence and the pitch black darkness made it impossible for Lydia to know when day became night. She had tried counting, at first. But her mind kept drifting, no matter how hard she tried to control it. Now, all she knew was this place. The cold that had buried its way deep inside her bones. The darkness that had invaded her mouth and throat until it filled every part of her. These things, she knew, would stay with her when she was finally let out of here.

It was called the Box, although really it was just a stinking, deep hole that someone had dug into the ground and covered with a stone slab. A ladder led from the surface down into the darkness. Lydia remembered the first time she'd been forced down here. After that, she had sworn to herself she would do anything to avoid being sent here ever again.

This time, it hadn't even been her fault. Peter had been hurting her. She'd cried out, begged him to stop, but he'd kept going. Her stomach twisted as she remembered how he'd looked. Like he was enjoying it. She remembered, too, the surge of anger that had risen through her body. A burning hot rage that felt so good she had given herself over to it, letting it grow bigger until it exploded into a punch straight into Peter's face.

She'd felt the crunch of bone beneath her fist, and the spray of warm blood on her cheeks. She would have hit him again if she'd had the chance. But Mother got there first, screaming and dragging Lydia off the bed, beating her with the stiletto heel of her shoe and calling her a stupid little bitch.

'Bitch' was a bad word, but Mother could say it without fear of Punishment because she was God's chosen child. At least, that's what everyone else believed. Everyone except Lydia, who believed Mother was a crazy fraud and as soon as Lydia got out of here she was going to tell the whole world what life here was really like.

First, she had to get out of this dark hole. She opened her mouth to scream, but her throat was too dry and no sound came out. She had screamed earlier, when she'd first been forced down here, yesterday or the day before that or whenever it had been. She'd screamed until her throat was raw, but no one had come to let her out.

There wasn't enough space to stand up. Her muscles were stiff and aching. She worried that she wouldn't be able to stand up ever again. That her body would be stuck in this hunched over position, her clothes sticking to her. Wet from wee that had been warm at first and felt good for a few minutes, until it cooled and turned her clothes to pieces of ice glued to her skin.

She heard scratching sounds. Rats and mice. Nibbling at her wet clothes, crawling over her skin and into her mouth, eating her eyes. Maybe her eyes were gone already. She blinked three times, but it made no difference. She couldn't see a thing through the thick blackness. She was blind and dumb and she was going to die down here. And maybe that's what she deserved. Mother was right. Lydia was an evil sinner and every time she misbehaved it made God cry and that's why Mother hurt her. When you made God cry you had to be punished.

More scratching sounds. She put her hands over her ears, but she could still hear them. The rats crawling around the inside of her head, eating bits of her brain and body. She screamed again, but still no sound came out. Even if she could manage to make some noise, there was no one to hear her. No one to rescue her and hold her close until she was warm again.

Later, minutes or hours or days, she didn't know, it was over. She was back in her room. Someone had taken off her dirty clothes and she was under the sheets, shivering.

'Lydia?'

She recognised Martha's voice and opened her eyes. Saw Martha standing by the side of the bed, her face creased in worry. Little Martha, who had turned seven last week, which meant she had nine years before she was forced to start making babies for Mother.

'Are you sick?' Martha asked.

'Yes,' Lydia whispered, because what else could she say? She couldn't tell Martha about a place like the Box. Because Martha never misbehaved and, along with Hannah, was Mother's favourite.

'You're cold.' Martha put a hand on Lydia's shoulder. 'Let me make you warm.'

Before Lydia could stop her, Martha had pulled back the sheet and was climbing into the bed beside her.

'It's okay,' Martha whispered. 'Mother asked me to take care of you. I've been with you since you came back. I had to give you water to drink and wash your clothes.'

She wrinkled her nose, but didn't mention what the clothes had smelled like and Lydia was grateful to her for that.

'Don't you remember, Lydia?'

When Lydia shook her head, Martha sighed.

'You said you'd remember, but I knew you wouldn't because you were shaking and crying and you were saying things that I didn't understand.'

'I'm sorry,' Lydia said. 'But I'm glad you're here now.'

She wrapped her arms around the little girl's body, letting her warmth seep into her own cold bones.

Martha started talking, telling Lydia a story about one of the cats. Lydia half-listened, luxuriating in the sudden, unexpected warmth. Her last, lucid thought before sleep claimed her was that she would find a way of getting away from here. She would do it, or die trying.

Chapter 11

Present

For the next few days, I move around from place to place. Scared, all the time, that Arnie will find me again. Last night, I arrived here in Maidstone. I've found a B&B on the outskirts of the town that let me pay cash for my room. I went to bed early and slept heavily.

When I wake up, I'm confused for a moment as I try to work out where I am. Then I remember and lie back on the pillow, relieved I'm somewhere safe. Despite a good night's sleep, I'm tired. Exhaustion has worked its way deep into my bones.

But I know I won't be able to go back to sleep, so I pick up my phone and start scrolling through Nuala's social media feeds. She's tried to call and text so many times I've had to block her number. But I can't stop myself from checking up on her every free moment I have.

She hasn't posted much recently, so it's a surprise to see a new post at the top of her Instagram feed. And even more of a surprise when I see what the post is about.

> Coming soon, another episode of Black Valley Farm.

I click on the link that's included with the post. It takes me to a recording of Nuala's voice.

> Hello, Nuala Fox here — creator and presenter of the award-winning true crime podcast Black

Valley Farm. Those of you who have listened to the podcast know that I made it because I wanted to uncover the truth about the deaths of nine people at a remote farmhouse in Lincolnshire. I also wanted to find a woman called Lydia, who the police always believed had something to do with the deaths at the farm.

During the making of the podcast, I learned that the people living on the farm had been lured there by a woman called Rosemary. Many of the women who ended up on the farm were fleeing abusive relationships. They were vulnerable and it's possible that Rosemary exploited this vulnerability.

Nuala pauses and takes a deep breath before continuing.

Over the last few weeks, something has happened that's forced me to make a confession. I lied during the making of the podcast. To find out what I lied about, and why, you'll need to tune in to a new, one-off special episode which will be available very soon.

Before then, I want to make an appeal to Lydia: I know you're scared, but I promise I don't want to cause you harm. I let you down when I lied before. I want to make that up to you. I want the whole world to know the truth about a certain politician and how she's connected to what happened at the farm. I'm sure you know who I'm talking about and I swear to you that any conversations we have will be completely confidential.

If you don't want her to find you – and I don't think you do – I'll make sure that doesn't happen. This is your chance to finally tell the world the truth. Call me. I'll never let you down again.

The recording ends there. No farewell from Nuala, no closing music. Just silence. I hit rewind, and listen to the whole thing again. And again. By now, my heart is beating fast and my tummy is fizzing with a mixture of fear, excitement and anger.

I see Nuala Fox and Mother, their faces separate then blurring together until it's impossible to know who is who. Nuala lied, Mother lied. I'm lying, too. Nuala says she's sorry, she wants to tell the truth. So do I.

I sit up so fast, I feel dizzy and have to wait for my head to stop spinning. When it does, I unblock Nuala's number on my phone and send her a message.

It's me, I type, *I'm ready to talk*.

When I'm done, I go for a walk to a nearby park. The sun is rising behind the trees, red and pink and orange light flooding the empty park. I sit on a bench, watching the sun rise higher in the sky as the colours pale and fade.

When my phone starts ringing, I don't answer right away. It will be Nuala calling, and I know as soon as I answer everything is going to change. And even though that's what I want, I wait a little longer, because once this moment is gone, I'll never get it back.

Chapter 12

When Nuala wakes the following morning, there's a moment before she remembers what she's done. Then it all comes racing back and she sits up, adrenaline spiking through her body. There's no going back now, even if she wanted to. Which she doesn't. For the first time in a while, she's done something she's proud of. It's a good, if unusual, feeling.

She has an urge to call Liz and tell her what she did last night so Liz will realise Nuala isn't a bad person after all. She could call on the pretext of wanting to speak to Josh, but she spoke to him last night and arranged to speak with him again tonight. If she phones now, Liz will think Nuala's up to something.

As it turns out, Nuala doesn't have to wait until this evening to speak to Liz. She's in the kitchen, making a pot of coffee, when her phone rings. She sees Liz's name on the screen and her heart skips several beats. Something's happened to Josh. There's no other reason Liz would be calling her now.

'What's wrong?' Nuala says before she's even managed to get the phone to her ear.

'I heard the trailer,' Liz says.

Not what Nuala had expected to hear and, as Liz continues speaking, she gets a giddy, tingly feeling that spreads from the pit of her stomach through the rest of her body.

'I can't believe you did it.' Liz gives a small chuckle. 'You're a constant surprise, Foxy.'

'Is that a good thing?'

'It can be.'

Nuala smiles. Suddenly, she wishes she could pack up and drive to Dungeness. Spend the next few days hanging out with Josh and Liz, playing on the beach and eating fish and chips while the sun sets in that big, wide open sky they have down there.

'What happens now?' Liz asks.

'Have you heard of Andrea Leach?'

'Right-wing, homophobic, racist?'

'That's her. She's got something to do with what happened at the farm.'

'You're shitting me,' Liz says.

'I'm definitely not shitting you.'

'Wow.' There's a pause and Nuala knows Liz is considering whether or not to point out that Nuala hadn't needed to lie after all. But because Liz is a better person than Nuala will ever be, she doesn't go there.

'That's great,' she says instead. 'Really bloody great, Nuala. Well done. So what happens next?'

'Well, I'm hoping Lydia will hear the trailer and get in touch. With her help, I'll be able to make sure Andrea Leach's political career is dead in the water.'

'Let's hope Lydia contacts you, then. People like that crazy bitch need to be stopped. Do you think Andrea had something to do with the murders?'

'I think it's possible, yes.'

In her mind, Nuala sees the message from *truthfinder*, with the photo of her boy. 'Are you still okay to have Josh for a few more days?'

'I was planning to have him at the end of the week, anyway,' Liz reminds her. 'So of course I'm happy for him to stay. But make sure you're able to pick him up on Saturday as agreed. I'm going out that night.'

'Of course.' Nuala refrains from asking where Liz is going and – more importantly – who with.

Liz puts Josh on the phone then, and hearing her son's voice pushes away dark thoughts of Liz dating other women. Josh

183

is the reason, after all, that the podcast happened in the first place. Everything Nuala's done since the moment she first saw him has been about keeping him safe and giving him a life that's as different in every way possible from her own, miserable childhood.

But she can't use Josh as an excuse for what she did. That was all down to her own poor judgement. The worst part of it, worse even than breaking her own journalistic code of ethics, is the irreversible damage it did to her relationship with the only adult who's ever really mattered to her.

When Josh eventually runs out of steam, Nuala says goodbye to him before he passes the phone back to Liz.

'He's a delight,' Liz says. 'It's been great having him here.'

'I'm glad,' Nuala says. Then, because she's never actually said this before, 'Liz, I'm so sorry for what I did.'

'I know.'

Not, Nuala notes, *it's okay* or *I forgive you*. Just *I know*. She wants to say more, to ask if there's any chance that Liz might one day forgive her. But she already knows the answer to that question so she says nothing.

'Well then,' Liz says, when it's clear Nuala is done speaking, 'I guess I'd better go. See you Saturday.'

'Yeah.' Nuala's eyes prick with tears which she brushes away, glad Liz is not here in person to witness this pathetic sign of self-pity.

'Thanks, Liz.'

But she's speaking to herself, because Liz has already hung up. This habit of Liz's – to end a conversation abruptly, ensuring she always has the final word – used to annoy the hell out of Nuala. It might have done now too, but before Nuala has time to get annoyed, her phone pings with an incoming text message.

The message is from Lydia. It's short and direct and everything Nuala could have hoped for.

It's me. I'm ready to talk.

'Yes!'

Nuala punches the air. This is it. A chance to finally tell the truth and, in doing so, destroy Andrea Leach and everything her appalling Progress Party stands for.

Chapter 13

Before

Today was Lydia's seventeenth birthday. So far, the day had passed like any other. Birthdays were recognised on the farm in the form of a prayer for the person whose special day it was. Apart from that, there were no presents or any other celebration.

It was a whole year since Lydia had started trying to make a baby with Peter. So far, she hadn't got pregnant but Mother insisted she keep on trying. Aunt Sarah had given birth to Robert earlier this year and the boy had become the new focus of Mother's affections. Lydia knew she should love Robert. But each time she looked at him, all she could think of was Aunt Sarah and Peter together and she wanted to throw up.

Aunt Katherine had been pregnant at the same time as Aunt Sarah, but her baby had been born dead and Peter had taken it into the woods where he buried it. Since then, Aunt Katherine had been moving around the farm like a ghost. Lydia knew she should feel sorry for Aunt Katherine but, each time she saw the woman's miserable face, all she felt was contempt.

This evening, Mother had come into the kitchen while the aunts were preparing dinner. As everyone else gathered around baby Robert, saying how big he was getting and what a beautiful child he was, Lydia slipped outside.

It was a warm summer's evening and she stood for a moment, enjoying the feeling of the sun on her skin. She saw Leo down in the field, leading the cows in for milking. He wasn't by himself, of course. No one was allowed outside the perimeter of the fence by themselves. Peter always had to go with you, taking the gun with him to make sure you didn't try to run away. Watching him now, keeping the gun pointed at Leo while he locked the gates, Lydia had to bite down on her lip to stop herself screaming with rage and hate and frustration.

Once Leo was in the shed and the gates were locked, Peter walked back to the annex where he lived with Mother. Lydia waited until he'd gone, before making her way down the garden to the milking shed.

'You want a hand?' she asked, sidling into the stall where Leo sat on a stool, his hands on the teats of the older, bad-tempered cow who always tried to bite Lydia.

'You shouldn't be in here,' Leo said, without turning to look at her.

'I've finished my work,' Lydia said. 'It's okay if I say I came to help you. Mother would rather I'm working than sitting around doing nothing.'

'I don't want you to get into trouble again.'

He looked up at her then, and she almost wished he hadn't because the pain in his eyes was difficult to see.

'I thought you were going to die this time, Lydia.'

'Well, I didn't. I'm here and I'm fine and if you'll stop behaving so stupidly I'll help you get the milking done so we can have half an hour to ourselves before evening prayer.'

'We can't be seen together.'

'Tell you what,' she said. 'I'll go down to the vegetable garden and pull out the weeds. I heard Aunt Sarah saying yesterday they're starting to take over again. When you're finished with the cows, come and join me. No one will see us there.'

He looked as if he might say no, but after a moment he gave a quick nod of his head before turning back to the milking.

'I'll find you when I'm done.'

Despite the warm day, the ground was hard. Trying to remove the weeds with the small trowel was difficult, but she kept going. Aunt Sarah had spotted Lydia leaving the shed and asked what she was up to. When Lydia had told her she wanted to help with the weeds, Aunt Sarah had handed her the trowel and told her she would be down later to inspect Lydia's work.

'You'd better do a good job, Lydia. I don't want you using this as an excuse to skive off your responsibilities. The vegetable garden might be out of sight, but you're still expected to work when you're there. Is that clear?'

Lydia kept her head down the way she'd been taught, and promised she would do her very best to get rid of all the weeds. Now, as she dug the trowel into the hard ground, she imagined she was sticking it into Aunt Sarah's round, white face.

She felt like she'd been digging forever when she finally heard the clink of the iron gate opening and footsteps on the paved path that led to this part of the garden.

'I was starting to think you weren't coming,' she said, as Leo drew up alongside her.

'I nearly didn't.'

'Why not?'

'You know why, Lydia.'

His hand reached out and brushed against hers, sending a thrill of hot electricity through her body. Whenever she was with him, there was an aching deep inside her that she didn't understand except she knew it had something to do with needing to be close to him.

When they'd been younger, Lydia and Leo had spent a lot of time together. As the oldest two children on the farm, it was only natural. They'd sat side by side in class, and were given different, more difficult exercises than the younger children. Often, they were given the same jobs, including caring for the other children during the long, hot summer days.

They knew, without ever being told, that Mother didn't like any of the children to become too close. They had learned early on to hide how much they liked, and needed, each other's company. Things between them had been fine, until about a year ago when Lydia started to get these weird feelings. Whenever she tried to analyse how she felt, the closest she could get was that it was like she was hungry for him. Even though that didn't make any sense because Leo was a boy, not a meal.

She'd thought it was only her who felt this way. But now, the way he was looking at her, like he wanted to see inside her and know everything about her, made her think maybe he felt it too. The thought made her head spin and her skin tingle and her tummy flutter with thousands of tiny butterflies.

His hand was still touching hers. Somehow, as if her body was a thing that was separate to her brain, her fingers reached out and wrapped themselves into his until both their hands were intertwined. His skin was rough and warm and she knew all of this was wrong, yet if it was, why did it feel so right?

Abruptly, he pulled his hand away and whispered at her that she was never to do that again. 'Touching is forbidden. You know that.'

'You touched me first,' she said, angry with him for being so difficult to understand.

'I shouldn't have done that. I'm sorry.'

'So why did you?'

'I think there's something wrong with me,' he said. 'There are all these things happening to my body, and I know it's bad but I don't know how to stop it.'

'When we get feelings we don't understand,' Lydia said, 'we're supposed to tell Mother about them.'

'What if I like the feelings and I don't want to tell her because she'll make them stop?'

'Then you'll burn in hell.'

'No.' Leo shook his head, his cheeks red and his face angry. 'It's not true. All this stuff they tell us, it's a load of crock. I was eleven when we moved here. I've been thinking about that a lot lately, remembering what life was like out there. Mother's always telling us the world outside the farm is bad. But you know what, Lydia? It wasn't bad. People were happy, and they touched each other all the time and they laughed and listened to music and danced and sang songs that weren't hymns. And nothing bad happened to them because of it.'

'How do you know all those people haven't died and are right now burning in hell for their sins?'

'I don't,' Leo said, 'but I'd like to find out. Wouldn't you?'

Her heart was beating hard and fast, and when she answered she'd never been more sure of anything in her life.

'Yes, I would.'

They were standing so close she could feel the heat of his body. And when he leaned down and his lips touched hers, it felt as if she'd been waiting her whole life just for this moment.

Chapter 14

Present

The phone rings for so long, Nuala doesn't think Lydia is going to pick up. She gets ready to leave a voice message when, suddenly, she hears a voice.

'Hello?'

Her voice is low, barely more than a whisper, but it's her. Finally. Nuala closes her eyes, lets out the long breath she's been holding.

'Lydia, hi. It's Nuala Fox here.'

'I know.'

'Sorry, of course. Um… listen, I'm so glad you got in touch. Thank you.'

'Did you tell Arnie how to find me?'

'Who?'

'Arnie Cummins.'

'I have no idea who that person is,' Nuala says.

'I don't believe you.'

So far, the conversation isn't exactly going the way Nuala had hoped. At this rate, she's going to lose Lydia before she's had the chance to persuade her Nuala can be trusted.

'I swear to you,' Nuala says, speaking quickly in the hope she can say enough to persuade Lydia not to hang up. 'I don't know who Arnie whatever-his-name is. Even if I did, how could I tell him where you are when I have no idea of that myself? I saw you briefly that day in London and that's it. Why do you think I know where you went after that?'

'My phone,' Lydia says.

'What about it?' Nuala's starting to wonder if Lydia's a bit simple.

'You had my number,' Lydia says.

'So what?' Then, when she doesn't get a response: 'Lydia, you can't track someone from their phone number. The only way to locate a person by their phone is with a Find My Phone app, or by monitoring the masts that a phone connects to.'

'If you didn't tell him where I was, why did he turn up the same day I sent you my phone number?'

'I have no idea,' Nuala says. 'Who is he, anyway?'

'And what about Andrea Leach?' Lydia says, ignoring Nuala's question. 'How do you know her?'

'I was making a TV documentary about her,' Nuala says. 'Until she fired me, that is. When she first approached me about the film, she said she wanted to work with me because she thought I'd done a good job with the podcast. I soon realised there was more to it than that.'

Nuala pauses, unsure how to continue. She gets why Lydia doesn't trust her, but she's suddenly aware of the fact that maybe she shouldn't trust Lydia, either.

'In your trailer,' Lydia says, 'you said something about a politician being connected to the farm. What did you mean by that?'

'Maybe we could talk about that when we meet up?'

'Tell me what you know about her first.'

'Okay,' Nuala says, deciding she's got nothing to lose by telling the truth. 'For now, this is only theoretical. But I think there's a possibility Andrea Leach might have been one of the women living on the farm.'

'Which one?'

Nuala thinks of what she learned about the farm and the people who lived there. A group of women, all persuaded to leave their husbands by a charismatic and beautiful woman called Rosemary. Then she thinks of Andrea, beautiful and charismatic and utterly amoral. And she knows, with absolute certainty, that the answer she's about to give is the right one.

'Rosemary,' she says. 'I don't know her surname, or why she changed her name to Andrea. But I think that Rosemary and Andrea Leach are the same person. Am I right, Lydia?'

'Yes.'

Nuala's been sitting down during this conversation, but she stands up now. She needs to move around while her mind races ahead, already planning out the episode.

'So now you know,' Lydia continues, 'you don't need me any longer, do you?'

'Oh, I really do,' Nuala says. 'Because as soon as I tell people I lied, they won't believe another word that comes out of my mouth. I need to get you on the podcast, telling everyone what life was really like on the farm and how Rosemary survived. Andrea Leach is a dangerous woman. This is our chance to destroy her.'

'Why should I help you?'

'Because I saw you that afternoon in London,' Nuala says. 'You were terrified, that's why you ran. I thought you were running from me, but you weren't. It was Andrea you were scared of, wasn't it?'

Down the line, Lydia is silent for so long Nuala worries she's hung up. She wants to say something, but if Lydia's still there she doesn't want to risk scaring her. So she waits, and her patience eventually pays off.

'I'll need time to think about it,' Lydia says. 'I want to help you, but I'm scared. I've been hiding for a long time. I don't know if I'm ready for what comes next if I decide to speak to you.'

It's not what Nuala wants to hear, but she senses if she puts too much pressure on Lydia she might lose her altogether. And she can't risk that, because what she told Lydia is true. Without Lydia, there's nothing stopping Andrea pointing out that Nuala's lied once before and this is nothing more than another lie aimed at her ex-employer.

'Take as much time as you need,' she says. 'I'll be here when you're ready.'

'Thank you.'

There's a click and Nuala realises Lydia has hung up. More than anything, she wants to call her back and keep her on the phone until Nuala has brow-beaten her into agreeing to meet. To stop herself from doing that, she switches her phone off and sits at her computer to start planning the new episode. She has no idea whether Lydia will agree to meet up or not. But she has to hope she will eventually. If she doesn't, this final episode may never happen.

Chapter 15

Two days later, I'm in Ashford in Kent. My money is running out fast, but it doesn't matter because I've agreed to meet Nuala Fox. I called her back and we're meeting here in Ashford tomorrow. It's not like I've got a choice. I'm done with hiding, pretending to be someone else. Louis was right. Prison can't be any worse than this half-life I've been living.

I don't care about politics or the Progress Party. But I do care about finding out what happened. If Mother didn't die that night, I need to know for sure who did. I've spent a lot of the last few days looking at the photos from the farm. There's one, in particular, I keep going back to. Two girls, dressed in identical white clothes, standing side by side. The outline of the farmhouse just visible behind them. We called each other sisters, even though we weren't actually related. But she was my sister in every way that mattered and I've spent the last ten years believing she's still alive. If she died, I want to know who killed her and why. That's why I called Nuala and told her I'm ready to talk.

We've arranged to meet tomorrow, in the park near the B&B I'm staying in. Tomorrow feels like an age away, though. Somehow, I'll have to fill the time between now and then. I have a sudden urge to speak to Kath. I don't know if she's even heard of Nuala's podcast, but I can't bear the thought of her listening to the new episode and hearing the truth about me before I've had a chance to tell her myself.

I call her before I can change my mind.

'Hello?'

I open my mouth to speak but no words come out. There's an ache in my chest and a lump in my throat that won't go away even when I swallow.

'Clare? Is that you?'

'Yes,' I whisper.

'Oh, thank God. I've been so worried about you. Tell me where you are and I'll come and get you. I know you're in trouble. You'd never have taken that money if you didn't need it. I don't want you worrying about that, or thinking I'm angry. Whatever's going on, we can fix it. Just let me help you. Please.'

My chin wobbles and my eyes fill with tears. I realise, too late, that I should have told her the truth. All she's ever shown me is kindness, and all I've ever given her in return is a bunch of lies.

'I'm okay,' I tell her. 'I've made a lot of mistakes, but I'm going to make up for everything. I never meant to keep your money. I'll pay you back, every single penny.'

'I don't care about the money. I've got too much of it, anyway. I'd rather you have it than see it sitting in my bank doing nothing.'

I know she means it, but that doesn't make me feel any better. I stole from her. There's no avoiding that simple fact.

'Can I see you?' she says.

I close my eyes, as if that will block out the pain I'm feeling. 'I can't.'

'I know who you are.'

'What do you mean?'

'You're Lydia, aren't you?'

I didn't realise, until this moment, how difficult it's been never being able to tell people who I really am. Suddenly, I want her to know everything, not just the bits she thinks she's worked out. Because the truth's more complicated than she could ever imagine.

'Sort of,' I say.

'Either you're her, or you're not. And I think you are. I listened to the podcast when it first came out, you know. But when I met you, a few months later, it never occurred to me you could have been that poor girl. For some reason, I'd assumed Lydia was older. Then I saw an interview in a magazine with the woman who made the podcast. Oh, what's her name? I can't remember now.'

'Nuala Fox.'

'Nuala, that's it. Well, the magazine had photos from her investigation and I recognised you immediately. Your hair's different now, and you're older, but I knew it was you.'

'When was this?' I ask, because in all the time we've known each other she hasn't once given me the slightest clue she didn't believe I was who I said I was.

'About a month after you moved in.'

'You never said anything.'

'Why would I?' Kath says, as if the idea of her telling me she knew I wasn't really Clare Brown is ridiculous. 'I knew you well enough by then to know you couldn't have killed those people. So I decided to stay quiet and let you carry on living your life the way you wanted to.'

'What about Arnie?'

'Arnie? What's he got to do with this?'

'You told him about me.'

'I wouldn't do that, Clare. I haven't told a soul.'

'Is he with you now?'

'Well yes, but he's in the other room. As soon as I realised it was you on the phone, I came into the sitting room because I didn't want him listening in. Ah, he's coming now. Probably wants to know why I'm being so secretive. Hang on a sec.'

Her voice goes muffled and I imagine her speaking to Arnie, telling him she'll be with him in a minute.

'Sorry,' she says, a moment later. 'Arnie was wondering where I'd got to, that's all.'

'Listen to me, Kath. You can't trust Arnie. He's dangerous. I don't think you're safe with him.'

She says something, but I don't catch the words because I'm still speaking, telling her she needs to get out of the house now. But my words are cut off by a scream from Kath, the sound too loud and too sudden.

'Kath,' I shout, but it's already too late. The line has gone dead. When I try calling her back, I get her voicemail. I call again, and again, until I realise there's no point. Her phone has been switched off.

Chapter 16

Desperate, I dial 999. Almost immediately, a woman answers.

'Hello, emergency service operator. Which service do you require? Fire, police or ambulance?'

'Ambulance. I think. It's for my friend. She's had an accident and she's not answering her phone.'

'Can you tell me where you're calling from?'

'Ashford. Except my friend isn't here. She's in Sheffield. We were on the phone and something happened to her. She screamed and her phone was cut off. I've tried calling her back but she's not picking up and I'm worried about her.'

The woman interrupts, asks me for my friend's name and address. When I give them to her, she tells me to hold while she transfers me to the ambulance service. After a few seconds, I'm speaking to a man and I have to repeat the whole thing again. It takes an age until he seems to get that this is a real emergency. He promises he'll send someone to Kath's house, and asks if there's anyone who can stay with her until they arrive.

The only person I can think of is her neighbour, Libby. I give him Libby's name, and tell him which house she lives in. He thanks me and says someone will call me back once they've been to Kath's house. He can't tell me how long it will be before they can get there and, after he hangs up, I feel like I need to do more.

I run through the list of people Kath knows in Sheffield. She has lots of friends but I've always done my best to avoid them. I don't know most of their names and have no clue where any of them live. Suddenly, I think of someone who might be able to help. I stop walking, put my bag on the ground and root around inside until my fingers find what I'm looking for. It's a business card, crumpled from being at the bottom of the bag.

I dial the number on the card, holding my breath when the call connects, willing her to pick up quickly.

'DI Robins.'

A scatter of memories flash in front of me. Car horns hooting, the woman screaming, the heat of the bus as it screeches towards us.

'It's Clare,' I say. 'We met a while back when your boy ran onto the road? You said I could call if I ever needed help.'

'Clare, of course. Hello. I've been thinking of you a lot since that day. What can I do for you?'

'My friend's in trouble. Her name is Kath Dinsdale, and she's got a boyfriend who's dangerous. We were speaking on the phone a moment ago when he attacked her.'

I'm going a bit OTT, but I need her to know this is important and she has to do something. 'I'm not in Sheffield, otherwise I'd go over there myself. I heard him attack her and I haven't been able to get through to her since. I called 999 and they said they'll send an ambulance over, but it could take ages. I'm really worried about her.'

'Give me her address,' DI Robins says. 'I'll drive over there now.'

'What if she isn't able to answer the door?' I ask.

'Is she friends with any of her neighbours?'

'She's friends with everyone,' I say. 'Although Libby in number seven is probably her closest friend on the street.'

'Okay. If Kath doesn't open the door for me, I'll try Libby at number seven. She might even have a spare key.'

She tells me to try not to worry, and promises she'll call me back as soon as she's been to Kath's house. I thank her and hang up because the longer she's on the phone to me, the longer it will take her to get to Kath.

Two whole hours pass before DI Robins calls me back.

'Have you found her?' I ask.

'I'm afraid not,' she says. 'No one answered when I rang the bell. So I spoke to the neighbour, Libby Fitzgerald. When I told her who I was and why I was there, she gave me a key to Kath's house and I went inside.'

'And?'

'The house was empty, Clare. But there were some signs that an altercation of some sort had taken place.'

'A what?'

'There was an overturned chair in the sitting room,' she says. 'And a broken mug on the floor.'

I stop walking and squeeze my eyes shut, while she continues speaking.

'Do you have any idea where Kath might have gone, Clare? Or any information about her partner? I'd certainly like to have a chat with him and see what he tells me.'

'His name's Arnie. Arnie Cummins.'

'Arnie Cummins? You're sure about that?'

'Yes. He volunteers at the Sunrise Homeless Shelter. That's where they met. I'm not sure if he's working today but someone there should be able to tell you how to find him.'

'Clare, you should probably know something. Shortly after that video appeared online, a retired detective from Greater Manchester contacted me. He was asking about you. His name was Arnie Cummins.'

My stomach clenches. Although this news shouldn't surprise me, it does. I feel sick, thinking it's my fault he came into Kath's life.

'What did you tell him?'

'There was nothing to tell,' DI Robins says. 'I only knew your first name, and had no idea who you were or where you lived. But now you tell me he's your friend's boyfriend, I'm wondering what the hell he was doing asking questions about you.'

'I don't know. I mean, the first time I met him was three or four weeks after the video was posted.'

'So you've no idea why he was trying to find you?'

'None.'

'I doubt that's true,' she says after a moment. 'But right now finding out why you're lying to me isn't as important as finding out what's happened to your friend. I'll go over there again later, and call you back as soon as I can.'

'Thank you, DI Robins. I really appreciate your help with this.'

'You saved my son's life,' she says. 'This is the least I can do. And please call me Helen, okay?'

Before she hangs up, she tells me to try not to worry, but we both know I'm not going to stop worrying until I know Kath is safe and well. I also know there's nothing I can do now except wait.

Chapter 17

Before

It was November. A cold month. When Lydia had woken up this morning, she'd found ice on the inside of her bedroom window. The clothes they were forced to wear were thin and worn, nowhere near thick enough to keep them warm. Like the others, Lydia spent most of the winter months aching with the cold that seeped through her thin blouse deep into her bones. The only times she wasn't cold were when she was with Leo. Then, her body burned up with an intense heat that spread through every part of her until her fingers and toes were tingling.

These last few months, every waking moment was taken up with Leo. When she wasn't with him, he was all she could think about. In the brief, stolen moments when they were together, her body and mind were consumed with needing to touch him and be touched by him. She had never wanted anything so badly, hadn't known it was possible to feel this way.

What they were doing was dangerous, but exciting too. All these new feelings were scary and wonderful. Her body had become something she had no control over, consumed with a desperate longing that only disappeared when she was with him and he was touching her and she was touching him and their bodies were entwined with each other, like they were now.

He was beautiful. She could have spent every moment of every day looking at him, taking in the curve of his jaw, the hard flatness of his stomach and the sheer wonder of the thing between his legs that caused such a joy of sensation inside her.

Mother told her that making a baby was a miracle. But when Lydia was with Peter it felt like the opposite of a miracle, disgusting and painful, and when she thought about it she felt sick. Now, Lydia finally understood what Mother had meant.

They were in the cow shed. This damp, smelly shed was the only place they could be together without being seen. People on the farm were closely monitored. Each morning, the bell woke them at five o'clock for meditation and prayer, followed by chores and breakfast. After breakfast, there were lessons for the children and chores for the adults. The afternoons were devoted to prayer and more chores. Dinner was at six thirty, lights out at nine thirty. Their rooms were locked at night and all the windows had thick metal bars across them, making it impossible to get out.

The only time they could be together was when one of them was given the job of milking the cows. When this happened, the other one would do their best to get their chores finished early so they'd be able to have a few precious moments together in the shed. There was always a risk they'd get caught but, so far, no one had noticed.

Today, they were lying together, wrapped around each other and Lydia wished she could stay here forever.

'We need to get away from here,' Leo said.

'How?'

Three years ago, Aunt Paula had left the farm with two of the children. A week after they left, Peter found their bodies. They'd been murdered, exactly as Mother had said would happen. Because life outside the farm wasn't safe. There were bad people, waiting to do bad things to anyone who was foolish enough to try to run away.

'We can't stay here,' Leo said. 'There has to be something better than this.'

For a moment, she allowed herself to imagine them living somewhere else, being in a place where they could be together all the time without worrying what would happen if someone saw them. The more time she spent with him, the more time she wanted to be with him. It was the opposite of most other things in her life that made her feel good – heat and food and sleep being the top three. With those, there was always a point when she'd had enough. Being with Leo was different. She could never get enough of him.

Lydia rolled onto her back, looking through the gaps in the roof at the dull grey sky. The idea of leaving was as exciting as it was terrifying. Everyone living on the farm knew how dangerous the outside world was. It was why Mother had chosen to create this community, so that they could be safe and never have to worry about violent husbands or angry gangs of young men with knives wanting to stab you like they had done to Aunt Paula and her two children.

'Lydia?'

'All we do is talk about it,' she said. 'We never actually do anything.'

'That's where you're wrong.'

Her stomach lurched. She sat up, pulled her knees to her chest and looked at him.

'Peter's going to teach me to drive.'

Lydia couldn't see him properly in the dim light, but she knew by his voice that he was smiling.

'Why?'

'He needs help with the deliveries,' Leo said. 'The aunts aren't allowed to drive, so Mother suggested me. She says I'm old enough now, and it would do me good to start helping Peter out a bit more. He's got a dodgy knee and it hurts worse when he drives.'

Once a week, Peter drove into the nearby town to sell the wooden ornaments the aunts made, and to buy food.

'How long will it take?'

'He says maybe a month, if I learn quickly.' Leo reached out and pulled her down so she was lying on top of him. 'So I'm thinking, what if I managed to sneak you into the back of the van? All we'd need to do is go into town with Peter and, as soon as we're there, make a run for it. He can't shoot us in the middle of town in front of other people. There won't be a single thing he can do to stop us.'

She closed her eyes and imagined them leaving this place and never coming back. It made her head spin thinking about it. She threw her head back and laughed, as the fire started inside her again. She knew it was the same for him because suddenly he was kissing her, and she was kissing him back, and they were pulling at each other, and his breath was hot against her skin and this was all she ever wanted or needed for the rest of her life.

When the door burst open, she didn't notice at first. Or maybe she noticed but she didn't care. Until she became aware of the voices, loud and angry, and the hands on her body, lifting her away from him.

In an instant, everything that had been perfect was ruined. She tried to get away, but someone was holding her hands behind her back. Then she heard Leo scream, the sound too loud and too long, slicing through her heart as she was dragged, writhing and wriggling and kicking and screaming.

'Silence.'

She turned towards the voice and a fist smashed into her face. She stumbled sideways but didn't fall because she was still being held up. She could hear Leo, screaming her name. She screamed back, before she was hit again, in the stomach this time. The person holding her let her go and her body crumpled to the ground.

She tried to get up, scrabbling away on the cold, hard ground, but they were all around her now, kicking her in the stomach and head and back. She closed her eyes, wrapped her arms around her head to protect herself. In her mind, she was in the van with Leo. Speeding away from here into the warm light of an orange sun setting slowly over the long shadows criss-crossing the green fields.

Chapter 18

Present

Nuala jolts awake. Eyes open, heart pounding. Her body on high alert. At first, she thinks it was a bad dream that woke her. Until she hears the familiar creak of the sitting room door being pushed open. There's a brief moment when she thinks Josh is up and about. Then she remembers he's still in Dungeness, and she's hit with a rush of fear so overwhelming she can't breathe.

Through the roaring inside her head, she hears a footstep. Then another, a little closer this time. Whoever's out there is coming towards her room. Biting back a scream, she slides out of the bed, pulls up the duvet, and tip toes across the room to the built-in wardrobe.

This is where Josh comes when they're playing hide and seek. Every single time, he ends up in here and Nuala has to pretend to be surprised when she finds him hiding behind the rows of her clothing. She holds her breath as she opens the door, willing it not to make a sound as she sneaks inside and ducks down behind her dresses and jeans. As she reaches out to pull the wardrobe door shut, a shaft of light brightens the room. The last thing she sees before the door clicks shut is the silhouette of a man standing in the doorway of the bedroom.

She clamps both hands over her mouth, too scared to breathe or move, as she hears him come into the room. Her heart is pounding so loud and fast she's sure he must be able to hear it. As his footsteps move closer to the wardrobe, part of her almost wants him to pull open the door and find her. Because anything would be better than this unbearable waiting for it to happen.

'The flat's empty.'

Her first thought: he's speaking directly to her. Her second, more terrifying thought: there is more than one of them. The floorboards creak as he moves around the room.

It's pitch black inside the wardrobe. She can't see a thing but there's something sharp sticking into her bum and, when she puts her hand down, she realises it's a wire hanger that's fallen off the rail. Slowly, she pulls it out from beneath her body and starts to unwind the wire.

On the other side of the door, he's speaking again.

'Her phone's here on the table by her bed, and the pillow's warm. Hang on, that means—'

She doesn't wait for him to finish his sentence. With a scream that comes from the deepest part of her, she shoves the wardrobe door open and lunges. She holds the unwound piece of wire in front of her, like a weapon, and races towards the man with every last bit of force that's left in her body.

She has the advantage of surprise, but he's much bigger than she is, and he recovers quickly. His arm goes up to protect his body, just as she thrusts the hanger into him. The wire pierces his lower arm, but it's not enough to cause any real damage. She sees his fist coming towards her and dodges left. Feels the whoosh of air, as his hand swipes past her face, before she turns and races for the bedroom door.

She makes it into the corridor, is almost at the front door, when she's grabbed from behind. He lifts her off the ground, crushing the air from her body as his arm wraps tight around her middle. She squirms and wriggles and screams, but it's like trying to fight a piece of steel. He's too strong and she is utterly helpless. She manages one final scream before his hand clamps across her mouth and nose.

She smells sweat and onions, before her body goes into panic mode. She can't breathe. When she tries to claw his hand away from her face, he shakes her until she stops. The flat swims around in front of her, as her mind floods with memories.

She sees her mother, the one time Nuala can remember her being happy, the day Uncle Brendan took them to the seaside. Nuala and Marion each held one of Mam's hands as the three of them ran in and out of the freezing cold waves on the beach at Enniscrone. Then her mother's and sister's faces disappear, replaced by Josh running in and out of the waves on the beach at Brighton.

She wants to hold onto this memory with everything she's got, but it's already starting to fade beneath the darkness that's closing over her. In the distance, far away, she hears a bell ringing. The line of a poem runs through her head. Another long ago memory. Standing at the front of a classroom reading John Donne. The classroom disappears, she searches for Josh's face but there's nothing there.

Chapter 19

Before

Lydia stood in the kitchen peeling potatoes, only vaguely aware of the conversation going on behind her. The other aunts were talking about something Robert had done in class, wondering whether or not to say something to Mother. Lydia didn't care what Robert had been up to this time. Whatever it was, it would be bad because Robert was like Lydia herself had once been. He broke the rules, over and over. No matter how often or badly he was punished, he seemed incapable of learning that it was better to stop caring and empty yourself of all feeling and simply accept things for what they were.

Lydia had finally realised this eight years ago, the day she learned Leo had died. It was three weeks after they'd been found together in the shed. She'd spent the first few days in the Box and, by the time she came out, Leo was gone. At first, no one seemed to know where he was, or what had happened to him. Then one afternoon, Peter and Mother came back from town and announced Leo's body had been found. He'd drowned in the river that ran through the town.

Lydia refused to believe it at first, convinced Peter and Mother were lying because they couldn't admit that Leo had managed to escape. But later, when they had his funeral and she saw his coffin being buried in the woods behind the farm, she knew it was true and that was the end of the person she'd been before.

Today, she could barely remember the angry young woman she'd been back then. These days, her feelings were muted, like a piece of music playing with the volume turned down so low you'd barely know it was there. She knew, now, she was never going to leave the farm. She would grow old here, and then, one day hopefully not too far away, she would die.

When she was finished in the kitchen, Lydia went upstairs to toilet. The door was locked and she was about to turn away, when she heard a noise coming from inside. She recognised the sound, and paused for a moment before shaking her head. What did she care who was crying in there? Yet when she turned to go, she found she couldn't do it.

'Hello?' she knocked gently on the door and waited.

Someone sniffled, then a mumbled voice told Nuala to go away.

'Martha?'

'No.'

'I know it's you,' Lydia said. 'What's wrong?'

'Like you care,' Martha said.

'Let me in,' Lydia said. 'Please. I want to help you.'

She thought Martha would refuse. After all, the two of them were no longer close the way they'd once been. Lydia had cut Martha off, along with everyone else, in the months and years following Leo's death. So it was a surprise when she heard the lock on the door click.

'I heard you crying,' Lydia said, when Martha opened the door. 'Has something happened?'

Silently, Martha undid the top buttons of her blouse.

'Oh God.' Lydia put a hand over her mouth as she saw the pattern of purple bruises across Martha's small breasts. She knew immediately where the bruises had come from. Martha had turned sixteen a few months earlier. Since then, their regular prayers had included a plea to God to grant Martha with the gift of a child.

'Peter did this to you?'

Martha nodded.

'I don't like it, Lydia. He hurts me so bad.'

Anger uncurled in the pit of Lydia's stomach, hot and fierce. The shock of feeling something after all these years of emptiness was strange at first. But the more she focused on it, let it rise up inside, the more she knew this was what she needed. A reason beyond herself to do what she should have done years ago.

'It's okay.' Lydia reached out and touched the younger girl's shoulder. 'It's going to be okay, I promise.'

Chapter 20

Present

The buzz Nuala had after finally speaking with Lydia is gone and she can't get it back. In its place is a bone deep darkness that she hasn't been able to shift since last night. She's tried telling herself that her attacker hadn't been planning to kill her, but she knows that's not true. If it wasn't for Dylan, who lives in the upstairs flat, Nuala doesn't think she'd be alive now. No matter how hard she tries, she can't stop her mind repeatedly going back over what happened.

Dylan heard Nuala screaming and came racing to her front door to try to help. The ringing sound she'd heard was her own front doorbell. Dylan told her later, after he'd smashed down the door and found her lying unconscious inside her flat, that he'd caught a glimpse of Nuala's attacker running out through the back door. Dylan chased after the man, who he described as being 'built like a brick shithouse', but hadn't managed to catch him.

Like Dylan, Nuala hadn't seen the man's face so there was little either of them could tell the two police officers who responded to Dylan's 999 call. Nuala tried to convince the police that the attack was linked to the podcast and Andrea Leach, but it was clear they didn't believe her. Partly, because she was semi-hysterical and not making much sense at that point, but also, as they kept telling her, there'd been a spate of burglaries in this area recently. The break-in at Nuala's flat was just another in a long line of similar break-ins.

Her phone and laptop were the only items stolen. Further proof, in her opinion, that this wasn't a random break-in. The police, on the other hand, remained convinced that Dylan had simply interrupted the burglar before he could steal anything else. At Nuala's insistence, the two officers promised they would interview Andrea Leach but Nuala already knows how that conversation will go. Andrea will switch on the charm and convince them that Nuala is delusional and can't be trusted. Which is exactly why Andrea had to fire her.

In Nuala's opinion, all police are right-wing bastards and the ones she spoke to have probably already decided to vote for the Progress Party in the next election. Although when she said this to Dylan the following morning, he told her there are many police officers who think the Progress Party, and its leader, are abhorrent and would never vote for them. Nuala wasn't sure this was true but conceded that, as a serving police officer, Dylan's opinion might count for something.

Her flat, normally her sanctuary, is now a crime scene. She spent the night on Dylan's sofa and the police have told her to limit her movements inside the flat until the Crime Scene Investigator has checked it for fingerprints, DNA and anything else that might identify the intruder.

This morning, she got up early and took a train to Canary Wharf where she bought herself a new phone. She's ordered a replacement SIM card from her phone provider, but that won't arrive for a day or two. Luckily, her emails and contact details are all stored in the cloud. Once she'd set up the new phone, she instantly had access to her contacts.

She's going to take the train to Ashford, travelling from London Bridge. On her way to the station, she calls Liz. When the call goes to voicemail, she leaves a message.

'Hey, it's me. I lost my phone yesterday so I've got a new number until my replacement SIM arrives.'

Nuala reels off the new number, asks Liz to give her love to Josh and hangs up. Next, she calls Lydia to make sure she's still okay for meeting up today. When that phone call is over, Nuala finds a coffee shop and drinks two shots of espresso. She buys herself an egg mayonnaise sandwich but can only manage a couple of mouthfuls before giving up. Her stomach's in knots and the food only makes it worse.

She realises, too late, that the coffee was a terrible idea. She's jittery as hell, getting spikes of anxiety that are difficult to control. She can't stop thinking how much worse last night might have been. In her mind, she sees Josh coming out of his room, sleepy and bleary-eyed. She imagines the shock and fear on his little face when he sees what's happening. And she hears him crying out in pain as that big brute swings his fist at him.

She leaves the coffee shop and enters London Bridge station. It takes an effort to push through the dark mood that's weighing her down, but she has to do it. Because today is the day she's going to blow it all up. She's going to tell the truth. Finally.

Seventy minutes later, the train pulls into Ashford International. It's a fifteen-minute walk from the station to the park where they've arranged to meet. Lydia has suggested meeting by the fountain in the centre of the park. When Nuala arrives, she's twenty minutes early. She finds a nearby bench and sits down to wait for Lydia.

It's a chilly day. A cold wind is chasing thick clouds across a grey sky. But Nuala has come prepared, she's layered up and barely feels the cold. She closes her eyes and empties her mind of everything except the steady in-out of her breathing.

Her body starts to relax, her shoulders loosening and the tight knot at the back of her neck slowly unwinding. She feels a sense of purpose that she hasn't had for a while, certain she's doing the right thing and determined to see this through to the end. Because she's getting close now, the different strands of her story are finally coming together.

She opens her eyes, looking around for Lydia in case she too has arrived early. They agreed to call each other when they arrived and, when Nuala's phone starts to ring, she thinks it might be Lydia. But when she checks the phone, it's Liz's number she sees on the screen.

'Hey,' she says, taking the call. 'You got my message then?'

'Nuala, I'm so sorry.'

Fear fills every part of her body. When she tries to speak, to ask Liz what's happened, Nuala's throat and mouth don't do anything. And when Liz continues speaking, the words don't make sense the first time round. It's only when Liz keeps talking, repeating herself as she tries to explain the inexplicable, that Nuala finally understands what Liz is telling her.

'He's disappeared, Nuala. He was playing in the garden. I had the back door open and I swear to God I only took my eyes off him for a moment. I've searched everywhere, but he's been gone for almost an hour. I'm so sorry. The police are on the way, but you need to come too. As soon as you can.'

Chapter 21

Nuala's racing towards Ashford International station when a car screeches in front of her. Black tinted glass means she can't see who's inside, but she doesn't need to. She already knows. When the passenger door swings open and she sees a patent red shoe with a heel, her stomach curdles.

'Nuala, what a pleasant surprise.'

'What have you done with my son?' Nuala hisses.

'He's fine,' Andrea says. 'Or, rather, he will be. As long as you do what I say.'

In her mind, Nuala is picturing the different ways she will injure and maim Andrea Leach. She is going to destroy the bitch if it's the very last thing she does with the rest of her life. But first, she has to do whatever Andrea tells her to because Andrea has Josh.

'What do you want?'

'Where's Lydia?' Andrea says.

Nuala thinks about lying, telling Andrea she has no idea what she's talking about, but she can't risk it.

'I'm meant to be meeting her in Victoria Park in a few minutes.'

Something flashes across Andrea's face, brief but unmistakable. Relief.

'Why?' Nuala says. 'What is she to you?'

'That's none of your business,' Andrea says. 'Call her. Tell her the meeting place has changed. Say that rain is on the way so she should meet you in the coffee shop down there instead.'

She nods at the road to her left that runs along the edge of a river.

'What then?' Nuala says.

'If you do as I say, your boy will be returned to your London home this evening at six o'clock.'

'No.' Nuala shakes her head. 'You need to return him now. I can't wait six hours before I see him.'

She thinks how scared he'll be, trapped somewhere with strangers who don't care about him. They won't know that he gets tummy cramps when he's anxious, or what to do if he gets one now. Sometimes, the cramps cause diarrhoea. She can't bear the thought of him sitting in soiled trousers for the next six hours.

'Call Lydia,' Andrea says. 'Now.'

She knows she should refuse. That it's wrong to set Lydia up like this. But the truth is, she's too scared not to do exactly as Andrea tells her.

The fear for Josh is so all-consuming, Nuala can't do anything except take out her phone and make the call. When she hangs up, she can't even remember what she said to Lydia.

'Give me your phone.' Andrea holds her hand out.

'Just tell me where he is,' Nuala says, handing the phone over. 'Please. I need to know he's okay.'

'I told you he's fine.' Andrea's voice is cold and emotionless. 'There's a Hampton by Hilton hotel near the station. It's a fifteen-minute walk from here. Roger's waiting for you in the bar. He'll wait for twenty minutes. If you don't show up in that time, you'll never see your son again.'

She says something else, but Nuala doesn't stop to listen. She's already running towards the hotel. Luckily, she spotted it earlier when she was leaving the station so she knows exactly where it is.

Within twelve minutes of leaving Andrea, she's crossing the hotel lobby to the bar. But when she steps inside and scans the faces of the few people who are in here, she doesn't see Roger.

Panic flares inside her chest and she swings around, searching every corner of the place for Roger. But he's not here.

She hasn't got her phone, so she can't call Andrea or anyone else to tell them she's done exactly what she was told to do. Somehow, she manages to locate the reception desk and asks the young woman working there if there's another Hampton by Hilton hotel nearby. But the woman tells her this is the only one.

There's a clock on the wall above the woman's head. It gives the time as eight minutes past twelve. Which means Nuala's got approximately four minutes to find Roger.

'Is everything okay?' the woman asks. But Nuala doesn't answer. She turns away, searching the lobby and the bar and the area outside the hotel. But she can't see Roger anywhere, and if she can't find him...

'Nuala.'

His voice is so close, so unexpected, she bites back a scream. He's standing right behind her. When he speaks again, she can feel the heat of his breath on her neck.

'I assume you're looking for me?'

'You're meant to be in the bar,' she says, when she trusts herself to speak without roaring her rage into his ugly face.

'I was checking our room.' He holds up a plastic key card with the hotel's logo embossed on it. 'We're on the top floor. Great views from up there.'

She stares at him, unable to move or speak.

'What's the matter, Nuala? Cat got your tongue?'

'I'm not going into any hotel room with you.'

'That's exactly what you're going to do,' he said. 'Unless you don't care what happens to your son. If that's the case, feel free to leave and get on with your life. Believe me, I don't care in the slightest what you decide.'

He's staring at her, like he's daring her to turn around and leave. She swallows hard, and nods her head. She'll go up to the room with him, and she'll do whatever he tells her. She'll do it for Josh, and she'll think of him while it's happening.

219

In the lift, he stands too close to her again. When the doors ping open, she steps out and waits for him to tell her which direction they're going in. It's too quiet up here, no sounds from any of the other rooms or anywhere else in the big hotel. She could scream her head off up here and she doubts anyone would hear.

'This is us.'

He stops at a door midway along the corridor. Using the key card, he opens the door and stands back, indicating that she should go into the room ahead of him. She walks past him, every cell in her body screaming that she should run as fast as she can in the opposite direction. Inside the room, she stands by the window and doesn't look around as she hears the door click shut.

'Have something to drink.'

She hears him pull open the mini bar, and the clink of glass.

'I'm not thirsty.'

'I don't give a shit if you're thirsty or not.'

She listens to liquid being poured into a glass and watches his reflection in the window as he crosses the room to where she's standing.

'Drink this.'

He puts a glass tumbler in her hand. When he stays standing right behind her, she moves away. She's trembling, head to toe shivers that she can't control. She has to use both hands to lift the glass to her mouth. The whiff of pure alcohol clears her mind, and she drinks the contents of the glass in a single go. It's vodka, or maybe gin, that burns as it works its way down her throat and into her stomach.

'Sit on the bed and take your shoes off,' Roger says.

He's staring at her, eyes moving across her body as she does what he tells her to do. The drink swills around inside her stomach and she knows if he touches her right now, she will throw up all over him.

She bends down to untie her trainers. When she's done, and she sits back up, he's still staring at her.

'I need to know Josh is okay,' she says.

Roger's eyebrows shoot up, but he doesn't speak.

'I'll do anything you want,' she continues, 'but not until I know my boy is safe.'

'You don't get to call the shots here,' Roger says. 'We've got the kid and he's safe until you fuck up. If that happens, he stops being safe. That's all you need to know.'

'Please.'

She hates herself for begging, but her need to know Josh hasn't been harmed is greater than anything else.

'Say it again. But mean it this time.'

You fucker, she thinks.

'Please, Roger. Let me know he's okay. That's all I'm asking. Please?'

His hand goes to the pocket of his navy Chinos. For one terrible moment she thinks he's touching himself. But he's getting his phone.

'Here.' He holds the phone out, turning the screen towards her.

It takes a moment for her eyes to focus. When they do, she moans in anguish and relief. It's a photo of Josh. He's sitting on a bed, knees tucked up to his chin, watching something on TV. He's got a bag of crisps on the bed beside him. He looks okay. A bit scared, maybe, but he doesn't seem injured in any way.

'Thank you,' she whispers, her fingers tracing Josh's outline until Roger takes the phone away and puts it back in his pocket.

'Lie down on the bed,' he says.

No, she wants to say. No, no, no, no, no. Please not this.

But she lies back, as he tells her to, and she grits her teeth together as she waits for whatever is about to happen to begin.

Chapter 22

The following morning I wake early. The first thing I do is check for any new messages from Helen Robins, but there's nothing. When I send her a text, asking for an update, she replies straight away.

> Nothing yet, but I won't give up until I find your friend. In the meantime, try not to worry.

Easy for her to say. Not bothering to reply, I climb out of bed and get dressed. I have hours before my meeting with Nuala Fox. After a quick coffee, I leave the B&B and spend the rest of the morning wandering around Ashford, looking at clothes I can't afford in shops I'd never have the courage to step inside of.

Two hours before we're due to meet I get a phone call. I'm so sure it's Helen Robins I don't bother to check the number. It's a shock, then, when I hear Nuala's voice.

'Lydia? It's Nuala. I lost my phone yesterday. Long story, which I'll tell you about when we meet. This is my new number. I wanted to make sure you had it, in case you need to contact me. You're still okay for today?'

She sounds different this morning. Yesterday, her voice was like it is on the podcast: calm and happy-sounding. This morning, she's speaking too fast and she sounds stressed. Really stressed.

'What happened to your phone?' I ask.

'It's not important,' she says. 'I just wanted to make sure you've got this number. And to check you haven't changed your mind.'

It would be so easy to turn around, go back to my room in the B&B and do nothing. But I think of how hiding makes me feel. Like I'm slowly dying, and every day another piece of me disappears. And I know if I carry on living the way I've been doing, one day soon there'll be nothing left of me at all.

'I haven't changed my mind,' I tell her.

The next two hours drag by. It's a cold day. Grey sky and a sharp wind that cuts through me. I've arranged to meet Nuala outside but as soon as she shows up, I'm going to suggest we go somewhere warmer.

Finally, it's time. I start walking towards the park and I'm almost there when Nuala calls again.

'Lydia, where are you?'

'Nearly at the fountain. Why?'

'The weather forecast says it's going to rain, so I've found a coffee shop near the park where we can meet instead.'

She gives me directions for the coffee shop and says she's there already so she'll order me something to drink. I ask for a Diet Coke and tell her I'll see her soon.

After I've hung up, I check the name of the road Nuala gave me on my phone's map. It's less than five minutes away. As I head in that direction, the first drops of rain start to fall and I'm glad Nuala's found us somewhere else to meet.

The road the coffee shop is on isn't what I expected. It's a semi-rural path that runs along the banks of a river. As I turn into it, my phone buzzes with a notification. I've got a new voicemail. A message from Helen Robins, who must have called when I was on the phone to Nuala.

'Clare, it's Helen. I've got some news about your friend. Can you call me when you get this message?'

I'm halfway through calling her back when I see a flash of yellow out of the corner of my eye. I look up, see Nuala Fox.

She's on the other side of the road, running in the opposite direction to where she should be going – away from the coffee shop, not towards it. In her hurry to get away, she doesn't even notice me.

Something's wrong. The knowledge sits in my gut, hard and heavy. I should never have trusted Nuala. She doesn't care about me, or the truth. All that matters to her is her stupid podcast. I look left and right, trying to work out the safest way to go. I've got three options: turn and go back to the park, follow Nuala and see where she's going, or continue down the path that runs along the banks of the river. The park, I decide. Nuala doesn't want me there so that's where I'll go.

The rain is heavier now. I push my wet hair back from my face and start to run. At the same moment, someone grabs me. A hand is clamped across my face, an arm wraps around my stomach and my feet are no longer touching the ground. My bag falls off my shoulder. Flashes of colour as I'm lifted off the ground. Grey sky, yellow tufts of grass at the edge of the footpath, the pointed edge of a red shoe. Then the black inside of a car boot with its hood open.

I try to get away from whoever's holding me, but I'm not strong enough. The last thing I see, before I hit the bottom of the boot, is the silhouette of someone standing over me. The boot closes and the silhouette disappears along with everything else.

Chapter 23

Before

Lydia lay in bed with her eyes wide open, waiting. It was happening tonight. She was going alone, not taking Martha as she'd promised. After giving it a lot of thought, she'd decided it was too dangerous. Everyone else who had tried to leave the farm had ended up dead. Lydia was willing to take that risk for herself, but she couldn't put Martha's life in danger too.

She hadn't told Martha she was leaving. Instead, she'd told the girl they couldn't try to escape just yet. Said it was too dangerous. The conversation had gone badly. Martha had become angry, screaming and crying and telling Lydia she hated her. That had been two days ago. Since then, Martha had refused to speak to her.

It was never quiet on the farm. Even now, while everyone else was sleeping, the night was full of sound. Breathing and snoring from the other aunts she shared the room with. The intermittent hooting of an owl outside the window, and the blood-churning screams from the foxes that roamed the countryside during the quiet hours when the humans were sleeping.

Most nights, Mother locked the bedroom doors from the outside. All the bedroom windows had thick metal bars on them, which meant there was no way out until Mother unlocked the doors in the morning. If you needed to use the toilet during the night, you couldn't. Anyone unable to hold on until morning, who had an accident during the night, would be punished.

But a few nights a month, Mother and Peter retired to their rooms early and Aunt Sarah was in charge of locking the doors. Once she'd locked the others in, she'd lock the door of their room, before getting into her bed and slipping the key under her pillow.

Tonight was one of the nights Aunt Sarah had locked up. After Aunt Sarah had climbed into bed, Lydia lay awake, waiting until she was certain everyone else in the room had fallen asleep. There were no curtains on the windows so Lydia was able to see the sky from her bed. She had worked out, from nights of lying here watching the moon move across the sky behind the metal bars, that the deepest part of the night was when the moon had reached the right side of the window.

Tonight there was a full moon that seemed to move so slowly she wondered if it had stopped altogether. But it hadn't stopped because, just as she thought she couldn't stay awake a moment longer, the moon was suddenly where she needed it to be.

She threw back her blanket and sat up. Then she froze, terrified at what she was about to do. But she had no choice. She wasn't doing this just for herself; if she was, she didn't think she'd have the courage to go through with it. She was doing it for Martha too, who would end up empty and broken like Lydia had been for too long. She had to go, and she had to do it now.

Aunt Sarah was lying on her back, little snoring sounds coming from her open mouth. In the grey light, her face was white, like a ghost. Holding her breath, Lydia leaned down and slipped her hand beneath the pillow. Aunt Sarah groaned and rolled over onto her side; Lydia held her breath, waiting for Aunt Sarah to open her eyes. But after a moment, Aunt Sarah settled once more and Lydia was able to push her hand further beneath the pillow until her fingers touched the key.

Slowly, slowly, she pulled it out. Once she had it in her hand, she squeezed it tight. She was about to cross to the door when she heard something. A muffled sound, like someone was crying beneath their blanket. Her first thought was Martha, who had recently moved into this room with the aunts. But when Lydia went over to Martha's bed, the girl was curled up on her side fast asleep.

Lydia stood for a moment, watching Martha and thinking how much she was going to miss her.

'I'll be back soon,' she whispered, leaning down to give Martha a gentle kiss on her cheek. Then she turned to go before she lost her nerve and changed her mind. When she put the key in the lock, it rattled once then stuck and wouldn't go any further. She tried twisting it back and starting again, making more noise each time but hardly caring now. Her desperation to get out overriding everything else.

She gave the key one final twist, harder this time. There was a loud click and suddenly the lock gave. The door creaked as she opened it, and again as she pulled it shut behind her. On the landing, she paused, her ears straining for any sign that someone had heard. But all around her the house was still.

Mother locked the front and back doors each night, taking the key with her to the annex where she lived with Peter. The only window in the house with no bars on it was the one in the bathroom over the toilet. Lydia assumed that was because the window was so small and high up, Mother didn't think anyone would be able to get through it. Even if they managed, the drop to the ground below was so far, it would be crazy to try to get out that way. But crazy was all Lydia had left.

To reach the window, she had to climb onto the edge of the bath. The window was closed but, when she pushed it, she was able to open it without any problem. It took all her strength to pull herself up and through the gap until the top half of her body was leaning out, looking down to the ground below. There was a drainpipe running down the side of the house. She'd planned to grab onto this and use it to swing herself out and down. But when she reached for it, she could barely graze it with the tips of her fingers.

She shoved herself forward a little more, reaching for the drainpipe again. Almost there. She stretched as far as she could, the left side of her body aching from the effort. Her fingers almost grasped the pipe. Her body wobbled on the edge of the window. She tried to wrap her hand around the pipe but instead she was propelled forward, out of the window and hurtling towards the ground.

Somehow, she managed to land sideways, her right shoulder and elbow taking the weight of her body as she landed on the damp grass. Pain shot through her, bright and hot. For a long time, all she could do was lie there, panting and waiting for the worst of the pain to pass.

When she sat up, she had to lean on her left arm because her right arm was loose and useless, damaged in some way she didn't understand, but she wasn't going to let that stop her.

She hurried around to the side of the house where Peter kept the van. For the last few weeks, one of Lydia's jobs had been to help unload the van when Peter returned from a trip to the town. From this, she learned that he didn't bother locking the van after it was unloaded. She guessed he didn't think there was any need, because he kept the key attached to his belt.

Lydia knew that when they woke up tomorrow morning and discovered she was gone, Mother would send Peter off in the van to see if he could find her. All Lydia had to do was hide inside the van. Then, once Peter was far away from the farm, she could climb out the back and make a run for it. The plan wasn't ideal, far from it, but she'd gone over it countless times, exploring the different ways she could try to escape, and this seemed like her best option.

Earlier this evening, Lydia had sneaked out here and put her bag into the back of the van. The bag contained clothes and some photos from the photo album in the sitting room. When she got out of here, she wanted the photos to show people how they were forced to live on the farm.

Her biggest worry had been that Peter might have locked the van at some point. But when she reached it and tried the door at the side, it slid open immediately. Lydia leaned against the side of the van, breathing out a sigh of relief. Until this moment, she hadn't realised how worried she'd been that the door wouldn't open. She was about to step inside when a sudden yank to the back of her hair dragged her backwards.

She lost her balance and fell to the ground. Stunned, she tried to get up but a weight pressed down on her stomach making it impossible to move.

'Get up,' Mother said, her voice cold and angry.

The pressure on her stomach disappeared and Lydia tried to scrabble backwards. She didn't see Mother's foot lashing out, but felt the impact of the kick to her side. A pain so intense that she forgot, for a moment, about everything else. She rolled onto her side, and Mother kicked her again. In the back this time. Lydia curled up smaller, but the kicks kept coming. To her back and her arms and legs and the side of her face.

Abruptly, the kicking stopped. She moaned, too scared to lift her head to see what Mother was planning next. Then she heard a different voice, sweet and familiar.

'Lydia? Are you okay?'

Chapter 24

The rain thunders against the car, the sound so loud it's impossible to hear anything else. The car moves slowly at first. By the time I notice it's speeded up, I've lost track of how long I've been in here. It feels like forever, but it could be anything from five minutes to five hours. Each time we turn a corner, my body slams into the metal sides of the boot. My back and shoulders are bruised and battered.

Later, the rain stops. The smooth sound of an engine replaces the roaring of rain battering the bonnet of the boot. It's cold and pitch black. I've stopped being able to tell if my eyes are open or closed. I've screamed until there's nothing left to scream, and I've kicked and punched the sides of the boot until my feet and hands are too sore to keep going. Nothing I do makes any difference.

The cold has buried its way deep inside me. I can't stop shivering, tremor after tremor rolling through my body. Snapshots of memories appear, then disappear. The elegant building in Blackheath with the red and black Progress Party logo on the gatepost. Nuala's yellow coat, moving along the Lewisham streets. Andrea Leach's face on the Progress Party's website. The pointed toe of a shiny red shoe.

And my sister. Ten years later and I can still feel her hand in mine, our fingers interlaced, as we raced across the fields that last night, laughing and wild beneath the silver moon. Running so fast it felt as if we were flying, our feet barely seeming to touch the ground. We could have run forever. The more distance we put between ourselves and the farm, the stronger we became. Or maybe it wasn't like that at all. Because I don't know anymore which memories are true and which are imagined.

The car slows down, turns another corner. As my body slams against the side of the boot again, the engine stops. The silence that follows is unbearable. I hold my breath, waiting for something to happen. I hear voices, too low for me to catch the words but I think there's a woman and a man speaking. Then footsteps, followed by a moaning that reminds me of an animal in pain. It takes a few seconds to realise the sound is coming from me. I squeeze my eyes shut, willing the car boot to stay closed. And it does.

Footsteps fade, then disappear completely. I don't know how many people were in the car, but one of them has left. Moments later, the engine starts up again. This time, the drive goes on forever. As my body rolls from side to side, my mind drifts until it's like I'm two separate things: my body, here in the car, and my mind flying high into the sky up, up and up until I've found my sister and we're together again, racing across the green fields. Wild and happy and free at last.

Hours pass. The car slows down, then stops. I hear the door open, feel the weight of the car shift as the driver gets out. Then footsteps, walking away from the car.

'Hello?' I shout, seized with a sudden fear that I've been forgotten. 'Hello? Let me out.'

Time passes – seconds, minutes, maybe longer – and still no one comes for me. My hands are bleeding but I keep punching the walls of this black prison, kicking although my legs and feet are aching and exhausted.

Suddenly, there's a burst of light so bright I have to cover my eyes.

'Get out.'

The voice strips back all the years since I last heard it. The fear that's never left me rears up inside me, along with the pathetic need for her to love me and take care of me. She grabs my arm, hauls me up and lets me do the rest. She knows I won't resist, because that was never who I was. Always the good girl, the one who wanted to please her and be loved by her. I half-climb, half-fall onto the grass that's wild and overgrown and brittle against my face.

I lift my head and look around. I already know where we are. Maybe I knew all along that this was where she'd take me. It's almost as if all the years since I left never really happened – almost, because although everything looks the same, it's different too. The garden is longer and narrower. The roof of the shed has fallen in, and one of its walls is leaning sideways, like it's about to fall over. When we lived here, there were always people about, but today it feels like the loneliest place in the whole world.

She's wearing the same perfume she always wore and, as I breathe in the familiar scent, a longing grows inside me. More than anything, I want her to hold me and tell me how special I am. To feel her arms tight around my body, while I bury my face against her. I want it so much that when it doesn't happen the disappointment is crushing.

I look up, taking in every inch of her. Red shoes, narrow ankles, black skirt and a white blouse with the collar turned up. Her hair is different, blonder than before and tied into a knot at the bottom of her neck. Gold and blue earrings, and lipstick the same colour as her shoes.

Finally, our eyes connect. A spike of fear pierces my chest, and I remember this too. The fear and the longing mixed together so I never knew how I was really feeling, or what I really wanted. She smiles, but it doesn't reach her eyes, which are like shards of ice. When I drop my head, because I can't bear to look at her, she crouches down, puts her index finger under my chin and forces me to look back at her as she speaks.

'Hello, Martha.'

Chapter 25

Before

'Lydia?'

It was Martha speaking, and Martha's face, scrunched up with concern.

'What are you doing out here?' Lydia whispered.

'I think I've killed Mother. I didn't mean for her to die. I was trying to stop her hurting you.'

Lydia's head was pounding, her whole body aching. She looked around for Mother, saw her lying on the ground a little further away.

'I knew you were planning to leave,' Martha said, speaking so fast Lydia could barely keep up with her. 'You kept your clothes on when you went to bed tonight. You thought no one noticed, but I did because I notice everything. I know that Aunt Sarah and Aunt Elizabeth hate each other, even though we're not allowed to hate anyone. I know that Mother and Peter eat different food to the rest of us, and Mother's rooms have a fire and a heater so she doesn't get cold in winter like we do. And I know where Aunt Elizabeth keeps the spare key for the front door because I've watched her when I've been working in the kitchen. She's like you. She thinks she can do stuff without anyone noticing. It's because neither of you think I'm important. You don't see me, but I see you.'

'Martha,' Lydia said, interrupting the flow of words. 'I'm sure you haven't killed her.'

'I don't want her to be dead,' Martha wailed. 'Am I going to burn in hell?'

'No one's burning in hell.' Lydia could see the rise and fall of Mother's stomach as she breathed in and out, which meant she was definitely still alive. 'It's okay, Martha.'

Right then, she heard a sound that made her freeze – the creak the front door made as it opened, followed by footsteps hurrying across the yard. Lydia squeezed her eyes shut, unable to imagine the horror that was about to unfold.

'Martha? Is that you? What on earth has happened?'

Aunt Elizabeth. Some deep forgotten part of Lydia was glad. Before she remembered that this woman had chosen not to be her mother the moment they'd come to live here. Then she felt a hand on her arm and saw her mother's face as she leaned down towards her.

'Come on, let's get you up.' As Aunt Elizabeth helped Lydia to stand, she asked again what had happened.

The light from the silver moon made Aunt Elizabeth's face seem whiter than ever, her eyes like two giant dark pools as she waited for Lydia to speak. But Lydia didn't know what to say, so she shook her head and said nothing.

'It was me,' Martha said. 'I saw what Mother was doing to Lydia so I ran into the kitchen and got the knife and I stabbed her and now she's dead.'

'She's not dead.' Lydia looked at the woman who'd once been her mother. 'None of this is Martha's fault. It's all down to me.'

She waited for the familiar hardening of Aunt Elizabeth's eyes, and the thin line of her mouth. Instead, Aunt Elizabeth lifted her hand and placed it gently on Lydia's cheek.

'My dear child,' she whispered. 'My dear, beautiful girl. You need to get away from this place.' She looked at Martha who, Lydia could see now, was still holding the knife and had dark stains of blood across her white blouse. 'You both need to go.'

Aunt Elizabeth stared at Lydia for a moment longer, before crouching down and patting Mother's clothes. She pulled a keyring, with several keys on it, from one of Mother's pockets and smiled up at Lydia. 'Let's go.'

She told Martha to drop the knife, then gestured for them to follow her to the big gate with the barbed wire across the top.

'Run,' Aunt Elizabeth said, as she unlocked the padlock and heaved the gate open. 'As fast as you can, and don't stop running until you're far, far away.'

Even though this was what she'd wanted, now the moment was here, Lydia couldn't do it. All the love and loss she'd felt for her mother bubbled up inside her. The thought that she might never see her again was, suddenly, unbearable.

'Go.' Aunt Elizabeth put her hand on Lydia's cheek. 'Please, Lydia. Before it's too late. I love you.'

There was so much Lydia wanted to say, but there would never be enough time to say it all. So she did what she was told. She grabbed hold of Martha's hand, and she started running.

Together, they raced across the rolling fields, barely noticing the hills. They ran so fast it felt more like flying than running, bathed in the silver-grey light of the moon that made the world look beautiful. Lydia's chest, her whole body, was bursting with a thousand thoughts and feelings. She started laughing, a loud, crazy sound that made her so breathless she had to stop running. She lifted her face to the moon, tears pouring down her cheeks. They'd done it. Finally, they were free and could start living their lives.

'Lydia?' Martha's voice brought her back down from wherever she'd been.

'We need to change our names,' Lydia said. 'What name would you like, if you could call yourself anything?'

Martha's face crumpled and she looked as if she was going to cry again.

'It's okay,' Lydia said quickly. 'You can carry on being Martha if you want to. Or any other name you want to give yourself. You can be me if you'd like. Wouldn't that be fun? From now on, you can do and say and think all the things you want to and no one is ever again going to tell you off for it.'

'I'm a bad person,' Martha whispered.

'You are not.' Lydia grabbed Martha by the shoulders. 'Listen to me, Martha. You saved me. You did the right thing and I'm so grateful to you. Mother's going to be okay, I promise.'

But Martha shook her head and burst into tears.

'It's okay, Martha.' Lydia wrapped her left arm – the one that was still working – around Martha's shoulders and told her, over and over, that everything was going to be okay.

'Let me go!' Martha screamed. 'Let me go, let me go, let me go.'

She lashed with her fists, punching Lydia in the jaw. As Lydia stumbled back, Martha whispered something.

'What did you say, Martha?'

'I told you.' Martha's voice was so low Lydia had to strain her ears to hear. 'The other day when you said we weren't leaving the farm. I told you how angry I was, but you wouldn't listen and I wanted to punish you. When I saw you get out of bed tonight, I went downstairs and switched on all the gas hobs in the kitchen. Aunt Sarah told me if you leave the gas on, it will cause a big explosion. I was so mad, I didn't care about anything except making you come back. I thought you'd hear the explosion and you'd find us all dead and you'd feel really bad for what had happened. But now I don't want you to feel bad. I want to go back to the farm and turn the gas off so no one gets hurt. Because I'm not angry anymore. I'm scared and I'm sad and I don't want to leave because I'll miss everyone too much.'

'Aunt Elizabeth will smell the gas and switch it off.' But even as Lydia said this, she wasn't completely sure that was true. What if her mother didn't smell the gas? The giddy joy disappeared as Lydia remembered that final moment at the gate. Her mother's hand on her cheek and her words. *I love you.*

'Can we go back, Lydia? Please?'

'I'll go,' Lydia said. They hadn't come far. There was still time. 'You stay here and wait for me. I won't be long. All I need to do is run back and switch the gas off before anyone wakes up.'

It was the last thing she wanted to do. The thought of it filled her with a sick dread, but she couldn't see any other way.

Martha started to argue but Lydia spoke over her.

'Listen to me, Martha. You need to do as I tell you. I'm going to go back, and you're going to wait for me. Right here. Don't you dare move, not even a step. Do you hear me?'

When Martha didn't reply, Lydia grabbed her by the chin and squeezed tight, forcing the girl to focus. 'You're covered in blood. Even if I tell them it was me who stabbed her, they won't ever forgive us. It's why Aunt Elizabeth told us to go. She knows what they'll do to us if they find us.'

Martha's eyes were big and scared, but she nodded her head.

'Do you promise you won't try to follow me?' Lydia said. 'You've got to promise, Martha. Because if you don't, I'm not going back there and then they really will die.'

'I promise.'

'Good.'

Lydia let her go and forced herself to turn back in the direction they'd just escaped from. The moon had moved further across the sky. It would be light soon. There wasn't much time.

Running back, it seemed to take three times as long to cover the same distance. She could feel the tiredness now, exacerbated by the throbbing pain down the right side of her body from her fall earlier.

When she saw the shadow of the farm rear up in the distance, her courage almost failed her. But she had to keep going. She hated the farm and most of the people living there, yet she would never be able to forgive herself if she let them die knowing she could have saved them. So she ran on.

She hadn't thought what she'd do if the gate was locked but, as she drew closer, she saw it was still open. Running through the gates into the yard, she saw the body. Except it had moved, wasn't where it had been when Lydia had left. Then she realised the person lying on the ground – by the gates, her white blouse stained black across her stomach – wasn't Mother. This person was taller, with silvery fair hair like Lydia's own.

'No.' Lydia shook her head, heard her voice repeating itself as she crossed the yard. 'No, no, no, no, no, no.'

Aunt Elizabeth, her real and only mother, who had sung songs to Lydia when she was a little girl and had cuddled her and told her she was the most precious thing in the entire world, who had grey eyes that were the exact same colour as Lydia's. Grey eyes that looked black now, as they stared up at the night sky.

Memories flashed back and forth through Lydia's mind. The attack and the knife in Martha's hand. Aunt Elizabeth's hand on her face as she told Lydia to go.

'No, no, no, no, no, no.'

But her voice was lost beneath the sudden roar of an engine bursting into life. She swung around, following the sound, just in time to see the beam of the van's headlights as it raced past her towards the open gate.

At the same moment, a little girl's face appeared at one of the upstairs windows and peered out at Lydia through the bars. It was Daisy, little Daisy with the blonde hair and the lisp. Daisy was shouting something, her fists banging against the glass.

Lydia ran across the yard to the house. The front door was locked. There was no point asking Daisy to let her in. The girls' bedroom would be locked. Daisy wouldn't be able to come out until the door was opened later this morning.

When Lydia tried the back door, that was locked too. She could smell smoke now, and when she peered through the window into the kitchen she saw an orange glow from the flames licking up the skirting board and along the wall.

The back door had two thick glass panels on them. If she could find something to break those, she might be able to get inside the house and save the people in there. She raced down to the shed, grabbed the stool they sat on to milk the cows, and carried it back to the house. Lifting the stool over her head, she charged towards the door and shoved the stool into the glass with every bit of strength left in her body, ignoring the roaring pain from her right side.

The glass shuddered, but didn't break. She lifted the stool to try again, and that's when it happened. First, the bang. So loud it eclipsed everything. Then the shock of her body, flying through the air, soaring upwards towards the silver moon. A burst of bright light, so crazily beautiful she wanted to laugh. Before the pain ripped through her, and she hit the ground and was gone, along with all the others.

Chapter 26

Present

Nuala is lying face down on a bed, unable to move. Her hands are behind her back, the muscles in her arms aching. When she tries to move her arms, nothing happens. There's something thick inside her mouth, pressing against her tongue, making it difficult to breathe. For a terrifying moment, she thinks she's paralysed. She's had a stroke or a brain haemorrhage, or she's been in some sort of accident.

Then it all comes rushing back and she starts to panic, thrashing helplessly on the bed. But her efforts are useless, because her hands have been tied behind her back, wrists bound with something that's too tight and is digging into her skin, and she's been gagged. The material in her mouth is too thick, pushing down into her throat and making her choke. She fights harder, struggling to draw breath through the one nostril that's not blocked.

Pinpricks of white light dance in front of her eyes. The only sound she's capable of is a jagged choking at the back of her throat. Then, when she truly believes she's going to die, there's a sharp rush of pain as the tape across her face is ripped off, the thick material is removed from her mouth and suddenly, mercifully, she's able to breathe again.

'Here.'

It's Roger. He's rolled her onto her back and is pulling her head forward, pushing a glass towards her mouth. She shakes her head, tries to turn away from the glass but he forces the liquid into her mouth. The glass bangs against her teeth as she splutters and coughs. Gradually, she realises it's just water, and relaxes a fraction. Then a little more as he cuts the tape binding her wrists and moves away from the bed.

As she sits up, rubbing her aching arms, she has another memory. Earlier in this room, the burn of alcohol as she swallowed it down before he made her lie down. The fear and rage at what she'd thought was about to happen. But she's got all her clothes on, and she'd know – wouldn't she? – if he'd hurt her. Apart from the pain in her arms and the stinging heat across her face, the rest of her seems to be uninjured.

'What time is it?' she croaks.

'Almost four.' Roger has walked away from the bed and sat down on the only chair in the room.

'You drugged me?'

'I didn't have a choice. I couldn't stay with you all afternoon, and I couldn't risk leaving you awake.'

Her head feels fuzzy, like it's filled with sludge, and she has a thumping headache.

'Was it you who broke into my flat?' she asks.

'Not me personally,' Roger says. 'One of my men did it. We needed to access your laptop and phone to see what you were planning.'

'They're password protected,' Nuala says.

Roger shrugs, like that's irrelevant. 'I have someone who can break into any device. She couldn't crack the code on your phone but she was into your laptop in five minutes.'

So they would have read the files. Her habit of documenting every encounter with anyone related to the podcast had been her downfall. She'd taken notes of the two phone conversations she'd had with Lydia, including their plans to meet in Ashford today.

'I need to see my son.'

'I might be able to arrange that.'

'Tell me what you want,' Nuala says. 'I'll do anything. Just let him go.'

'I want to know about Andrea.'

She hadn't expected that, and isn't sure how to respond.

'She's your partner,' she says eventually. 'Surely you know a lot more about her than I do.'

'I don't know why she sees you as some sort of threat.'

'Is that what I am?'

Roger doesn't answer. Instead, he lifts his phone off the table beside him and holds it up for Nuala to see.

'One phone call is all it will take,' he says. 'If you give me everything you have on Andrea, I'll tell my man to let the boy go. If you decide to fuck around, you won't see your son again. I don't care either way.'

The icy fear that grips Nuala then is beyond anything she's ever felt. She tries to tell herself he wouldn't hurt Josh, who's only a child, after all. But this man is a monster. He's capable of anything.

'What exactly do you want to know?' Her voice sounds small and scared, but she can't help it.

'Everything. I've invested a significant amount of money in my beloved Andrea. I've done that because I think she has what it takes to become Prime Minister of this once-great country. Before sharing my plans with her, I did every background check I could find. They all came back squeaky clean. But if she's not got anything to hide, why is she so desperate to get you and that other woman, Lydia, out of the way?'

'I'll tell you,' Nuala says. 'But only if you let me speak to Josh first.'

'No.'

'Then how do I know you haven't already killed him?' She nearly chokes on the words but, somehow, manages to get them out. 'Please, Roger. I swear, if I can hear his voice, I'll tell you everything I know.'

She thinks he's going to say no, and she's accepted that if he does she'll tell him anyway. But after a moment, he makes the call.

'Put the kid on the phone.'

Then, like a miracle, he's handing her the phone and she hears her son's beautiful, perfect voice.

'Mummy? Where are you?'

A sob escapes her mouth.

'Josh, darling. Are you okay?'

'I want to go home, Mummy. Will you tell Harry to take me home? Not to Liz's house. I want to be back in London with you and all my things. I miss you.'

'I miss you too, darling. I'll be seeing you really soon, I promise. You just need to stay with Harry until I get there. Do you think you can do that?'

'Will we go home then?'

'Absolutely. I promise. And we can get chips from the takeaway and you can sleep in my bed tonight if you want.'

She wants to say more, but Roger takes the phone away.

'Speak to me,' he tells her after he's ended the call.

Nuala nods, and starts talking.

'*Black Valley Farm* is a true crime podcast about the murders that took place in a farm of the same name ten years ago. Nine people were killed. Four women, one man and four children. One of the victims, a woman, had been stabbed to death.'

'I know all this,' Roger says impatiently. 'I listened to your podcast when we were deciding whether or not to hire you.'

'Well, then you'll remember that the last episode featured an interview with a woman called Marianne. During this interview, Marianne told me the woman who'd been stabbed was Rosemary. From my research, I'm pretty sure Rosemary was the woman in charge of whatever scene they had going on at the farm.'

'And?'

Nuala swallows. Here comes the hard bit. She wonders if it will get easier the more times she says it. Probably not.

'The interview was a hoax. A friend of mine is an actress. I wrote Marianne's script and persuaded my friend to pretend to be her.'

'Fuck me,' Roger says quietly.

Nuala doesn't say anything, waiting for him to piece it together.

'Fuck me,' he repeats. 'What about the rest of the podcast?'

'That was all real,' Nuala says. 'The only bit I made up was that final interview.'

He doesn't ask her why she lied. He jumps ahead instead. Straight to the same place Nuala's already got to.

'So if that interview's a hoax,' he says, 'then maybe this Rosemary character is still alive, right?'

He looks at her and she can see he's worked it out. Even so, she spells it out for him because she said she'd tell him everything.

'Rosemary wasn't killed that night. She survived and reinvented herself as Andrea Leach.'

Chapter 27

Mother lets go of my face and takes a step back. I'm still on the ground. I need to get up, run away from here, but I can't move. I'm a child again, completely at her mercy. After all this time, she has as much power over me as she ever did.

'You broke my heart, Martha.'

'Sorry,' I whisper. 'I'm so sorry.'

'I dedicated my life to the people who lived here,' she says. 'I was trying to save you, but you didn't want to be saved. You and Lydia and Sister Elizabeth. Do you know how much it hurt to be betrayed like that? I might have expected it from Lydia. But you were my special child, Martha. My good girl. I loved you.'

I start crying, because I know she's right. I'd loved her too. I'd loved her and hated her and feared her. But now I'm here with her again, it's the love that's rising above the other feelings. I want her to wrap her arms around me and tell me that she loves me more than anyone else in the world, and that the bond between us is so strong it can never be broken.

When she crouches down in front of me, I hold my arms out. Ready for an embrace that never comes. Instead, she unbuttons the sleeve of her blouse and rolls it up.

'Look.' She holds her arm out, shows me the scar on the soft skin beneath her inner elbow. 'Each time I see this, I think of what you did to me that night and my heart breaks all over again.'

I look at the scar, then up at her face, trying to understand.

'What's wrong, Martha? Are you going to tell me you don't remember sticking that knife into me?'

I try to sort through the jumbled scramble of memories from that night. I remember the weight of the knife in my hand, the warm rush of blood and the look on her face as she fell. But these memories don't match what she's showing me. If I'd stabbed her more than once, I'd remember. Wouldn't I?

She rolls her sleeve back down and buttons it, before standing up.

'Where have you been all these years, Martha? I've never stopped looking for you, but you were impossible to find. I'd almost given up hope of ever seeing you again.'

A surge of joy rushes through me. All this time I thought she was dead, that I had killed her. But she's here, and she isn't angry. If she was angry she wouldn't have tried so hard to find me, would she? I can't remember now, why I'd been so scared of her. She loves me, and I love her, and I know why she's brought me back here. So we can start again, and this time we'll do everything right.

As if she knows what I'm thinking, she holds out her hand. When I take it, she pulls me up until we're standing facing each other. So close I can feel her breath on my face when she starts to speak again.

'My darling Martha,' she whispers. 'What on earth am I going to do with you?'

I want to say something, but my mouth won't work. My head is filling up with memories, too many of them, pushing against the sides of my brain. Mother and Lydia and Peter and the Box, and endless days full of fear and dread. My brother, Leo, who ran away even though he knew the risks. Who left because death was better than having to spend another day in this place with this woman. Dear Lydia, who I haven't seen since that night but I've always believed is still alive.

I know now she's dead.

There were eleven people living here. Nine of them died that night, which means only two of us survived. Me and Mother.

As this truth sinks in, something else does too.

'You never loved me,' I tell her. 'You've never loved anyone except yourself.'

She slaps me across the face, so hard I stagger and almost fall. Before I have a chance to recover, she punches me in the stomach. All the air leaves my body. I stumble, gasping for breath. She punches me again. In the face, this time. Pain explodes across my nose. White dots dance in front of my eyes.

The ground rises towards me as I fall. I reach out, trying to grab hold of something, but there's nothing there. I land on my stomach. A foot presses into my back. The pressure from her heel bores through my sweatshirt, cutting my skin. Her hand grabs my hair and pulls my head back. *She's going to kill me.* The thought flashes through my mind. Replaced by another. *Not if I kill her first.*

Something cold and hard pushes into my cheek.

'If you don't stop moving, I'll pull the trigger.'

It takes a moment for the words to sink in. A gun. She's got a gun and it's pressed against my face. Part of me wants her to do it, end it once and for all. I think of how peaceful it would be, to never be scared again, never have to hide or pretend or lie all the time about who I am and the life I've had.

Then I see Lydia's face, that last night as we ran from this place, laughing like I'd never heard her laugh before. I remember the feeling of giddy joy, the sudden shock of freedom. Not knowing what we were running towards but not caring either. If I die now, Mother will have won. I can't let that happen.

'Stand up.' She pushes the gun harder, the inside of my cheek grinding against my teeth.

I nod my head slowly, and she takes a step back. I can't see her, but I know she's behind me, pointing the gun at me, daring me to make a wrong move. When I'm standing, I hear her move towards me, and I feel the gun against the back of my neck.

'Start walking, Martha. Towards the end of the garden.'

I don't want to, because I know what's down there. But she presses the gun harder into my neck and my feet shuffle forward, as if they're separate from the rest of me. The garden is overgrown with weeds and wild flowers. The carefully planted beds of vegetables, the stone path that ran along the centre, and the long wooden chicken coop have all disappeared beneath the wildness of nature.

Only one thing remains unchanged: the dark gaping hole in the ground at the back. We've reached it now and I can see the top of the ladder that leads down into the darkness. We called it the Box, although it's nothing more than a hole dug into the ground. The stone slab that covers it has been dragged back, cutting a curve in the long grass that's been squashed beneath it.

'Get in,' Mother says.

'I'll do it, whatever you tell me to,' I say. 'But first I want to know the truth. What really happened that night? I thought I'd killed you. But you're still alive. So if it wasn't you, who was the woman whose body was found outside the house?'

There's a long silence, so long I wonder if she's even heard me. But then, when I've almost given up hope of an answer, she starts speaking. 'I had to kill her. She betrayed me.'

I think, at first, she's speaking about Lydia. But when she continues speaking, I realise she means Aunt Elizabeth.

'I watched her unlock the gate and let you go. I was lying on the ground bleeding, yet she stole my keys and left me there. I gave her a home, a safe place to live. If it wasn't for me, she'd never have left her husband. She had no backbone. None of those women did. They needed me to lead them to safety. I thought they understood I was their saviour. But as I lay there that night, I realised how mistaken I'd been. Because if Elizabeth could betray me like that, who's to say the others wouldn't do the same one day?'

'So you killed her.'

By now, I've turned around so I'm able to see her face as she's speaking. She looks like she's enjoying telling me what actually happened.

'Yes. And when I'd finished with her, I went inside, gathered my things and left.'

'And Lydia?'

'She came back.' Mother laughs. 'After all the effort she put into escaping, she couldn't stay away.'

'She came back because I left the gas on,' I tell her. 'She was trying to save everyone.'

'What are you talking about?'

'I was angry and I turned the gas on. That's what caused the fire.'

'Is that what you've thought all these years?' Mother says. 'You poor, simple child. I didn't know who had left the gas on, and I didn't care because it gave me an idea.

'Once I'd finished packing, I gave the gas a helping hand. You see, Martha, even if the gas had been left on all night, it might not have been enough to cause a fire. Not by itself. So I set fire to the net curtains in the kitchen and I locked the front and back doors before I left.

'I was driving off when I saw Lydia. She couldn't get inside because the front door was locked. I saw her running around to the back of the house right before the explosion. It was rather beautiful, you know. The whole sky lit up.'

The anger that's been bubbling inside me explodes, like the house exploded that night. I charge at her. She's still holding the gun but I'm too fast for her. My head collides with her stomach, throwing her back. We hit the ground hard, me landing on top of her. I can feel her squirming beneath me as I punch her in the face. Twice. Nothing has ever felt this good.

I lift my fist to punch her again. There's a roaring sound inside my head, blocking out the screaming that might be coming from me or her or both of us.

Something hard smashes into the side of my face. I fly side-ways, landing on the ground beside her. She's standing over me now, a dark shadow blocking out the sun. She's holding the gun in both her hands, pointing it at my face.

'Get up.'

I shake my head. I spent too many years doing everything she told me to. Never again.

'Don't you dare disobey me.' She kicks me in the stomach and all the air leaves my body. I roll onto my side, gasping for breath. She kicks me again, in the back this time. I try to crawl away, but she presses her foot on my back, grinding me into the ground. Dirt and grass in my mouth, her heel cutting my skin.

She grabs my hair and pulls my head back so far I think my neck's going to crack.

'Get up. Now.'

'No.'

She smacks the gun against the side of my face. I hear a crack, feel the powdery pieces of a tooth on my tongue. Out of the corner of my eye, I see her fist swing down. I reach out, grab it and pull with every last piece of strength I've got. She topples sideways, screaming. I roll over, out of the way.

Somehow, I manage to drag myself up. Around me, the garden is swaying in slow, hazy circles. I spin with it, trying to work out which way I need to run. Then I see the burnt-out house and, behind it, the rolling green hills that rise and fall all the way to the grey sea.

I shuffle forward, towards the hills. A hand grabs my ankle, pulls hard. My body flies backwards and I fall, down down down, into the dark hole. I scream, but no sound comes out. I land on my back, winded and unable to move. I can see the sky above me, grey and cloud-covered and disappearing as the stone slab is dragged over the top of the hole until there's nothing left but darkness and pain.

Chapter 28

'But how?' Roger says. 'My background checks were thorough. There's an agency I use for this sort of thing. A proper professional operation. Andrea Leach is a real person.'

He stops speaking and shakes his head, as if he's still trying to work out how he could have been duped so easily. If he wasn't such a grade A arsehole, Nuala might feel sorry for him.

'I have a detailed file on her,' he says. 'Are you telling me all that information is made up?'

'The women who lived on the farm all looked alike,' Nuala says. 'I think Rosemary chose them for that reason. She wanted women who looked like her. If Andrea was one of the women who died, it wouldn't have been too difficult for Rosemary to take her ID and use it for herself.'

'She wanted women who looked like her?' Roger frowns. 'Why the fuck would she do that?'

'I don't know,' Nuala says. 'But it explains how Rosemary became Andrea. The real Andrea Leach was an only child and both her parents were dead. There was no one left to miss her if she suddenly disappeared. Or reappeared.'

'She almost got away with it,' Roger says. 'Probably would have, if it wasn't for you.'

'It would have come out eventually,' Nuala says. 'Once you'd registered the party with the Electoral Commission, Andrea would have become more high profile. More journalists would have started digging into her background. If I was able to discover the truth, other people would have too.'

'Why you?' Roger asks. 'You know more than anyone about what happened at the farm. I'd have thought you'd be the last person she'd want to work with on the documentary.'

'I've wondered about that too,' Nuala says. 'I think she needed to find out exactly how much I knew. Plus, she probably thought she could use the documentary to keep me in line. It's no secret I've struggled to find work recently. My guess is Andrea thought that, even if I worked out who she really was, she could persuade me to keep quiet in return for the chance to rebuild my career.'

'Makes a sick sort of sense, I suppose,' Roger says.

'You promised if I told you what I knew that I could see my son.'

She thinks he's going to refuse, or find some other reason to keep her here, but after a moment he nods his head.

'Okay. Let's go.'

'Really?'

'Yeah. We'll get a taxi. The kid's back at the house.'

'And when we get there, you'll let us go?'

'You promise to keep quiet about all this?' Roger says.

'It's not like I have a choice, is it?'

'Not if you don't want to spend the rest of your life wondering if your son's safe.'

At first, she's so relieved she doesn't think any further than the moment she's reunited with Josh. But on the slow drive across to Blackheath, doubts start crowding in. Roger is a fixer. And there's no doubt that Nuala is a problem that needs fixing. Knowing what she does about Andrea, Nuala could bring down the entire Progress Party and everything Roger Constantin has worked so hard for.

By the time the taxi emerges from the Blackwall Tunnel, Nuala is certain that Roger isn't going to let her go. She runs through the different options available to her – everything from screaming at the taxi driver to pull over so she can jump out, to taking out the ballpoint pen in her bag and thrusting it into

Roger's eye – but before she can do anything, she has to get to the house in Blackheath to make sure her son is okay. Once she's with Josh, she will work out how to get away from Roger. Until then, she'll have to stay quiet and pretend she's taken in by this charade.

Josh isn't the only reason she keeps quiet. There's Lydia, too. Nuala set Lydia up, led her straight to Andrea. Each time Nuala thinks of what she did, she hears Liz's voice telling her she's messed up again. The only way to shut Liz up is to find Lydia before it's too late.

When the taxi finally pulls up outside the elegant Regency house, Nuala can't get out quickly enough. On shaking legs, she runs towards the front door, pounding on it and calling out her son's name.

'Stop making such a racket,' Roger says. 'The kid's fine. You'll see him in a second.'

He leans over her, puts his key in the lock and opens the door. Nuala rushes inside and, immediately, knows she's made a mistake. If Josh was here, she would have felt his presence straight away. But the house is too still and quiet.

She swings around to Roger, fear for her son overcoming any fear she has for herself.

'Where is he?'

Too late, she sees Roger's hand reach out. She tries to duck out of the way, but he grabs her by the collar of her blouse and shoves her back until she's pressed against the wall. She can't fight him off, because he's bigger and stronger than she is. His hands wrap around her neck, squeezing tight as he lifts her so her feet are no longer touching the ground. The pressure is unbearable, his thumbs digging into the front of her neck. She claws at his hands, desperate for it to stop. Her lungs screaming for air that isn't there.

She kicks out with her feet, feels one foot connect with his shin. He doesn't seem to notice and she knows he's not going to stop. Everything in her life has narrowed down to this moment.

Roger's eyes boring into her, his hands squeezing the life out of her body, her head slamming against the wall because he's shaking her like she's nothing, like she's already dead.

She has failed, because the only thing she was put on this earth to do was create her beautiful son and keep him safe. Now, she'll never be there for him as she'd always said she would. Through the darkness and the pain, she sees his face and she hears his voice, telling her that he loves her. And she wants, more than anything, to tell him she loves him too. But there are no words left.

Then suddenly, mercifully, the hands around her neck are no longer there. Without them, there's nothing holding her up. She slips to the ground and curls into a ball, choking and coughing as air rushes down her burning throat. A hand touches her back and she jerks away, terrified because it's not over, it's about to start again and she can't bear it.

'It's okay.'

Not Roger's voice. Someone else's. She's too scared to look up. Better to lie here with her eyes closed, focus on trying to breathe and ignore the collar of burning pain around her neck. Then she remembers Josh. If he's not here, she needs to find him. She needs Roger, because he's the only person who can tell her where Josh is.

She opens her eyes. Realises, with a shock, that she's seen this man before. The last time was when he was running out of a community hall in south London.

'I've got your son,' he says.

Chapter 29

I can hear them. Lydia and Leo, just like I heard them all those years ago. Whispered voices from inside the shed. No one apart from me knows this is where they go. I spotted her last week, walking quickly away from the house and looking over her shoulder, like she was making sure no one could see her. I waited until she was inside the shed before I followed her. They were speaking in whispers, so I couldn't hear what they were saying. But they sounded happy. Every few seconds Lydia laughed, in a way she never normally does. It made my tummy feel funny hearing them. Leo was my brother, not hers, and if he was going to meet anyone in secret it should be me.

I want to go into the shed now and laugh with them, but when I try to move towards the door my body won't move. I can't hear Leo and Lydia anymore, either. The only sounds are the chitter-chatter of my teeth and a scratchy, rasping noise that I realise is my breathing. The shed is gone, too. There's nothing except this pitch black darkness and the cold and my shivering, dying body.

Later, Lydia is back. I can feel her breath as she whispers in my ear. It's icy cold, not warm like breath is supposed to be, and I know that's because Lydia's dead and this is her ghost.

'Get up, Martha. You can't stay here.'

She's wrong. This is the only place for me to be. Because this is what's always been waiting for me. My Punishment.

'You didn't kill them,' Lydia says. 'It was Mother, not you. She lit a fire and she locked the door to make sure they couldn't get out, even if they tried. It's her fault. And if you don't get up and get out of here, she'll never have to pay for what she did.'

I shake my head, because Lydia doesn't understand. There's another reason I deserve this, something I did that she can never, ever know about.

'Get up.'

When she shakes my arm, it feels so real I reach out to touch her. But there's no one there.

I think of Kath, how I'll never know now what happened to her. I hope Helen Robins keeps looking for her. And I hope she finds Arnie, too, makes him tell her the truth about who he is.

It was rather beautiful, you know. Mother's voice inside my head, gloating like she was proud of what she'd done. All those people she killed and the terrible things she's done and she's going to get away with it. Something flutters inside me. I put my hand on my stomach, searching for the flicker of warmth, the tiny part of me that's still alive.

The feeling spreads, into my chest and along my hands into my fingers. I lift my right hand, move it slowly until it touches the bottom rung of the ladder above me. It's high, but not so high that I can't wrap my fingers around it. By the time I manage to stretch up to grasp it, my arm is exhausted, the muscles aching with the need to let go of the ladder. But I don't let go. I hold on tight, waiting until I'm strong enough to pull myself up.

I'm still cold, but I'm sweating too. Heat and ice melding as every part of me is focused on the next step. I swing my right foot as high as it will go. It's not enough. I try again, and again. On the third attempt, my foot connects with the metal rung. Drawing on every last piece of strength I've got, I swing it up one last time. It hits the rung and stays there.

When both feet are on the ladder, I pull myself up to the next rung, and the one after that. The pain is excruciating, but I keep going until I'm almost at the top. If I stretch up, I can touch the stone slab. I stretch my right hand up, feeling for the next rung. I pull hard, putting all my weight into it, to drag myself up. The metal creaks, then snaps, and suddenly I'm falling backwards, screaming.

I try to grab the ladder as I fall, but it's impossible. The last thing I see, as I hit the ground, is a flash of sky above me and Leo appears, holding his hand out and calling for me to join him. I close my eyes, relieved it's finally over, and picture my soul leaving my body and rising up through the darkness towards the bright light.

Chapter 30

Nuala scrabbles away from the man, needing to put some space between them.

'It's okay,' he says, stepping back. 'I'm not going to hurt you, I swear.'

But it's not okay. He's just told her he has Josh. Which means he's working for Roger and Andrea. So why is Roger lying in a heap on the ground? Unconscious, or worse.

She wants to demand he tells her where Josh is, but her throat is on fire and it's impossible to get any words out through the burning. He seems to understand because he disappears and returns a few seconds later with a glass of water.

'Here.' He holds out the glass. 'Just tiny sips to start with. Anything more than that will make it feel worse.'

She takes the glass and does what he tells her. The first few sips are agony. She coughs and splutters and spits the water back up. But after a few attempts, she's able to swallow some. Then a bit more. When she's drunk as much as she can, she stands up. But her body is weaker than she realised and she falls back, against the wall.

'You need to sit down,' he says.

She shakes her head. She doesn't want to spend another second here in this house, but she can't leave until she finds out where Josh is.

'My son,' she croaks.

'It's okay,' he says again, and she swears if he says that one more time she'll punch him.

'Where is Josh?'

Instead of answering, he takes a phone from the pocket of his denim jacket and makes a call.

'All clear here, Harry. Can you put him on for me?'

He leans towards Nuala, causing her to flinch, then puts the phone into her free hand and gently guides the same hand to her ear.

'Mummy?'

The relief and joy are so huge she starts to sob. The crying makes her throat hurt like hell but she doesn't care because she can hear his voice, asking when he can see her.

'Hello baby,' she whispers.

'Where are you, Mummy? I know you had some important work to do, but Harry said as soon as that's finished you're going to come and get me.'

Nuala has no idea who Harry is, and she doesn't give a shit. All that matters is he's with Josh and he's keeping him safe and stopping him from becoming scared because he's in a strange place with a stranger.

'That's right, darling,' she says. 'I'll be with you soon. I promise.'

'Your voice sounds funny.'

'I've got a sore throat.' She wants to remind him of the time, last winter, when she lost her voice and could only speak in a croak for four whole days. But there's no way she's capable of saying that many words right now. So she whispers, instead, that she loves him, and tells him – again – that she'll see him soon.

'Harry wants to speak to you,' Josh says.

Nuala opens her mouth to say she doesn't want to speak to Harry, but it's too late because Harry is already speaking to her.

'You've got a good kid there,' he says. 'I'll make sure he's safe until you get here. Try not to worry.'

There's something familiar about his voice, something that triggers a warning. She isn't safe yet. Neither is Josh.

'Where are you?' she says.

'Leo will tell you.'

The line goes dead and Nuala looks at the man she assumes is Leo. Questions are spinning through her mind, so many things she wants to ask him but she starts with the only one that matters.

'Who the fuck is Harry and what's he doing with my son?'

'Harry's a friend of mine,' Leo says. 'A good friend. Josh is safe with him, I promise you. They're in a hotel in Canterbury. We're going to go there now.'

She looks at him without speaking, trying to get her thoughts into some sort of order. There's something about him – his height and the way he's standing with his hands in the pockets of his jeans – that triggers another memory. The evening she took Josh to the park. This is the man they saw across the road. The one Josh described as 'the bad man', but Nuala now realises is known to her by another name: *truthfinder*.

'It's you,' she says. 'You've been watching my son, taking photos of him in the playground and using them to threaten me.'

He doesn't try to deny it. Instead, he tells her he's sorry but she didn't give him any other choice. Rage makes her reckless. She takes a step towards him, her hands clenching into fists.

'No matter what I did,' she snarls, 'it doesn't justify you using my son like that.'

'Maybe not,' he says, 'but I didn't know how else to make you admit you lied.'

'You could have simply asked me straight out, instead of acting like a psycho stalker.'

'Would you really have admitted what you did?'

'Maybe,' she says. 'I don't know. Either way, it doesn't give you the right to kidnap my son, you wanker.'

'That was Andrea's doing,' Leo says. 'Lucky for you, I'd already got Harry working for her. I doubt anyone else would have taken such good care of your boy.'

Harry is one of Roger's goons. Nuala knows now why she recognised his voice. The thought of that man being anywhere near her son makes her want to puke.

'He's a good guy,' Leo says, as if he knows what she's thinking. 'The Harry you saw when he was working here? That's all an act. We had to make sure his cover was credible. Otherwise, there's no way Andrea and Roger would have kept him on.'

'Who the fuck *are* you?' she says.

'Leo.'

'Duh. I already know your name. I mean who are you, and what's your connection to the farm?'

'I'd like to tell you, but I'm not sure I trust you enough.'

'*You* don't trust *me*?'

'No.'

The simple way he says it makes her skin flush with shame. She shouldn't care what he thinks of her, yet, somehow, she finds that she does.

'What should we do about him?' Leo asks, nodding at Roger's crumpled body.

Nuala shivers. She doesn't care what they do, as long as it doesn't involve any more violence.

'Can't we leave him?'

'He tried to kill you,' Leo says. 'If we leave him, he'll wake up eventually or someone will find him. Then he'll make up some bullshit story about walking in on a burglary and getting attacked. The police will believe him, and he'll get away with everything.'

'Not if we tell the truth about Andrea.'

Leo looks at her properly then, and she realises it's the first time he's done that. She realises, too, that he's remarkably handsome and has to remind herself of all the reasons she shouldn't feel attracted to him.

'You'd be willing to do that?'

'I was going to do it anyway.'

He smiles then, and it's a damn good smile that transforms his face.

'You ready?' he asks. 'It's time I took you to your son.'

He turns to go, opening the front door and stepping outside into the grey evening. Nuala hurries after him, resisting the urge to give a quick kick to Roger's head as she sidesteps his body.

Chapter 31

'So let me get this straight,' Leo says. 'You called Lydia and told her you'd changed the meeting place. Then you ran off and let her walk straight into the trap that woman had set for her?'

'Andrea had my son,' Nuala says. 'I didn't have a choice.'

'Josh was never in any danger,' Leo snaps. 'I would never have let anything happen to him.'

'I didn't know that, did I?'

'You're a piece of work, Nuala Fox. You really are.'

Leo sounds disgusted with her, and Nuala can't really blame him.

'I panicked because I was scared,' she says. 'It's a shitty excuse, but it's the only one I've got.'

'And you've no idea where they are now?' Leo asks.

Nuala shakes her head. 'No.'

She's sitting in the passenger seat of Leo's car, a red Tesla with cream leather seats that are insanely comfortable. They're driving along the A2 towards Canterbury, the seconds ticking by agonisingly slowly.

So far, she's told Leo how she ended up working for Andrea and everything leading up to the attack by Roger at the house earlier. Given the way he's been practically stalking her these last few weeks, she'd expected him to focus on the podcast and her reasons for lying. Instead, all he seems to care about is what might have happened to Lydia.

'Who is she to you, anyway?' she asks. 'Lydia, I mean. And why are you so worried about what Andrea might do to her?

When I saw you that afternoon at Craggy Vale, it was Andrea who looked scared of you, not the other way around.'

'She was scared because I'm one of the few people left who knows she's not who she says she is.'

'You know her from the farm,' Nuala says, reaching the only conclusion that makes any sense. 'You were there. Oh God. It was you. All these years, everyone assumed it was Lydia. But you were there too and you didn't die that night, which means it was you who killed those people.'

She's in the car with a crazed killer, who also happens to be holding her son hostage.

'I had nothing to do with any of that,' Leo says, just as Nuala's considering whether or not to throw herself from the moving Tesla. 'I'd left the farm years before the fire.'

'You expect me to believe that?'

'Believe it, or don't believe it. It makes no difference to me.'

'If you don't care what I think,' she says, irritated, 'why go to all this trouble? Why create a fake ID – with a totally *crap* username, by the way – and send me those threatening messages. Was that just for kicks, or was there some other reason?'

'I've already told you, I wanted you to admit that you lied.'

'But why?' she repeats. 'I don't get it. You said yourself, you were there on the farm. You know Andrea Leach isn't who she says she is. Why do you need me?'

'Because,' he says, speaking slowly, as if she's so dumb she won't understand otherwise, 'I haven't got a single shred of evidence to back up what I know. It would be my word against hers.'

'You could still do a lot of damage to her reputation,' Nuala says. 'Maybe that would be enough.'

'Enough for what?'

'To stop her,' Nuala says. 'Any reputational damage, at this stage in her career, would probably be enough to make people doubt her.'

'That's not enough. I want to destroy her. That woman did unspeakable damage to people I loved. She tried to ruin my life, and she very nearly succeeded.

'When I first read about the fire, when I realised all those people were dead, I thought I could finally put that part of my life behind me. I assumed, stupidly, that she'd died that night along with everyone else. Then I listened to your podcast and I heard Marianne confirm that she really was dead, and I was so relieved. You have no idea, Nuala, what it felt like to know – absolutely and completely – that she was dead and she could never hurt anyone again the way she hurt me and so many others.

'Then last month, I saw her. I recognised her immediately, and realised you had lied. Your award-winning podcast was a load of bullshit.'

Nuala stays silent, too tired and ashamed to defend herself.

'Lydia's my sister,' Leo says, after a moment. 'Although her real name is Martha. We haven't seen each other for years, not since I left the farm.'

Nuala's stomach contracts as she thinks of her own sister and what it felt like after Marion had been killed. She understands, now, why Leo was so upset when she'd told him how Andrea had made her call Lydia and lie about the meeting place.

'I'm so sorry, Leo.'

'About trapping my sister or lying on your podcast?' Leo asks. 'Speaking of which, why did you do that, Nuala? I've been trying to work it out, ever since I listened to that last episode. The rest of the podcast was so good. Why ruin it with a big fat lie right at the end?'

'I was desperate,' she says quietly. 'The podcast was good – you're right about that. But it didn't do what I'd set out to do, which was find out what really happened the night those people died.'

'So you went ahead and made something up?'

'Yes.'

'How did you get Marianne to lie? More to the point, how could you be absolutely sure she wouldn't one day turn around and tell everyone what you'd done?'

'Because I knew the woman I chose would never, ever do that.'

Nuala pauses because, speaking about it, knowing how badly she messed up, isn't easy.

'My girlfriend at the time was an actress,' she continues. 'Well, she'd more or less stopped acting by then because she never got any parts. I persuaded her to do it. I knew she loved me and I knew she'd do it if I kept nagging her until it was easier for her to give in and say yes.'

'Wow.' Leo lets out a low whistle. 'That's quite something to ask someone to do.'

'Yeah, well. It got me what I wanted with the podcast, but she never forgave me for it. We're not together anymore. And if you don't mind, I'd rather talk about something else now.'

'We can do that,' Leo says. 'What would you like to talk about?'

'Your friend, Harry,' she says. 'How do I know my son is safe with him?'

'Harry's my closest friend. I'd trust him with my life.'

'He works as a bodyguard for a far-right, racist organisation,' Nuala says. 'You sure you're comfortable being friends with someone like that?'

'You were going to make a documentary for the same far-right, racist organisation,' Leo points out. 'Besides, Harry only took the job because I asked him to. I needed someone on the inside. Clearly, I couldn't do that myself, so Harry did it for me.'

'So all that macho tough guy stuff,' Nuala says, 'that was an act?'

'Not exactly. I mean, Harry's as tough as they come. But he's also left-leaning in his politics and he'd never hurt anyone unless they deserved it.'

'That's reassuring.'

She looks out the window, watching the countryside race past, willing time to pass as quickly. Suddenly, she has an over-whelming urge to see Liz. When Nuala had borrowed Leo's phone to call her earlier, Liz had told her the police were at her house.

'They've been trying to get hold of you for most of the day,' Liz said. 'I've been going out of my mind with worry, and now you call and tell me it's all okay? What am I supposed to tell the two police officers currently sitting in my kitchen?'

'I'm sorry,' Nuala replied. 'I can't tell you anything else, Liz. Not yet.'

She'd hung up then, and now Leo's phone is switched off because Liz kept trying to call back. At some point, Nuala will have to speak to the police, but for now she's got more important things to sort out. Like being reunited with her son. And finding Lydia.

Finally, they reach Canterbury. Leo turns the car into the car park of a hotel on the outer edges of the city. As he finds a place to park, Nuala sees a flash of colour. A little boy is running out of the hotel entrance. He's wearing a Marvel DC sweatshirt with an image of Thor, the hammer-wielding god, on the front of it.

Not bothering to wait for the engine to be switched off, Nuala pulls off her seat belt, opens the car door and runs, faster than she's ever run before, across the car park to her son. Josh sees her, his little face lighting up, as he throws himself towards her and jumps into her outstretched arms.

Chapter 32

I'm back on the farm, working in the garden with Lydia. In the background, there's the murmur of voices as Aunt Elizabeth and Aunt Sarah prepare the evening meal. There's something important I need to tell Lydia, but I can't remember what it is.

'I've got a secret,' Lydia says. She's smiling and she looks happier than I've ever seen her look before. 'Do you want me to tell you?'

When I nod my head and say yes, she leans forward and whispers in my ear:

'Leo and I are in love. He's my boyfriend and we love each other and we're going to run away from here and live together forever.'

Before I can say anything there's a bang, then a burst of orange light and Lydia is screaming as she's lifted into the air. I try to reach for her, but she's too far away. Her body explodes, little bits of her floating higher and higher into the orange and black sky.

'Hey, wake up.'

A man's voice and a hand on my shoulder, shaking me. I open my eyes, see a face I don't recognise staring down at me. I bite back a scream as I scrabble to sit up. Every movement causes sharp shots of burning pain in different parts of my body. My back, legs, shoulders and head.

I'm on a bed in a room I don't recognise, although the view from the window looks familiar.

'You were dreaming,' the man says.

My mouth is dry and I can't speak. I lick my lips, swallow a few times, but nothing seems to make any difference. As if he knows what the problem is, he lifts a glass of water to my lips. Cool water trickles into my mouth and down my chin. I grab the glass, and drink some more until he stops me.

'Not too fast,' he says. 'You'll make yourself ill.'

He has pale brown eyes, that look golden in the dim light of the bedroom. Outside the window, the sky is so grey it's almost white. Completely covered with clouds, so I can't tell if it's morning or evening or somewhere in between.

'Who are you?' I ask.

'I'm Ben.'

I wait for him to tell me more, but he seems to think this is all the explanation I need. I'm about to ask him what I'm doing here, when it all comes racing back. The shock of it, playing out again in my head, causes a surge of panic. The room starts closing in on me. I need air but I can't breathe. Ben's face grows bigger as the room gets smaller. I remember seeing Leo with the white light behind him. I'm dead, I realise. None of this is real, or maybe it is. This is hell, where I always knew I'd end up one day.

'Breathe.'

He puts an arm around my shoulder, tight but not too tight, just enough to stop me disappearing into the darkness.

'It's a panic attack. It'll pass in a moment if you focus on your breathing and nothing else.'

As he says this, air rushes down my throat and everything starts to slow back down.

'Not surprising,' Ben says, 'given what you've been through.'

I need him to move his arm away. I shift sideways and he seems to get the hint. The heavy weight on my shoulders disappears.

'How did I get here?'

'I live next door,' he says. 'This house is a little further down the hill from the farmhouse. You can't see it from up there unless you lean over the wall that separates the two properties. I went out for a walk earlier and noticed the gates to the farmhouse were open. I thought someone had broken in, so I went to take a look. I noticed the grass by the stone slab in the garden had been flattened. I knew there was a hole beneath the slab. Soon after I moved in here, I spent an afternoon exploring what's left of the old farm.

'The flattened grass could only have been caused by someone dragging back the stone slab that covers the hole. It wasn't me, because I've made sure the hole is always covered so no animal falls down there by accident. I didn't know what I'd see when I pulled the slab back, but I certainly hadn't expected to find someone lying down there.'

I have a blurry memory of him helping me off the ground and getting me onto the ladder. He made me go first, told me he was right behind me and he'd catch me if I slipped. Somehow, I made it to the top but I can't remember anything after that.

'You collapsed before we could get inside. I had to carry you. I hope that's okay?'

'You saved my life.'

He shrugs, like it's no big deal.

'I found this too.' He lifts my bag off the floor and puts it on the bed beside me.

I remember it falling off my back as I was lifted into the boot of the car. Mother must have put the bag in the car too, presumably so no one would find it and try to contact its owner.

'Where was it?' I ask, opening it and searching through it for my phone.

'Behind the old shed,' he says. 'I noticed it earlier, when I went in to get some wood for the fire.'

'My phone is missing.'

'I haven't taken it,' Ben says.

'Sorry, I didn't mean to imply you had. At least the rest of my stuff is still there. Thank you.' I think of something else then, and look at him. 'You said this house is next door to the farmhouse. But there's never been any other house here.'

'This place was built three years ago, by the developer who bought the farm and the land around it. He'd intended to build an entire estate but he ran out of money. So there's only this house and what's left of the farm. Nothing else.'

'You know what happened there?'

He nods. 'Difficult not to with the number of people who come here to take a look. It's been worse than ever since that podcast came out last year.'

'What day is it?' I ask.

'Monday.'

It was Friday when we arrived here, which means I'd been down there for almost two days before he found me. I shiver, thinking how close I'd come to never being found at all.

'Morning or afternoon?'

'Mid-morning. I reckon you've been asleep for about fourteen hours. Listen, we should probably go to the police. And we should definitely get you checked out at a hospital. You don't seem to have any broken bones, but I'm not a doctor.'

When I don't say anything, he leans forward and asks, in a gentle voice, if I'm able to tell him how I ended up trapped inside the hole in the ground. Part of me wants to tell him everything, but there's so much to say and I'm not sure I know where to begin. And I'm tired, so very tired.

'Are you hungry?' he asks.

'I'm not sure.'

I should be starving. I can't remember when I last ate, but the thought of food doesn't appeal to me right now.

'Come on,' Ben says. 'Let's go downstairs. I'll make you some breakfast.'

I shake my head. 'I should probably get going.'

'Where will you go?'

'I need to find my friend, Kath. I think something bad has happened to her. If it has, it's because of me.'

'What can I do to help?'

'There's a detective who's helping look for Kath. I'd like to call her, but I don't have her phone number.'

'Do you know where she's based?'

'Somewhere in Sheffield,' I say.

'That's a start.' Ben smiles. 'My phone's downstairs. Let's go make a few calls and see what we can find out.'

'Thank you.'

'I recognise you,' he says. 'Sorry, I hope it's okay to say that. I'm never good at knowing the right thing to say to other people.'

'What do you mean you recognise me?'

'You're Lydia, aren't you?'

I could deny it, but I doubt he'd believe me. Besides, there's something about him that makes me want to tell him the truth.

'My real name's Martha,' I tell him. 'Lydia was someone else.'

I hear her voice in my head, so clear that for a moment it's like she's here in the room with me.

We need to change our names… You can be me if you'd like.

In the confusion of those first few days, I held onto those words. Each time a new person asked me my name, I gave them the same answer: *My name's Lydia. It means standing pool.*

'Well then, Martha. Nice to meet you. We'll go call your detective friend and have some breakfast. After that we can work out what to do next.'

'We?'

He smiles.

'I saved your life, remember? Don't you think that gives me a say?'

He holds his hand out, and I surprise myself by putting my own hand in his and letting him help me off the bed. My sleeve falls back, revealing the pattern of silvery scars on my arm. I see Ben looking at the scars, but he doesn't say anything and I'm grateful to him for that too.

I think of the men I've met before Ben, men like Jasper who only help you when they want something in return. I know I need to be careful, but there's a part of me that refuses to believe this man would do anything to hurt me.

As I follow Ben down the stairs, I hear the people who used to live in the farmhouse next door. Their voices mingle with my memories, the old feelings of fear and anger churning through me, burning brighter and whiter like there's a fire inside my body that will blow me up too if I'm not careful, taking Ben and this house and everything else with it.

Chapter 33

'Police have confirmed the identity of the man found dead in a house in south east London is Roger Constantin, co-founder of the far-right Progress Party. Mr Constantin was found dead in his house on Saturday morning. Police are treating his death as suspicious. A nationwide search has been launched for Andrea Leach, Mr Constantin's partner, who police are keen to speak to.'

Nuala leans forward and switches off the radio. Roger is dead. Murdered, if the news report is anything to go by. She's certain he was still alive when they left him. She can remember the rise and fall of his chest as she stepped past him. But she has no idea if the police believed her when she told them this.

The day they arrived in Canterbury, Nuala and Leo went to the police to report Lydia missing. Or Martha, as Nuala now knows is the woman's real name. Leo and Nuala each gave a statement, outlining everything they knew about the politician called Andrea Leach.

It's been three days since Martha and Andrea disappeared and the police don't seem any closer to finding them. In the meantime, while Nuala and Leo have been waiting for news, they've recorded a new episode of the podcast. Not once has Leo let his obvious concern for Martha's wellbeing distract him from giving his full attention to the podcast. His ability to compartmentalise is impressive, if a little weird.

The podcast is due to drop this morning at 9 a.m.. Nuala knows the episode is good, maybe even brilliant. It starts with an apology from Nuala, setting out what she did and why. Then she passes to Leo, who shares his experiences of life on the farm. Leo's account is shocking and moving in equal measures. Anyone listening to this episode will be in no doubt about exactly the sort of evil monster Andrea Leach really is. This, coupled with the fact that Leo Bailey is already a well-known entrepreneur, makes for an explosive episode.

Once she'd finished recording, Nuala came back to London with Josh who couldn't wait to come home. They've spent most of the weekend holed up in the flat, cuddling together on the sofa, eating junk food Nuala usually doesn't allow and watching too much TV. Now Monday's here, she is determined to get him back into his normal routine, starting with getting him to school on time.

She checks the time. Eight o'clock. Nine feels like an age away. Thankfully, she'll be busy until then getting Josh ready, out the door and into school for his eight forty-five start. Speaking of which, he's been remarkably quiet since going back to his room after breakfast to get dressed. Normally, he zooms in and out, talking to her at high speed while she tries to hurry him along. This morning, he hasn't come out of his room once.

'Josh?'

No answer. A hand grabs her chest, cold fingers of fear squeezing so tight she can barely breathe. She hurries out of the kitchen and along the corridor to his room. She's already imagining him lying unconscious on the ground, his head twisted sideways at an odd angle, spittle gathering at the corners of his mouth. But what she finds when she pushes open his bedroom door is worse than anything she could have imagined.

'Good morning, Nuala.'

Josh's face is white, whiter than she's ever seen it before. His eyes wide open and terrified. His chin wobbles when he sees Nuala. Apart from that he doesn't move. Frozen to the spot by the gun pressed against the side of his perfect little head.

Chapter 34

After several phone calls, I find the police station where Helen Robins works. But when I'm finally put through to her, I get her voicemail. I leave a message with Ben's phone number, asking her to call me back as soon as possible. When I'm finished, I go into the kitchen, where Ben is making breakfast.

There's music playing, Taylor Swift singing about champagne problems, the sound coming from a portable speaker on the worktop.

'You like Taylor Swift?' I ask.

Ben looks at me like it's the craziest question ever.

'She's a legend. Anyone who doesn't like her music is an idiot.'

'Hell, yes.'

We smile at each other and for a moment I forget about everything except being here with him while Taylor's voice wraps itself around us.

As Ben cooks and the kitchen fills with the smell of frying bacon and melting butter, he doesn't stop talking. It's like he's waited for ages to tell someone how he's ended up living here and, now he's found me, he's desperate to get it all off his chest.

'I found out the woman I was living with, who I was planning to marry, had been having an affair with my best friend. I needed to get away, so I quit my job and left London, ended up in Lincolnshire. This place had recently been built, and the landlord was looking to rent it out. He doesn't charge much and, in return, I keep it in good nick and scare off the ghouls and true crime fanatics who show up next door.'

He stops what he's doing and turns to look at me.

'They always ask about you, like I might know where you're hiding. You'll need to be careful, while you're here, not to be seen if any of them show up.'

'I'll bear that in mind.'

He smiles, then continues talking.

'I've been here almost two years. Didn't plan on staying that long, but the more time I spent away from London, the less inclined I was to go back. I live simply, grow my own vegetables and have a few chickens. You might have heard the cockerel earlier. He makes a right racket first thing in the morning.'

He's speaking quickly, the words pouring out of him with no sign of stopping. Suddenly, I need to get out of here. The smell of food cooking, the memories and the endless flow of words is all too much.

'I'm going outside for some fresh air,' I say, interrupting him mid-sentence.

'Sorry.' A red blush spreads across his cheeks. 'I talk too much. I should have realised you're tired. I'm sure the last thing you want is to listen to my boring life story. Go ahead. I'll call you when the food's ready. I promise to stay quiet when you come back in.'

'It's fine,' I say, feeling bad for him. 'I'll feel better once I've eaten something.'

I go out through the back door and look around me. A grey mist sits low across the fields, giving it a magical, mystical look. Another memory comes to me then. Holding Lydia's hand on a morning like this one, watching the way our breath steamed on the cold air while Lydia told me about the mist fairies who were almost invisible, but if you looked really hard and were really lucky, you might catch sight of one. It was only years later, long after I'd left the farm, that I realised there was no such thing as mist fairies.

The air is cold and damp. It seeps through my clothes and settles on my skin. When I rub my arms to warm my body,

I feel the bumpy pattern of goosebumps. And when I breathe out, I can see my breath, just the same as that morning with Lydia.

Ben's house is in a dip of land behind the original farmhouse that would have been inside the fence that once surrounded the property. The fence is now gone, along with the high metal gates that kept us locked inside the grounds. Apart from the stone wall that separates Ben's small garden from the bigger one next door, there are no boundaries around either property.

I walk up the hill and clamber over the wall into the other garden, searching for the exact spot I stabbed Mother. But it was so long ago, and my memories of that night are so confused, I'm not even sure where it happened. Was it here, near the front door? Or further away from the house? I have no idea. The only thing I know for sure is that I didn't kill her, and that means I can't trust my own mind. Because if I misremembered that, what else have I got wrong?

A sudden sound cracks through the still morning air, making me jump. I swing around, my senses on high alert, trying to identify what I heard. It sounded like the start of a scream, but it could have been an animal. Maybe a bird, even. I scan every corner of the yard, but can't see anything that shouldn't be there.

I stand stock still, waiting, but when nothing else happens, I start to relax. It's okay, I tell myself. I'm safe now. Nothing bad is going to happen. Ben is inside making breakfast and, later this morning, I'm going to find the nearest police station and tell the truth about who I am and what happened the night of the fire.

I'm hungry now, my tummy rumbling as I climb back over the wall and walk down the hill towards the open back door that leads straight into Ben's kitchen. Stepping inside the house, I become aware of two things at the same time. First, the smell. Fried bacon, fresh coffee and something else that I recognise but can't identify right away. The second thing I notice is the pair of feet, sticking out from the far side of the kitchen table.

From the angle of the feet, it's clear the body they're attached to is lying face down on the kitchen floor.

The feet belong to Ben. I recognise his trainers. I should go and see why he's lying on the ground, but I don't because right then I realise what the other smell is. It's cologne, cloying and clogging the insides of my nose and throat.

I swing around, but I'm not fast enough. A hand grabs the back of my head, causing me to stumble backwards. I feel the heat of his body behind me as he pulls me tight against him.

'Don't move or I'll cut your throat wide open.'

Cold metal against my neck. Arnie's breath warm and damp in my ear. I want to ask what he's doing here, how he found me and what's going to happen now that he has. But I can't speak, can't move, because he presses the knife harder. There's sharp pain, before I feel the first trickle of warm blood running down my neck.

Chapter 35

Josh is kneeling on the floor, still wearing his Spiderman pyjamas. He's so tiny, so vulnerable, it's unbearable. Behind him, sitting on his unmade bed, is Andrea. Legs crossed, the left one swinging slowly back and forth. One arm resting on her lap. The other holding the gun.

A wave of hatred rises up from the pit of Nuala's stomach and spreads through every part of her. She tastes it inside her mouth, bitter and thick, and feels the heat of it burning up through her stomach and chest, down her arms and into her fingers, which tingle with the need to grab Andrea by her scrawny neck and squeeze every last bit of life from her evil body.

'Let him go.'

The words sound far away, as if it's someone else speaking, not her.

Andrea gives a small shrug of her slender shoulders, like the decision isn't hers to make. A single thought lodges itself inside Nuala's head: *I will fucking kill you.*

'You don't know how lucky you are.' Andrea's voice is barely more than a whisper. Nuala has to strain her ears to hear what she's saying. 'A little boy of your own, Nuala. Do you know how many women there are who can't have children? Yet here you are, with your ready-made little family and you take it for granted. If I was in your shoes, if I had a boy as lovely as this one, I wouldn't waste my life with a job. I would devote every waking moment to being the best parent ever.'

Nuala doesn't take her eyes off Josh the entire time Andrea is speaking. It crosses her mind that this woman, holding a gun to her son's head, is insane. It's not a comforting thought.

'What do you want?' Nuala asks.

'I wouldn't kill a child,' Andrea says. 'Not by choice, at least. But it's not my choice, is it? That is down to you, Nuala. If you do what I ask, you and the boy will be unharmed.'

'Tell me what you need me to do.'

'This new episode of the podcast, what's on it?'

'It's an interview with someone who lived on the farm.'

'Leo, I assume,' Andrea says. 'It can't be Martha, because I've dealt with that particular disappointment.'

Josh has started crying, silent tears rolling down his face. Nuala longs to cross the room and take him in her arms but she's too scared to move. Terrified to do anything that might cause Andrea to pull the trigger.

'You need to stop the episode from being broadcast,' Andrea says. 'I've listened to the trailer and I know it's due to go live at nine o'clock. That can't happen. If you stop it, I'll leave you both alone and that will be the end of it.'

She smiles at Nuala, the same smile she used that very first time they met. Although this time, unsurprisingly given the circumstances, it doesn't have the same effect it did then.

'You'll do that for me, Nuala?'

'Of course.'

Nuala's mind has gone into overdrive. Even if she stops the episode, it won't end there. Andrea's not going to simply walk away and let Nuala carry on with her life. Andrea's clever. She will have worked out that Nuala has most likely already spoken to the police. Nuala guesses Andrea is planning to get the podcast stopped, then make sure Nuala can't give any more statements to the police or anyone else. She's not here just to stop the podcast. She's here to kill Nuala. And Josh, too.

But Nuala can't let that happen, so she needs to think. And she needs to think fast because, according to the clock on Josh's bedside table, it's now ten past eight. Time is running out.

'I can get it stopped,' she tells Andrea. 'But to do that, I have to make a phone call.'

Andrea shakes her head. 'No phone calls. I don't want anyone else involved.'

'I'll put it on speakerphone. You can hear exactly what I say. Come on, Andrea. Do you really think I'm going to do anything that risks my son's life? I'm not that stupid.'

'Who do you need to call?'

'Leo. I came back here to get Josh ready for school and left him in charge of making sure the podcast goes live at nine.'

The seconds drag by as Andrea considers what Nuala has said.

'I need to call now,' Nuala says. 'If I don't, it will be too late.'

She can feel the panic building inside her, becoming an unbearable pressure against her chest. She tries to breathe, tells herself over and over she has to stay calm. But how can she do that when there's a great big fucking gun pressed against her son's precious head?

'Okay,' Andrea says after an eternity. 'But on speakerphone, like you said.' She repositions the gun, pushing the end of it tighter into Josh's head. He moans and the rage inside Nuala burns brighter and stronger.

'My phone's in the kitchen,' Nuala says, forcing herself to speak slowly. Pushing down the urge to run at Andrea, screaming at the top of her voice.

'I'll get it.' Andrea stands up and takes hold of Josh's right arm. 'You stay here.'

'No.' Nuala's voice is sharper and louder than she'd intended.

'Excuse me?'

'Sorry. I'm sorry. He's upset and he'll get worse if you keep twisting his arm like that. Please, Andrea. Don't hurt him. Let him go. He can stay here. You won't move, Joshie, will you? If we leave you here in your room, you'll be a good boy for me?'

She's babbling, unable to stop now she's started. She sees the flash of anger in Andrea's face and it's enough to shut her up.

'For Christ's sake.' Andrea shoves Josh away from her.

He stumbles, but doesn't fall. Nuala starts to go over to him, but Andrea points the gun in her face.

'Leave him.'

'Okay.' Nuala holds her hands up. 'Whatever you say.'

Andrea motions for Nuala to go first, so she turns around and walks out of the room. Behind her, she can hear Josh crying and begging her to come back. Every step away from him is agony, but she has to keep going.

Her phone's on the worktop beside the kettle. As she picks it up, her fingers are shaking so badly it takes several attempts to find the number she needs and then dial it. When she hears the ring tone, she switches to speakerphone.

It rings six times. Nuala's almost given up when, suddenly, his voice fills the small kitchen.

'Nuala, is everything okay?'

'There's a problem with the podcast,' she says, speaking quickly so he doesn't have a chance to interrupt. 'I've got some new information, something important.'

Leo starts to say something but she speaks over him, raising her voice.

'I can't explain over the phone. But it can't go live at nine o'clock. We don't have much time. You're going to have to pull it. I'd do it myself but you're the only one with access to the software. Can you do it?' She lets her voice wobble, a half-sob escaping before she continues. 'Will you stop it the way I showed you? Please. It's really important.'

There's a long pause, during which Nuala completely forgets how to breathe.

'Okay,' Leo says. 'Yeah, sure. Do you want me to call you when it's done?'

The relief is so extreme she has to grab hold of the worktop to stop her legs giving way beneath her.

'Do it now,' she says, 'while I'm on the phone.'

Pretending to still be staring at her phone, Nuala risks a glance at her beloved chef's knife, lying flat on the draining board because she never lets it see the inside of a dishwasher.

'Just a sec.'

There's a pause, then the click–clack sound of a computer keyboard.

Slowly, Nuala slides her hand a fraction of an inch across the counter towards the draining board.

'All I do is enter the password and then click stop?' Leo says.

'That's right.'

If he was in the room now, she'd throw her arms around him and hug him. As it is, she has to content herself with watching the gap between her fingers and the handle of the knife, trying to work out how fast she'll be able to grab it.

'All done,' Leo says.

With a scream, Nuala grabs the knife, whirls around and throws herself across the room. She's moving too fast to stop. Even when she sees the gun rising, sees the finger pulling back on the trigger, there's nothing she can do except keep going. She thrusts wildly with the knife, feels it sink into some part of Andrea's body. At the same time, there's a blast of noise, a sudden, sharp pain in Nuala's left shoulder as her body is thrown up and back before falling onto the hard ground.

She tries to stand up, but her body won't do what she needs it to. The last thing she sees are Andrea's ice blue eyes, and the long dark tunnel of the inside of the gun that's pointing directly down into her face.

Chapter 36

'Why do you keep running away from me?'

As Arnie speaks, he keeps the pressure on the knife. I know my skin is cut, but I don't know how bad it is. I want to ask him what he's doing here, how he found me and why he's so interested in me. But when I try to open my mouth, nothing happens. His body pressed against my back, the stink of his cologne mixing with the smells of the breakfast Ben was cooking – it's too much. If it wasn't for Arnie, holding me up, I'd collapse onto the ground.

'All I've ever done is love you, Martha. I have devoted my entire life to trying to find you. Ever since your mother took you from me. Then, years later when I finally manage to track you down, you treat me like dirt. Like I'm nothing more than a piece of dogshit on the bottom of your shoe. You are my daughter and I will not put up with this behaviour from you.'

His voice rises and he shakes me so hard my teeth rattle together inside my mouth. I can't move or speak, but I'm crying. Tears rolling down my face, soaking into the collar of my shirt.

He drags me out of the kitchen into the hall. He's breathing heavily, sweating too. I can feel it through the back of my shirt. There's something so disgusting about the thought of his sweat soaking through my clothes and onto my skin that I retch. I taste bile, but swallow it back down because I'm too scared of what he'll do if I spit it out.

He swings us both around so we're facing the front door, which is open. A blast of cold air rushes towards me as Arnie shoves me forward. Then we're outside, in the front garden.

'Stop.' It comes out as a whisper and I don't think he's heard me, because he keeps pushing me forward.

I try to resist then, but he pushes harder. I stumble forward, feel the knife catch against my throat. In my head, I see the gash across my neck, the rush of red blood that bursts out of me, warm, sticky and endless. But it never happens. Somehow, he's still holding me and I haven't died. Not yet.

Different bits of information swirl around inside my head. Ben, lying on the floor in the kitchen. I wonder if he's dead. I wonder, too, if he's the reason Arnie's here.

You are my daughter.

At some level I'd worked it out that night he found me in London. We were only three when my mother ran away from him. Young enough so I have almost no memories of him. Just old enough to remember the bruises on her face and the constant feeling of being scared of him.

'I love you,' he says. 'Why can't you understand that? I never wanted to hurt you. All I've ever wanted was to bring you back home.'

Home. I doubt I'd even remember it, if it wasn't for the stories Leo told me. A three-bedroom, red-brick, semi-detached house in a modern estate on the outskirts of Warrington. Every surface kept spotlessly clean, every toy cleared up before he came home from work because he couldn't stand dirt or mess.

The few memories I have of my father are of a man overweight to the point of obese. Arnie is lean and muscled, but some things aren't so easy to change. Like his eyes. The first time I saw him, I felt a flash of recognition that I couldn't place. Now I know it was those eyes, pale grey with nothing except hate and loathing behind them.

He pushes me around to the side of the house where there's a car parked. I wonder how long he's been here, if he was watching me earlier as I walked up the hill and climbed the wall into the other garden. The passenger door is wide open, waiting for me. I won't go with him, but I can't work out how to get away from him. I need to think, but it's hard to focus when he's holding me so tight I can barely breathe, and the knife is pressing into my throat. He shoves me further towards the car.

'No.'

I struggle against him, desperate now. He's strong, but panic makes me brave. I lift a foot, swing it back and stamp down as hard as I can. I feel the crunch of something cracking across the top of his foot. He howls, both hands dropping away from me.

I twist around and run, across the long front garden towards the wide open countryside. He chases after me, screaming at me to stop. I'm almost at the gates when he grabs me. I stumble back, falling against him and we both crash to the ground.

I'm lying on top of him, but when I try to get up, he throws me onto the ground and now he's on top of me. He pushes his face so close his features blur, screaming at me.

'You're *my* daughter, *my* baby girl. Why did you let her take you away from me? I loved you, Martha. I loved you and I thought you loved me too, but you never did.'

It's bullshit. He hated me, hated all three of us. Shouting at us and setting so many rules we lived in constant terror of doing something wrong. Then taking his anger out on her, our mother, when he couldn't cope. He was the reason she stopped loving him. It's his fault, no one else's.

Inside, I'm screaming this at him but no sound is coming out of my mouth, because I can't breathe. My hands flail out either side of my body, flapping uselessly on the grass. When the fingers of my right hand touch something, I barely notice at first. But when it happens again, a word comes to me: *knife*.

I flap my arm again, feeling the edge of the knife's handle with my fingers. Above me, Arnie's face slips in and out of focus. I can feel the top of the handle, but it's just out of reach, too far for me to wrap my fingers around it. I try one last time, using every last bit of energy that's left in my body, and suddenly the knife is in my hand. As I lift my arm, it's like I'm back there that night and it's not just Arnie I'm trying to hurt. It's Mother too, and Jasper, and even golden-eyed Ben who lied to me because how else could Arnie have found me?

A scream roars out of me, every bit of fear and regret and loss and hatred spilling into the cold autumn air.

I see the blade as it plunges into the side of his body. There's a moment when nothing happens. Then he makes a sound, somewhere between a grunt and a sigh, and there's a rush of blood. It splatters across my arms, body and face. It feels warm and familiar, as if I've been waiting for it my entire life.

Chapter 37

When Nuala opens her eyes, the first thing she sees is Liz's face. Which means she isn't awake, after all, but is still dreaming. She closes her eyes again, wishing it wasn't a dream and Liz was really here with her.

'Did you see that?' Liz says. 'She opened her eyes.'

'Are you sure?'

A man's voice, familiar, but Nuala can't place it. Not yet.

'Of course I'm sure,' Liz says. 'Nuala? Nuala, love. Can you hear me?'

'It's a bit hard not to,' Nuala says, or tries to. In fact, the words come out as an incomprehensible croak. Her mouth and throat are unbearably dry. As she opens her eyes again, a sudden panic seizes her. She doesn't know where she is. This isn't her bedroom. She doesn't recognise this room, and she has no clue what Liz is doing here.

She tries to lift her head to see who else is here, but the sheer effort required to move is too much for her.

'Water,' she whispers.

Miraculously, Liz suddenly has a glass of water in her hand. Lifting Nuala's head with her other hand, she holds the glass to her lips, letting the water trickle into Nuala's mouth. When Nuala's had enough, she motions for Liz to take the glass away. As her head slumps back onto the pillow, she becomes aware of the sharp pain in her left arm. She tries to lift it but nothing happens and, when she twists her head to see what the problem is, she's surprised to see the upper part of her arm is hidden beneath layers of white bandage.

A series of images flash through her head. Andrea and the phone call to Leo and the gun. And Josh! With superhuman effort, she manages to sit up, looking frantically around for her son. She's in a hospital, she realises. And the man here with Liz is Leo. But there's no sign of Josh.

'It's okay.' Liz pats Nuala's good arm. 'Harry's taken him to the canteen to get something to eat.'

'The gun,' Nuala says.

'You took a bullet to the arm,' Liz says, 'but luckily your neighbour turned up at your flat before Andrea could finish what she'd started.'

'Dylan?'

'He was there when I arrived,' Leo says. 'I knew you were in trouble. All that nonsense about logging into the server and stopping the episode from being broadcast. As if I'd have the first clue how to do anything like that. I knew you were trying to tell me something was wrong. Then I heard you scream. We jumped onto Harry's bike and drove over to yours as fast as we could.

'You'd been taken away in an ambulance by the time we arrived. Dylan stayed behind with Josh. I'm afraid Andrea was long gone by then.'

'Josh thought you were dead,' Liz says. 'He's okay now, but he was in a bit of a state at first.'

Nuala's heart contracts in her chest. To think of her boy seeing her like that is unbearable.

'How long have I been here?' she asks.

'Two days,' Liz says. 'You lost a lot of blood and needed a transfusion. Plus you had to have an operation to remove the bullet from your arm. You're lucky to be alive, Nuala.'

Liz's voice cracks and Nuala can't bear it. All this pain she's caused to the people she loves most. She promises herself she will be a better person after this. She will devote her life to being a good mother and friend. Even if that means working as a temp from now on and giving up on her dreams. Because, let's face it, so far, following her dreams hasn't exactly worked out the way she'd hoped, has it?

She looks at Liz, who shouldn't even be here, yet she is. Dear, sweet Liz, who's a better person than Nuala could ever hope to be. The one who got away.

'I'm so sorry,' Nuala tells her. 'I fucked up, didn't I?'

'Yeah, you did. But you know what, Nuala? Fucking up is okay if you're big enough to admit what you did was wrong. And you did that. Not just to me, or Leo, but to everyone.'

'What do you mean?'

'The podcast,' Liz says. 'That last episode was incredible. You've gone viral, kiddo. There's even a piece about you in today's *Guardian*.'

A few weeks ago, this news would have sent her into a frenzy of hysterical excitement. Now, she finds she doesn't care that much at all. Funny how the thing you think you want often turns out to be different to what you actually need.

She thinks of something else then, and looks at Leo, almost too scared to ask. But she knows she has to.

'What about Martha?'

'She's okay.' Leo's face cracks into a wide smile. 'She's in Lincolnshire, but I'm meeting her later this week.'

'Andrea Leach is screwed,' Liz says. 'Apparently, the gun she used on you is the same gun that killed Roger. She's the main suspect in that murder investigation and, of course, she's now part of a wider investigation into everything that happened at the farm. The Progress Party's reputation is in tatters. No way they'll recover from this. That's all down to you, Foxy.'

'But none of it matters if she disappears again,' Nuala says.

'The police will find her.' Liz sounds more confident than Nuala can allow herself to feel. This isn't over until Andrea has been arrested and locked up.

'What I don't understand,' Liz continues, 'is how she ever thought she'd get away with it. She must have known that, sooner or later, someone from her past would recognise her.'

'She's a narcissist,' Leo says. 'I'm sure she one hundred per cent believed she could carry on pretending to be Andrea Leach for as long as she wanted. We know who she is now, Nuala. Her real name is Rosemary Fry. She grew up in Norfolk, but disappeared shortly after her parents died.'

'How did they die?' Nuala asks.

'There was a fire in the house they were living in,' Leo says. 'Rosemary managed to get out, but her parents didn't. The official verdict at the time was that the fire had been caused by an electrical fault. Given what we know now, the police are pushing for the case to be reopened. It's possible she'll be charged with the murder of both her parents too.'

Nuala stays quiet while she lets this information sink in, all the time thinking how close she had been to becoming another one of Rosemary Fry's victims.

'And Andrea Leach,' she says, 'did Rosemary kill her too?'

'Possibly,' Leo says. 'I was eleven when I moved to the farm. Shortly after I arrived, one of the women died. I never knew her surname, but her first name was Andrea. We were told she'd died in an accident.' He shrugs. 'Maybe that's true. I guess we'll never know for sure.'

And there it was. Nuala's guess had been correct. Andrea Leach had been one of the women who lived on the farm.

'Andrea grew up in Australia,' Leo continues, 'but her mother was English. After her parents died, she applied for a British passport. That's what she used to travel with when she left Australia. It would have expired after ten years. At some point after that, Rosemary applied to get the passport renewed using a photo of herself.'

There are thousands of questions chasing around inside Nuala's head. Something else too, an uneasy need to see Andrea – or Rosemary – again. Although if she was asked to explain why, Nuala didn't think she'd be able to.

But now is not the time to think about Rosemary Fry or anyone else, because the door to her room is opening and Josh is here. He pauses inside the door, like he's scared to go any further. But when he sees Nuala is awake, and she calls his name, his face breaks into the biggest smile she's ever seen and he charges towards her.

When he's close enough, she holds out her good arm, wraps it around him and pulls him close for a hug. As she buries her face in the top of his head, and breathes in his soft smell, she starts crying. Tears of joy because he's here, her boy, and no matter what trauma he's carrying from the last few days, he's alive and they're together and she will do everything she is capable of to make sure no harm ever comes to him again.

Chapter 38

'Are you okay?' Ben squeezes my hand and I return the pressure, grateful he's here.

We're in London, walking along the south bank of the Thames. Big Ben and the Houses of Parliament sit looking at us from the other side of the water. It's five days since Arnie attacked me, and a lot has happened since then.

The first thing is that Arnie didn't die. He survived the knife wound to his stomach and is in hospital, under police custody. Thanks to Ben, the police believed I'd acted in self-defence. Arnie has been arrested and charged with a range of offences, including actual bodily harm for his attack on Ben.

At first, I refused to see Ben. I thought he was the reason Arnie had found me. It was only after Arnie told the police how he'd managed to track me down – first in Hastings and then at the farm – that I realised Ben had done nothing wrong.

That day he'd found me in London, Arnie had managed to attach a tracking device to my bag. When the police told me this, and showed me the device that was no bigger than a button, I remembered Arnie handing my bag over after he'd grabbed me. The device had been in the small inside pocket of my bag ever since.

Arnie had been on his way to Ashford the day I was due to meet Nuala Fox. When Mother abducted me, he got a notification that I was on the move again. Following me to Lincolnshire, and the farmhouse, had been easy.

Later, Ben told me he'd done his best to persuade Arnie he'd made a mistake, that the woman he was looking for wasn't there.

But Arnie had seen my bag, hanging over the back of a chair in the kitchen where I'd left it, and knew Ben was lying. He'd attacked Ben, knocking him unconscious, right before I came back inside.

The second thing to have happened is Ben. We've spent the last few days together and I already feel like I've known him my entire life. He's kind and funny and easy to be with. In every way possible, he's the exact opposite of Jasper and the other men I've known. Ben wants to help me, not use me. All the time we've been together, I keep waiting for him to show me that he expects something from me but he hasn't done that.

Yesterday, when we went for a walk, Ben reached out and took my hand. He didn't say anything, and neither did I. But I could feel my face aching with a huge smile and, when I looked sideways at him, he was smiling too. Tiny sparks exploded in my tummy and it should have been scary, but it was perfect. We haven't kissed yet, or anything like that, but I think that might happen soon. At least, I hope so.

The third thing I found out is that Kath is okay. That day I'd called her, Arnie smashed her phone out of her hands when he realised who she was talking to. He couldn't risk me telling Kath he'd followed me to London. Unfortunately for Arnie, Kath is tougher than she looks. She'd been in the sitting room when he attacked her, and she grabbed the poker by the fireplace and chased him out of her house before he could hurt her any further.

After Arnie left, she decided to leave too. She didn't want to be alone in the house if he came back. She checked into a nearby hotel before going to her local police station and telling them what Arnie had done. It took several days, and a lot of work from Helen Robins, before Kath's statement was cross-referenced with the missing person's report Helen had filed in Kath's name. Once she'd made the connection, the rest was easy.

The final, and biggest, thing of all is finding Leo. My brother is alive! He's the reason I'm in London today. I'm meeting him at his apartment ten minutes from now. Ben and I got the train to London first thing this morning. The feelings inside me are too big, too intense to put into words. I'm nervous and excited and scared. I'm happy and sad and angry too, because of all the years we've already lost out on. And the guilt I've felt about what I did all those years ago is mixed in with everything else, making it impossible to enjoy today as much as I want to. I know I should tell Leo what I did, and maybe I will someday. But not yet, not when we're finally seeing each other after all this time apart. I need him to get to know me first, see that I'm not really a bad person. That way when I finally do tell him, maybe – just maybe – he'll be able to forgive me.

'This is it,' Ben says.

We stop walking and look up at the glass-fronted building of the address Leo gave me when we spoke yesterday. Leo Bailey is his new name. He changed his surname by deed poll, he told me, because he couldn't bear to have the same surname as our father. So he became Leo Bailey, replacing Arnie's surname with our mother's maiden name.

Leo's death was another one of Mother's lies. She couldn't bear to admit he'd escaped, that he'd got away from her and there was very little chance she'd ever find him again. So she'd invented a different ending for him, one which had the added bonus of breaking Lydia's heart all over again.

Leo escaped, ran away from the farm and never looked back. The first time we spoke, four days ago over the phone, he told me of the guilt he's carried with him all these years. How he'd always planned to go back for me and Lydia but, the more time that passed, the easier it was to focus on his new life and his future.

I've told him that's okay, that he was only a child too and we weren't his responsibility, but I don't think he believes that and I understand why. Because it doesn't matter how young we were, there are some things we'll never be able to forgive ourselves for. I'm pretty sure no matter how many times I try to tell my brother he has nothing to feel guilty about, it won't make any difference. That guilt at having survived, at still being here when so many of our family didn't make it, is something we'll both carry for the rest of our lives.

'Want me to stay?' Ben asks.

'It's okay,' I say. 'Thanks.'

'Call me if you need me,' he says. 'There's a pub at the end of the road. I'll go there and wait until I hear from you.'

And then Ben is gone and I'm alone, standing outside the building where my brother lives. I lift my hand to press the buzzer for his apartment, feeling suddenly shy. When I was little, he was the centre of my world. My hero older brother who could always make me laugh. Who made me feel safe in a place where nothing else was, until one day he was gone and I've never really felt safe since.

With my finger hovering over the buzzer, an image comes to me. His face one of the last times I saw him. We were in the garden, picking courgettes. I was angry about something and Leo was trying to cheer me up by making stupid jokes. I remember asking him why he was in such a good mood, what was making him so happy. He didn't answer right away. He was looking at something behind me, and there was an expression on his face I had never seen before. When I turned my head, I saw Lydia crossing the yard and I understood that what I'd seen on Leo's face was love.

I still haven't pressed the buzzer when the door to the building swings open and he's there in front of me. His face, as familiar as my own even after all these years, is looking at me now with the same expression it had that long ago afternoon in the garden. He opens his arms and I walk into his embrace. He holds me close, neither of us speaking. And it feels like I've finally come home.

Chapter 39

One month later

The bar has low lighting that suits her purposes. With her new hair – pixie cut and dyed black – she is almost unrecognisable. Almost, because it's not so easy to change her eyes or the shape of her face. Well, not if she wants to still look this good. Which she absolutely has to, because she's going to need some help getting herself out of this particular mess.

For now she's Dawn Connor, the name on the driving licence she stole two weeks ago. She'd spotted Dawn in a London bar, drunk and alone with her bag hanging open on the chair beside her. One drink was all it took for Dawn to trust Rosemary enough to ask her to look after her bag while she went to the toilet. By the time Dawn staggered back to her seat, Rosemary had left the bar – taking Dawn's driving licence with her.

Being Dawn is a temporary measure. It's only a matter of time before the real Dawn notices her driving licence is missing and orders a replacement. In the meantime, it has enabled Rosemary to secure a room in the luxury hotel she's currently booked into.

She's in Leeds, a city she's never been to before, which has turned out to be far nicer than she'd expected. This hotel, in particular, is a real find. A converted warehouse building overlooking the canal, it's discreet and luxurious. She'd never have guessed Nuala Fox had such good taste.

The message on Nuala's Instagram post last week couldn't have come at a better time. The press interest in Rosemary has started to die down. Whole days go by now without any mention of her. While she had grown tired of the lurid head-lines, the opinion pieces and the lies that had been written about her, there's a part of her that misses it. The flush of excitement each time she saw her face on the front cover of a newspaper or magazine. The knowledge that the whole country was talking about her and thinking about her – well, that was quite some-thing.

The real Andrea would have hated it, of course. That scared little mouse of a woman who'd realised, three weeks after leaving Australia, that she wasn't in any way equipped for trav-elling by herself. Luckily for Andrea, she wasn't alone for long. On her second day in London, she'd met Rosemary and the two women became inseparable.

It had taken Rosemary less than fifteen minutes to work out how Andrea felt about her. After that, it had been easy to get Andrea to do and say exactly what Rosemary asked of her. In some ways, it was thanks to Andrea that the farm ever came about. When Rosemary mentioned, in passing, her desire to have children of her own one day, Andrea had asked if she'd ever considered using a surrogate – someone who looked enough like Rosemary so the child might even resemble her.

At the time, Rosemary had discounted the suggestion because she didn't want just one child, she wanted lots. She had believed – wrongly, as it turned out – that having her own family, being surrounded by a brood of adoring children, might help to fill the empty black hole inside her. To fix what her father had broken.

Andrea had been excited, at first, when Rosemary laid out her plans for the farm. But soon after they moved to the farm, Andrea changed. She started asking questions, speaking up when she disagreed with decisions Rosemary had made. In the end, Andrea's moaning became too much and Rosemary had to get rid of her. She had taken no pleasure in killing Andrea – she wasn't a monster, despite the things that had been written about her – but there was no denying the buzz Rosemary got when she turned her dead friend into one of the UK's most talked about politicians.

Besides, it wasn't like she'd needed Andrea by then. Finding women to live on the farm had been almost too easy. Rosemary had a talent for scouting them out – vulnerable women with fear etched into their faces like a tattoo. Once she'd befriended them and spent endless hours listening to them moaning about their husbands, it was easy to persuade them there was somewhere better they could be. A haven, somewhere remote, where their husband would never be able to find them. In exchange, all they had to do was obey the rules of the farm and never question Rosemary's place as Mother and Leader. For a long time, it had been everything Rosemary had dreamed of. Until it all went wrong.

Pushing away thoughts of the farm, she takes a sip of her martini. Catching sight of her reflection in the mirror that runs the width of the wall behind the bar, some of the tension in her body eases. Despite the stresses of the last few months, she looks good. Especially in the low-lit bar which conceals the signs of age that no amount of Botox or surgery can fully eradicate.

She's never bought into the – frankly ludicrous – notion that you're meant to embrace old age, as if wrinkled skin and sagging body parts are something to be celebrated. A woman's face is her currency. Rosemary has grown so used to getting what she wants simply because of the way she looks, it's been quite a shock to realise that's not going to work for much longer.

She swivels her stool sideways so she can check out the rest of the bar. There are a few people in here, but none of them are Nuala Fox. She frowns, wondering if she might have somehow misjudged what's been going on between them. Surely not. She's always thought their similarities were one of the reasons she was so drawn to Nuala. Because when she first listened to Nuala's podcast, Rosemary recognised a kindred spirit. Someone who wouldn't think twice about twisting the truth if that's what it took to get what you wanted. Rosemary knows some people disapprove of what Nuala did, but she's certainly not one of them. As she's made clear to Nuala more than once since they reconnected last week.

The barman, lean and muscled with a cheeky grin, slides a fresh drink across the bar towards her. She's about to tell him she hasn't ordered another, when he nods at something behind her.

'The person over there bought you this.'

Andrea takes the glass, but doesn't look around. Not yet. Better to wait, savour this first tingle of anticipation before Nuala makes her move. She's barely taken the first sip from the glass when she sees Nuala's face in the mirror, sliding onto the empty stool beside her.

'Hello, Rosemary.'

Rosemary smiles. 'I was starting to think you'd stood me up.'

'I wouldn't do that.' Nuala holds her gaze as she speaks and Rosemary finds herself transfixed. There's a confidence about Nuala she hasn't seen before. It's intoxicating.

The moment she'd seen the post on Instagram, Rosemary knew what it was. A message, from Nuala to her. *We're going to make history, you and I.* It's what Rosemary had said the first time they'd met, in that bland hotel near London Bridge. And just in case the meaning wasn't clear enough, above the sentence there was a photo of two women's hands intertwined with each other.

Since then, there'd been a flurry of messages and phone calls. Rosemary had been cagey at first, unsure of Nuala's motivations. She'd needed to understand why Nuala had got in touch, and what she wanted. Because Rosemary knew Nuala wasn't chasing justice. Her goal was more ambitious, more selfish. Like Rosemary herself, Nuala Fox was motivated by self-glory, the need to shine in a world full of grey people. And it seemed that, for now, Nuala had decided Rosemary was still her best chance of getting that shine.

Nuala catches the barman's eye and orders a gin and tonic. After the drink arrives, she clinks her glass against Rosemary's.

'You look good,' she says. 'The new hairstyle suits you.'

'Thank you.' Rosemary smooths her hair behind her ears, glancing at her reflection in the mirror at the same time.

'So tell me,' she says, 'how is this going to work?'

'I've got all the recording equipment in my room,' Nuala says. 'We can go up there after our drinks and get started.'

She leans forward, her eyes glittering, and puts her hand on Rosemary's arm. 'It's going to be electric, Rosemary. Getting you on my podcast, giving you a chance to tell your version of events, will be amazing.'

'I take it I can trust you not to tell anyone where I am,' Rosemary says, although she already knows the answer to this. Just in case the message hasn't been made clearly enough, she takes out her phone and shows the photo that was sent to her earlier this afternoon.

As Nuala takes the phone, something flashes across her face – anger or pain, Rosemary can't be sure. The photo is of Nuala's son, Josh. He's sitting on the sofa in Nuala's London apartment with the man Rosemary has hired to stay with him until this is over.

'You promise he won't get hurt?' Nuala asks, handing the phone back to Rosemary.

'As long as you stick to our agreement,' Rosemary says. 'We do the recording, then you wait a day before releasing it. By which time I'll have moved on to a new town. You wait here until you get my phone call telling you Josh is safe and you can go back home.'

'How do I know your goon won't hurt him in the meantime?' Nuala asks.

Rosemary sighs. They've gone through this several times already.

'Harry won't do anything unless I tell him to. I trust him completely.'

After Nuala made contact, Rosemary knew she'd need help setting this up. So she'd called Harry, the only one of Roger's men she'd ever really had any time for. She'd explained what she needed, and how much she was willing to pay for a job well done, and Harry had jumped at the opportunity.

'Okay.' Nuala nods. 'There's just one thing I wanted to ask before we begin.'

'If you must.'

'The women who lived with you on the farm. Why were they there?'

'To have my children.'

'I don't understand.'

Of course you don't, Rosemary thinks irritably. No one could possibly understand what her life had been like.

'If I tell you, do you promise it won't be included in your podcast?'

'I promise.'

'I fell pregnant when I was nineteen.' Rosemary pauses. It's not easy speaking about something she's spent most of her life trying to forget. On the other hand, it's important that Nuala Fox, more than anyone else, understands her. 'My father forced me to have an abortion. He found a doctor who agreed to do it privately. After the abortion, I had another operation. I was told it was because something had gone wrong with the abortion. It was only later I discovered the truth. My father had paid that man to sterilise me.'

Nuala's hand goes to her mouth. She looks shocked.

'It's why I had to find another way to have children,' Rosemary says. 'And for a while everything was perfect. They had a good life, you know. Those women were living in fear before they met me. I got them away from their abusive partners, gave them a home and somewhere safe to live. They should have been grateful, but in the end it wasn't enough. They wanted more.'

'Is that why you set fire to the house?'

'It was all ruined by then,' Rosemary says. 'The discontent and ingratitude had started. I knew it would spread through the farm like a virus. I had to stop it.'

It was clear, from the way Nuala was looking at her, that Nuala didn't understand. Well, how could she? What would Nuala Fox know about making sacrifices, devoting your entire life to something bigger than yourself?

Nuala was no better than all those other journalists. The ones claiming, on the one hand, to be proponents of women's rights while at the same time writing reams of vitriolic bullshit about Rosemary. The only thing they haven't done so far is out her as a witch and call for her to be burnt at the stake. A bunch of hypocrites, the lot of them.

'Maybe this isn't such a good idea, after all,' Rosemary says.

She pushes her stool back and stands up to leave. The bar has emptied out while they've been talking. There were lots of people here earlier but there's no one here now except the two of them.

Something is wrong. The thought comes to her as the door to the bar swings open. A man and a woman appear, their faces stern, as they stride towards her.

'You'll never see your son again,' she hisses, turning to Nuala as she realises she's been set up. She expects Nuala to look scared, but Nuala smiles instead and tells Rosemary her son is perfectly fine. Which doesn't make any sense but Rosemary can't think about that now because the man who's come into the bar is talking to her.

'Rosemary Fry, I am arresting you on suspicion of murder. You do not have to say anything, but it may harm your defence if you do not mention, when questioned, something which you later rely on in court.'

'You bitch.'

She lunges for Nuala, but the man grabs her, twists her body around until she's pressed down on the counter of the bar. He yanks her arms behind her and she feels the sudden, shocking weight of handcuffs.

She struggles against him, rage making her want to claw his eyes out and watch the blood running down his cheeks. But she can't, because the two detectives have taken hold of her arms and are dragging her across the bar towards the open door.

Outside, there's a police car, blue lights flashing on the roof and the back door open, waiting for her. As they shove her into the car, her mind flashes back to the night Martha and Lydia escaped. She remembers watching them racing through the open gates and disappearing into the night. She closes her eyes, and she's there with them, throwing her head back, her laughter flowing up to meet the thousands of tiny stars dancing across the black sky.

Epilogue

One year later

It's Sunday afternoon and we're having lunch in Leo's apartment. On my way over here earlier, I'd been excited. I haven't seen much of Leo recently because he's been busy with work. I was looking forward to spending time together today, just the two of us. But he's also invited Nuala and Liz and their son, Josh; and Kath and Harry and Alicia.

Alicia is the director of the documentary film she and Nuala are making about Black Valley Farm. During the summer, when we were filming the documentary, I saw Leo all the time. I thought we'd continue seeing lots of each other once the filming was finished but that hasn't happened. He says he's busy with his job and the reality TV show he joined recently, but seeing him now with Alicia, I know the real reason he doesn't have any time left for me these days.

He's cooked a big roast for lunch. There's pork, and roast potatoes and massive Yorkshire puddings and three different types of vegetable, as well as gravy and apple sauce. It's all delicious but I can't eat much because each time I see the way Alicia and Leo are looking at each other, my stomach twists tighter and tighter.

'Are you okay, Martha?' Kath, sitting beside me, puts her hand on my arm.

'Fine.' I force myself to smile and pick up my fork. 'This food is delicious, isn't it?'

'If it's so delicious,' Kath says, 'why have you barely touched it?'

I shovel a forkful of roast potatoes into my mouth so I don't have to answer her. I still live with Kath, in the attic room at the top of her house. We drove down from Sheffield yesterday evening and spent the night in a hotel. I wanted to stay here, at Leo's, but that didn't happen. Apparently he had a work dinner last night so it wouldn't have been convenient.

'Have you thought any more about the song?' Nuala asks from across the table. Then, when I shake my head, 'Oh Martha, please do it. You've got a beautiful voice and think how special it would be to have you singing the song that goes with the opening and closing credits.'

'I agree,' Alicia says. 'It would bring something really special to the film.'

Alicia has pale hands with long, slender fingers. In my head, I see my own hand reaching out, sticking the fork into her hand and skewering it to the table. I imagine the red blood, staining the white tablecloth, and her voice as she screams in agony.

'Maybe you guys should stop pestering her about it,' Liz says. 'I'm sure if she wants to do a song for the film, she'll do it.'

'She's too modest,' Kath says. 'That's her problem.'

I can't bear to sit here a second longer, while they're all talking about me as if I'm not even here. I push my chair back and stand up, crossing over to the glass door that leads onto the terrace. Behind me I hear Kath, still speaking about me.

'It's a difficult transition for her. She needs time, that's all. This will get easier eventually.'

I shut the door behind me, blocking out their voices and their faux sympathy and their unthinking happiness. In this moment, I hate all of them, even Leo. Especially Leo. When I found out he was alive, I thought things would be different. I assumed I'd found someone who understood what it felt like to be me. But Leo doesn't understand. No one does. Leo's got his business and his successful life, and friends like Harry and now probably a girlfriend too.

I'd spent so many years imagining what my life would be like, if only I could stop hiding, stop pretending to be someone I'm not. I thought I would feel free and happy and be the person I was always meant to be.

For the first few weeks, everything was exactly as I'd imagined. I had Leo, I could stop hiding and pretending, and I had Ben too. Then Ben decided we couldn't be together because of my 'unpredictable moods' and my 'anger issues'. I'd wanted to move in with Leo when Ben and I broke up, but he said that wasn't a good idea. So I moved back to Sheffield instead. Kath always says her home is my home, but she doesn't mean it. I know I'm difficult to live with, and I'm sure she is biding her time until she finds the right moment to tell me I have to leave.

I've tried so hard to be someone different. I've changed the colour of my hair – blue, then pink, and now bleached blonde – and I've got tattoos and ear piercings, and I wear make-up every single day and brightly coloured clothes. But none of it changes how I feel inside. I'm still empty and lost and confused and angry. And I'm still sick with a guilt that never shifts.

It's cold out here. A breeze is whipping along the river, rippling waves across the surface. Leo's apartment is on the top floor, which means this terrace is really high up. I lean forward, pushing the top half of my body over the railing.

Down below, there are people walking along the path by the river. A couple holding hands. A woman with a tiny white dog on a long lead. Two girls speeding past on pink scooters. I lean forward a little more and close my eyes, picturing my body tipping over completely and crashing onto the hard concrete.

'Hey, Martha.'

It's Leo. His voice makes me jump. I straighten up and turn around, forgetting for a moment that I don't want to talk to anyone.

'I'm glad you came today,' he says. 'There's something I want to speak to you about.'

He's going to tell me he's fallen in love with Alicia and she's moving in with him, here into his lovely apartment. I dig my fingers into the palms of my hands, waiting.

'I'm opening a new bar,' he says. 'In Sheffield.'

'Oh, I see.' Except I don't, not really. It's cool, I guess, that there'll be a Bermondsey Beer pub in Sheffield, but I don't understand what that's got to do with me.

'It's going to be a live music venue, and I'd love you to be the first act we have there. If it goes well, I was thinking you could even have a permanent slot.'

I start to shake my head, but he holds his hands up and continues speaking.

'I know you're scared, Martha. Doing something new, especially after all you've been through, is terrifying. But sooner or later, you're going to have to take a risk. I understand, you know. I see how angry and lost you are. I see it, because I'm like that too.'

'You? You're nothing like me.' I wave my arm, indicating the terrace and the apartment that is proof positive his life is very different to mine.

'I'm better at hiding it, that's all.'

If he keeps talking like this, I'll start crying. I really don't want to do that, so I clench my hands tighter, force the sadness back down.

'I don't want to talk about this. I don't want to sing in your bar or have a permanent slot. Why does everyone think I want to change my life? Why can't you all just leave me alone?'

'Because we care about you.'

'Well you shouldn't,' I tell him. 'I don't deserve it.'

'That's not true.'

'Yes it is,' I shout at him. 'I am a horrible person. You don't realise how horrible I am. It was me, you know. I'm the reason you and Lydia were found that day. I knew what you were doing and I told Mother. I was so angry with you both. You were my brother, but she was the one you loved and the one you wanted to spend time with. It wasn't fair.'

As I'm speaking, those old feelings come rushing back: the jealousy and the anger and the feeling of being left out of the one good thing that was there in that place. Then I think of Lydia and how beautiful she was, and how kind she'd always been to me. I see her that last night, running back towards the farm to try to save everyone, and I start crying and I can't stop.

I'm glad I've finally told Leo what I did. He'll hate me forever but it's what I deserve. When he takes a step towards me, I tense, waiting for him to hit me, or grab hold of me and scream in my face, or shove me over the railings.

But he does none of those things. He wraps his arms around me instead. Holds me close and tells me it's okay.

'How is it okay?' I say into his chest. 'It was my fault.'

'You were a child,' Leo says. 'A damaged little girl who wanted to be loved. What happened that day wasn't your fault. You were as much a victim as we were. Besides, I've always known it was you who told Mother.'

'You have?' I step back and look up at his face to see if he's telling the truth.

'Yes. She told me herself. Said she had little Martha to thank for bringing the matter to her attention.'

'You don't hate me for it?'

'Martha, you're my sister and I will always love you. Whatever you did that day is nothing compared to what I did. I ran away and I left you. You've been able to forgive me for that, so why on earth are you finding it so hard to forgive yourself?'

I don't know how to answer that, so I stay quiet. Behind Leo, the terrace door opens and Josh comes running out.

'Uncle Leo, Mummy says you've got a pavlova for pudding. It's my favourite pudding in the whole world but she says I'm not allowed to have any until you come back inside. Will you come now? Please?'

Leo looks at me, and I nod my head.

'You go,' I tell him. 'I'll follow you in a bit.'

I wait until they're gone, then I turn and lean over the railings again. This time, I don't look down at the path, I look at the river instead, winding its way through the city on its endless journey towards the sea. There's a yellow barge bobbing along the surface and I imagine myself in there, heading off on a big adventure, travelling to some place I've never been before.

I think of Lydia, how she was that last night as we ran across the fields, her face bathed in the silver light of the full moon, her laughter loud and joyful. I close my eyes, and I make her a promise. I tell her I will live the life she should have had. I'll go travelling and I'll fall in love and I'll have children. If I have a girl, I'll name her Lydia. And as my daughter grows older, I'll tell her all about the other Lydia, the one who lost her own life so that I could live mine.

Acknowledgements

Thanks as always to my parents, for your ongoing support and your tireless work promoting my books at every opportunity. I know you're very proud of me, and that means so much.

As every author knows, it takes a team of people to create a finished book. This one wouldn't be in the shape it's in without the brilliant work put in by Siân Heap, who is wonderful in every way possible. Thank you too to Alicia Poutney, Chere Tricot and Rachel Malig for picking up all the typos, inconsistencies and errors through the editing process! Thanks also to the wider team at Canelo – you all work so hard and are such a joy to work with: Louise Cullen, Nicola Piggott, Claudine Sagoe, Thanhmai Bui-Van and Kate Shepherd.

I also want to thank my my super duper new agent, Sophie Gorell Barnes for your patience with my endless questions and your enthusiasm for my writing – you're fab!

A very special thanks to to the dedicated community of book bloggers who do so much to support and promote authors. Every review and every post from you guys means so much.

A big shout out to my fellow crime writers Lorraine Mace, Marion Todd, Rachel Lynch and Chris Curran. We keep each other going and I value your friendship enormously.

Massive, massive thanks to Claire Lyons and Kath Dinsdale for trekking down to Eastbourne for the party! We had a raffle for the brilliant charity, You Raise Me Up, and Kath won the prize of being a named character in this book. Kath, I know you had dreams of being a kick-ass secret agent – I'm sorry I couldn't do that this time!

Thank you, as always, to the brilliant group of people who run the UK Crime Book Club, particularly my pal Samantha Brownley.

Finally, love and thanks as always to the three people who mean the most: Sean, Luke and Ruby.

CANELOCRIME

Do you love crime fiction and are always on the lookout for brilliant authors?

Canelo Crime is home to some of the most exciting novels around. Thousands of readers are already enjoying our compulsive stories. Are you ready to find your new favourite writer?

Find out more and sign up to our newsletter at canelocrime.com